THE
EAGLE
AND THE
VIPER

BOOKS BY
LOREN D. ESTLEMAN

THE
EAGLE
AND THE
VIPER

A Novel of Historical Suspense

**LOREN D.
ESTLEMAN**

FORGE

A TOM DOHERTY ASSOCIATES BOOK • NEW YORK

THE EAGLE AND THE VIPER

Copyright © 2021 by Loren D. Estleman

All rights reserved.

A Forge Book
Published by Tom Doherty Associates
120 Broadway
New York, NY 10271

www.tor-forge.com

Forge® is a registered trademark of Macmillan Publishing Group, LLC.

Library of Congress Cataloging-in-Publication Data

Names: Estleman, Loren D., author.
Title: The eagle and the viper : a novel of historical suspense / Loren D. Estlemen.
Description: First edition. | New York : Forge, a Tom Doherty
Associates Book, 2021.
Identifiers: LCCN 2020051716 (print) | LCCN 2020051717 (ebook) |
ISBN 9781250258625 (hardcover) | ISBN 9781250258618 (ebook)
Subjects: LCSH: Napoleon I, Emperor of the French, 1769-1821—Assassination
attempts—Fiction. | GSAFD: Biographical fiction. | Alternative histories (Fiction)
Classification: LCC PS3555.S84 E14 2021 (print) |
LCC PS3555.S84 (ebook) | DDC 813/.54—dc23
LC record available at https://lccn.loc.gov/2020051716
LC ebook record available at https://lccn.loc.gov/2020051717

Our books may be purchased in bulk for promotional, educational, or business use. Please contact your local bookseller or the Macmillan Corporate and Premium Sales Department at 1-800-221-7945, extension 5442, or by email at MacmillanSpecialMarkets@macmillan.com.

First Edition: March 2021

Printed in the United States of America

0 9 8 7 6 5 4 3 2 1

The bullet that can kill me is not yet cast.

—NAPOLEON BONAPARTE

HISTORICAL NOTE

In 1789, France declared itself a Republic.

Four years later, it killed the royal family.

The next year, it killed its Republican leader.

Meanwhile, it imprisoned 300,000 citizens and killed 17,000 by way of the musket ball and the guillotine.

In 1799, an obscure Corsican artillery officer took over the government, the third in ten years.

The new First Consul brought order, but his own position was far less stable than the nation's.

Supported by England, which feared the spread of Republicanism to its shores, both the radical-Revolutionary Jacobins and the Royalists dedicated to the restoration of the monarchy plotted to assassinate the upstart.

By Christmas Eve, 1800, numerous attempts had been made on the life of the future Napoleon I, Emperor of the French.

I. HISTORICAL

THE CONSPIRATORS

GEORGES CADOUDAL, the mastermind behind the Royalist plot to depose Bonaparte and restore the Bourbon throne;

FRANÇOIS CARBON, a career sailor, Cadoudal's chief accomplice in the field, and the architect behind the atrocity that took place on Christmas Eve, 1800;

PIERRE SAINT-RÉJANT, a former general in the Royalist army, one of Carbon's partners in the Christmas Eve Plot;

JOSEPH PIERRE PICOT LIMOËLAN, a former Royalist general also, the third participant in the Christmas Eve Plot;

CHARLES PICHEGRU, another Royalist general, recruited later.

THE INVESTIGATORS

NAPOLEON BONAPARTE, First Consul of the Republic of France;

JOSEPH FOUCHÉ, Bonaparte's ruthless Minister of Police;

NICOLAS DUBOIS, Paris Prefect of Police, subordinate to Fouché.

SECONDARY CAST MEMBERS

JOSEPHINE BONAPARTE, the First Consul's faithless and fashionable wife, First Lady of France;

CÉSAR, Bonaparte's coachman, an accidental hero.

II. EXCLUSIVE TO THIS STORY

THE PAWNS

GEOFFREY RANDLE, fourth Earl of Rexborough and one of Cadoudal's many British sympathizers, financial backers, and fellow schemers;

CAROLYN RANDLE, Lady, Rexborough, married to Randle contemptuous of him, and a veteran of illicit affairs;

CHARLES ESLÉE, a village physician;

MARIANNE DEAUVILLE, a widow of the French wars;

JACQUES MALROUX, a country constable;

THE VIPER, a pioneer in the profession of hired assassin.

I

NIVOSE

(Month of Snow)

1

"This is no work for a soldier," said Saint-Réjant. "I joined the army to get out of farming."

"Did you gripe this much in the army?" Carbon asked.

"Only until they made me a general."

"You'd enjoy the work better if you'd served aboard ship. Once you've survived battle with the enemy, the sea offers you a second chance to die."

"It wouldn't make me any more wet."

The rain had begun at dusk and settled into a monotonous drizzle, icy and glutinous. It dripped off their slouch brims, their noses too, and the ropy mud of the boulevard clung to their boots and made them heavy as sledges. It turned a level stretch into an uphill climb.

The date was 24 December, 1800 (4 Nivose, Year VIII by the Revolutionary calendar). Traffic was heavy, despite the weather. France had cut the heads off priests and abolished religion, but after a dozen years of austerity, Parisians insisted on celebrating Christmas Eve. Twice now, Carbon had almost been run down by carriages bearing drunken revelers toward the Rue Saint-Nicaise. After the second near miss he'd cajoled Saint-Réjant and Limoëlan to step down from the cart and help him lead the lame, wind-broken mare.

Carbon, a naval veteran, and one admittedly inclined toward recklessness for the sheer thrill of it, nevertheless considered his companions bad risks. Saint-Réjant, most recently a common bandit, had found that occupation more to his liking than his late service to the King, at the expense of his commitment to the Cause, and Limoëlan's lust for vengeance was the very thing that had led the despised regicides to ruination. If this plan had a flaw, it was his partners.

"Shit!" Limoëlan stepped in a hole, turning his ankle and slamming him shoulder-first against the cart. It lurched. Something heavy shifted under the sodden pile of hay.

Carbon snatched his arm. "Watch your step, ass! You want to blow us all to ashes?"

A week earlier, on 17 Frimaire (December 17 to the rest of Europe), a grain dealer named Lambel had admitted to his shop in the Rue Meslée a thickset man with a blond beard and a large scar above his left eye. He walked with a rolling gait that spoke of years at sea.

The man paused, breathing in the sweet smell of oats and wheat preserved in barrels; an odor the merchant himself no longer noticed. "Will you hear a proposition?"

"That would depend on the proposition," said Lambel.

"I sell textiles. I recently came into possession of a shipment of brown sugar, which I hope to barter for bolts of cloth in Brittany."

"You'll have no problem selling that lot in Paris. The women in the Tuileries would scratch out each other's eyes for three yards of muslin. For silk they would do murder. I don't exaggerate."

"At the moment I have no way of transporting either the sugar or the cloth. I understand you have a horse and cart for sale."

"I have for a fact."

"Will you take two hundred francs?"

"I would."

Lambel was under no illusion that the man was trading in either cloth or sugar: He had been too quick to offer the money without inspecting the horse and cart. More likely his cargo was English Port, or some other product outlawed by government embargo. But the times were too uncertain to quibble over a fellow's motives, and Marguerite, the mare, was very old and had a cataract. He helped the man with the scar hitch her up and watched him lead her out of the barn behind his place of business.

The man with the scar stopped at a wine shop, where he bought a spare Macon cask large enough to contain sixty gallons. Once again the customer explained that he intended to transport sugar. The proprietor helped him load the cask aboard the cart. From there he went to a shed he'd rented in the Rue Paradis near Saint-Lazare. He drew the doors shut, but they were joined poorly, and neighbors had a largely unobstructed view of what went on inside.

One did not trespass, of course. Was a curious fellow resident no better than a *voyeur*? But there were few enough entertainments at the best of times, and most of them taxed by the Republic; a free show was not a subject for question.

The spectacle taking place across the narrow street was not without curiosity. When two more men appeared and set to work reinforcing the cask with ten stout iron bands, conversing in whispers all the while, it was assumed they were brandy smugglers, hardly an unusual sight that time of year, when a dram was just the thing to drive the cold from one's bones, even at black market prices.

The neighbors paid them little attention after that. The mystery was explained, and as for reporting the activity, there was no telling what miseries may follow any kind of contact with the authorities, however civic-minded. Madame Guillotine seldom distinguished between accuser and accused.

François Carbon was neither a cloth merchant nor a brandy smuggler, but a Brittany-born sailor who came by his fearsome scar when a line broke loose during a storm in the Channel and the frayed end struck him above the eye, gouging out flesh like a piece of grapeshot. He had no sugar in his possession. He'd trained in the proper use of firearms and explosives under Georges Cadoudal, a French Royalist who operated a camp for insurgent expatriates in England, on the estate of a British peer in sympathy with the restoration of the Bourbon monarchy in France. (Where, after all, might it end? George III in exile or executed, and the American parvenu Thomas Jefferson in charge of the Empire? As well a bishop!) Although still in his thirties, Carbon had seen the government of his adopted country change hands three times.

He was determined to make it four.

The two men seen working with him on the cask were Pierre Robinault de Saint-Réjant and a master cooper named Jardin, who'd been recruited to forge and fashion the iron bands. Jardin thought the cask stout enough for its purpose, the storage of wine; but a job was a job, and the man with the scar paid up front and in cash, not in promises or poultry. Saint-Réjant wore his civilian attire with the air of a uniform, snug and tidy and with nothing dangling loose, his handkerchief tucked inside his sleeve. He'd served as a divisional general under Cadoudal, and knew little of casks and cart horses.

A fourth man who visited the shed from time to time was later identified as Joseph Pierre de Limoëlan, an aristocrat who'd seen his father borne, fettered and beaten, past jeering crowds to the *Place de la Revolution* to have his head taken from his shoulders. Cadoudal, a conservative commander not given toward impulsive promotions, had made Limoëlan a major general after he returned from patrol swinging the head of a Jacobin leader by the hair. Individual initiative must be rewarded.

When the cooper left, Limoëlan stood watch at the door while Carbon and Saint-Réjant drew the sacking off two kegs and poured black powder into the cask, then scooped broken and jagged pieces of stone from a barrow and mixed them with the powder; "to slash flesh and pulverize bone," explained Limoëlan, who'd suggested the refinement, "and make as many good revolutionaries as possible."

On Christmas Eve, a street musician strummed a mandolin and sang the refrain of a Catholic hymn outlawed in 1789. He frowned at the small collection of coins in his upturned hat, slung it onto his head without spilling them, a gesture perfected through repetition, and trudged off through the drizzle. Behind him, his corner on the Place du Carrousel glimmered in the light of torches struggling against the rain in front of the Tuileries Palace. Through those same gates, eight years before, King Louis XVI's own gunners had escorted their sovereign to his place of imprisonment, and from there to his execution.

The musician passed three men loitering beside a shabby cart piled with hay, two of them knocking their heels against the wooden wheels to dislodge mud from the soles, a third squatting to feel the fetlocks of a bay mare that didn't look as if it would last to the end of the street.

"Poor buggers," he muttered to himself. All he had to look after was his mandolin.

A patrol of National Guardsmen came along a few minutes later in their blue uniforms and shining oilcloth cloaks, observing the trio still engaged in the same activity. The heightened presence of the sentries suggested that the man in the Tuileries—no king, this, Limoëlan thought; merely a contemptible clerk appointed to govern his betters—was preparing to venture out. The plotters' intelligence was sound.

The patrol slowed as it approached. Seized with a wicked whim, Carbon gestured with his short-barreled pipe; what the English called a bulldog.

"Have you a light?"

The guardsman hesitated, shook his head, and continued walking with his companions.

"Was that necessary?" Limoëlan was the bloodthirstiest of the three and therefore the most cautious.

"I judged it so. In another moment he'd have been searching the cart. This way he knows we have nothing to hide."

"What if he'd given you the light and searched it anyway?"

"Have you ever tried to get a spark out of flint and steel on a night like this?"

"You mistake audacity for valor. It will mean your death."

"Sound advice from a highwayman."

Limoëlan did not respond. If this plan had a flaw, the rash sailor was it; but Carbon was in command and so he swallowed his retort. He and Saint-Réjant had spent many such a dismal night waiting to waylay coaches on the stage roads along the coast—an unbecoming pursuit for generals; but even the great causes needed financing, same as mummery shows and ladies' wardrobes.

For Saint-Réjant, his alliance with Carbon, a sailor-adventurer unhinged from reason by a blow at sea, and Limoëlan, a fanatic who would usher in a new Reign of Terror, only with the executioners and the victims reversed in favor of the monarchy, was far from ideal. If this plan had a flaw, it was they.

The clouds were bottomless. Foul drizzle soaked the conspirators to the skin and chilled them to the bone.

Perfect weather, Limoëlan thought, for a funeral of state.

Moving quickly now before another patrol could appear, the men backed the cart into position, not quite blocking the street, but obliging any passing traffic to slow and swerve round it. Carbon and Saint-Réjant tilted the heavy cask while Limoëlan unwound the oilcloth from a twisted length of twine and inserted it in the hole drilled in the top. The fuse was impregnated with gunpowder: the fast-burning variety intended for muskets.

"How much time?" Saint-Réjant helped right the cask.

Carbon's teeth ground on his pipestem. "Who's to say? The cocksucker is always early. Ask the Austrians."

"I meant the fuse."

"Then say what you mean. Six seconds, give or take."

"Give or take what?" Limoëlan asked.

"Give or take the life of one Corsican more or less."

Saint-Réjant crossed himself, an automatic gesture.

Carbon smiled in the darkness. "Careful, my friend. We are surrounded by atheists."

Limoëlan did not smile. "In a little while they'll be surrounding themselves."

2

"It's *Creation*. Haydn's one of your favorites, isn't he?"

"I daresay Haydn is more popular with me than I am with him, since the surrender of Vienna."

"You bring politics into it only to confuse me."

Bonaparte scowled at his wife. It was the same expression he wore in Thomas Phillips' official portrait, and in fact would wear in the hundreds to come.

"In any case," he said, "the composer must survive without me for one night. I've been up since dawn, making laws, with imbeciles to tutor me in the language. They're essential, but no fit company for a man with even a spark of intelligence. I've been wailed at by castratos enough for one day."

"But you're expected at the opera! You can't disappoint your subjects tonight of all nights."

"They're citizens, like myself, not subjects. You talk like a Royalist. And what night are you speaking of?"

"Christmas Eve!"

"Christ is in exile, haven't you heard? It was in every broadside."

He was only pretending to be annoyed with his wife. She was at all events a pretty little thing, and especially fetching tonight, in snow-white ermine with her tiny hands buried in a muff to match, a creature impossible to hold a grudge against. He himself was in shirtsleeves. Without the high-collared tunic of rank, he might have been a common shopkeeper relaxing in his armchair at the end of a day of trading, and like any common shopkeeper, being badgered by his mate. He was six years younger than she, but looked older for his cares; it was no small thing for a man of thirty-one to govern a country.

"Don't debate with me, Bonaparte. I'm not one of the other Consuls. Your sister and Hortense have been looking forward to this evening for weeks."

"Then go, with my blessing. We both know you're quite capable of entertaining yourself without me."

"As are you, my little general; your every movement is an affair of state, and widely reported. But you'll find this a pleasant distraction."

They were in the drawing room, where he'd retired after bolting supper: "Versailles dining," with its endless courses and meandering conversation, broke his patience. Logs chuckled on the grate: Even they were amused by his displeasure at the prospect of leaving them on such a night.

He drained his goblet and brushed uselessly at a fresh crimson spot on his white waistcoat. "I see my blunder now. I opened with an argument based on exhaustion, offering my own weakness as a defense. The battle was lost before it was joined. I capitulate."

"Must everything be about war?"

"No. Yet it is." He smiled; knowing full well the perfection of his teeth and the disaster that was hers. "Don't furrow that child's brow with things beyond your understanding. Be quick with your toilet. I wouldn't wait for Murad Bey, and I won't wait for you."

She had no earthly idea who Murad Bey was, but flounced out on the heels of her victory, silk rustling against satin. Women, was there no defense against them after all these centuries? A single petticoat was worth a battery of cannon.

Fifteen minutes in his dressing room, with the expert assistance of Constant, his valet, saw him outfitted from the skin out in cologne, fresh breeches, crepe-soled pumps, Irish linen (pre-embargo), and a scarlet cloak, spun from fleece and brocaded in gold, with epaulets on the shoulders. That excellent servant adjusted his master's bicorne hat at the preferred angle and stood back to let him regard his image in the cheval glass.

"What a peacock I've become."

"Not at all, sir. You wear your clothes like the Prince of Wales."

"You alone could get away with the comparison. I cut a better figure in the rags of a half-pay general."

"Shall I ask if Madame First Consul is ready to depart?"

"Is César ready?"

"Yes, Citizen Bonaparte."

"She's had a quarter-hour to powder her nose. Tell her I'll see her in our box."

Constant bowed and withdrew. In the corridor that led to Josephine's dressing room, he shook his head. While it was certainly true, as had been claimed, that no man is a hero to his valet, he admired his master's ability to shatter a basic rule of marital accord with neither thought nor fear of repercussion.

César was drunk and disgruntled.

He'd been certain, despite popular expectation, that his master would be too exhausted by his labors on behalf of the people of France to venture out this evening. With no prospect therefore of leaving his quarters, the coachman had commemorated the Lord's birth with a bottle of wine.

Now, flushed and lethargic, he buttoned himself into his greatcoat and stroked the muscular neck of the white gelding he prized above the other five in the team; above all the other horses in the world, and most men he had had the misfortune to know. (Dumb brutes, he'd found, were more pleasant company than others of his genus; for instance, they never borrowed money, nor argued politics.)

"Bad news, old fellow. We go out into the worst of nights."

Mameluk tossed his head and shook his mane. He could be as irritable as his keeper and as imperious as César's master. The horse seemed to know its own importance in the scheme of things.

The burly driver, who affected the moustaches of an old campaigner, was one of the few men living who could make a horse understand as if he spoke its language, and the only one the gelding condescended to acknowledge the fact. César poured wine from the long-necked green bottle into his palm and let Mameluk drink. After that he took the bit without resisting.

"Small enough comfort," said the man, helping himself to another swig.

He dashed cold water into his face from the pump in the stable, breathed into a palm, smelled it, and frowned. He rummaged among his personal effects until he found a small sack of peppermints; a gift from the First Consul, who suffered from dyspepsia and assumed (not without justification) that the affliction was contagious among his intimates.

The coachman himself boasted a cast-iron stomach, but like most men partial to spirits he had a sweet tooth, and accepted the boon gladly. Now he helped himself to a handful, trusting pungent candy to wash his breath in the blood of the lamb.

Not that he ran risk of a sacking. He'd driven an ammunition wagon in the Marengo battle, and the First Consul knew that not a French life had been lost for want of a round in his musket.

He opened his battered footlocker, then changed his mind and tucked the sack under the footboard of the state coach instead. Beside it he placed the green bottle, securely corked. This was no night to enter without satisfactory provisions.

At the thought, César pulled at his moustaches, stimulating

the faculties of memory. What was it his master was fond of repeating so often? "An army travels on its stomach."

Just so; but it traveled just as far on its liver.

At last, activity took place before the palace.

Shadows crossed in front of the sputtering torches, the clink
of a bit-chain and the sonorous snort of a grenadier's horse regis-
tering its opinion of the conditions reached the ears of the three
conspirators: The little cocksucker was headed out.

Carbon withdrew himself to a safe distance. Limoëlan crossed
to the corner of the Place du Carrousel, leaving Saint-Réjant with
the mare and cart containing its seasonal greeting. From there he
could see to the end of the street. At first sight of the coach-
and-six, he would signal for the fuse to be lighted.

"What is the signal?" he had asked.

Limoëlan had replied by inserting two fingers into his mouth
and blew a note that split the ears.

A killer among killers! Between them, the others hadn't saliva
enough to raise a whistle.

Saint-Réjant, his breath smoking in the cold, stamped his feet
and bent to tie the rope halter to—

What? There was no post visible in the darkness or within quest
of a groping foot. None of them had thought to bring a picket.

He knew an icy thrill of panic. A fine group of assassins they
were! Marguerite, the quintessential "old gray mare" of lore,
surely would bolt when she caught the scent of a sparking fuse:
She was not, after all, *un cheval de combat,* a warrior steed versed
in the stink and racket of war. A comic-opera scene unfolded in
the imagination of the unfrocked general: a bucking horse towing
a burning powder keg the wrong way down the street, capturing
the attention of Bonaparte's coachman and causing him to haul
back on the reins while the vessel of destruction veered away.

Quel ridicule! A man could not be expected to strike flint and steel and hold a horse at the same time. Not in broad daylight, and certainly not in a monsoon, with every limb shaking from cold and anticipation. And what of the time necessary to establish distance? He did not aspire to become a martyr to a principle; let that honor fall to the enemy.

Curse Carbon! A true general foresaw everything, and remained on post for what could not be foreseen. Saint-Réjant wondered, disloyally, if this sailor, this Channel pirate, had after taking his leave commandeered a café as his forecastle. He might be swilling buttered rum this very moment, warming his toes before a hearth, while his compatriots shivered in the cold in what were more than likely the last moments of their lives.

At that moment he heard a footfall.

In the light reflecting from a puddle, he observed a gaunt female creature approaching, huddled in a cloak and carrying a basket of coal. The cloak was threadbare, the piddling amount of fuel obviously intended for some poor hearth, witness to a household scraping to survive. Why were palaces always built in the worst neighborhoods?

But one did not question Providence.

Saint-Réjant groped in a pocket, counting coins by touch. When the girl came near, he cleared his throat politely.

"Your pardon, *mademoiselle*." He lifted his hat.

The girl started, stopped, withdrew into herself, as if to create a smaller target for assault. Saint-Réjant knew that two hours in filthy rain had not made of him a stranger to inspire trust. And he saw then that she was even younger than he'd thought, a girl in truth. He could be her father. Her *grand*father, if he were but candid with himself; soldiers had opportunity to spread their seed earlier than most. But surely this scrawny thing could not have sprung from the loins of a warrior.

The girl said nothing, holding her basket tight to one bony

hip, as if it were the only thing on her person worthy of plunder.
Naïve creature! Did their mothers teach them nothing, even in
these times? He produced his handful of coppers.

"Would you be interested in earning six sous for the work of
five minutes?"

César was feeling indestructible.

They did not call wine "spirits" for nothing.

A final long pull on the bottle, another handful of peppermints,
and he was truly ten feet tall, physically and in temperament. His
perch atop the First Consul's grand ebony-and-mahogany coach
flying the Tricolor of the Republic from each corner placed him
precariously high above the ground, but he clambered onto his
seat as agile as a cat and slid the whip from its socket. The whip
was a fine supple one of braided calfskin, a Christmas gift from
his master, who forgot no one, general or scullery.

About him the grenadiers of the Consular Guard were mounting, and he felt a little less tall among those plumed bearskin shakos and bayoneted muskets propped upright on their saddles. At
least, the coachman thought, he wasn't the only one turned out
into this shithole of a night.

He blew his nose into the bend of his elbow. It was a preposterous display. The escort alone would outnumber the entire opera
company, and all for a quarter-hour trot that a man on foot could
have completed in the time it took to assemble the party. But logic
was the luxury of the lower classes.

Beneath him the coach shifted, sighing against its leather
braces, and he knew the First Consul was aboard along with Generals Lannes, Bessiers, and Lauriston, his aides-de-camp, like him
mere junior officers but for the Revolution. The presence of a second coach behind César's told him that Madame Bonaparte and
her party would be traveling separately.

A good coachman, the Madame's; although not on a par with César, or he would be sitting in his place, coddling the First Consul's testicles like eggs. That one man in a thousand should set out ahead of his wife while she dawdled at her toilet was the stuff of legend. César himself would as lief ask his beloved white gelding to pull a plague-wagon. The waiting ritual alone had been sufficient to keep him a bachelor all these years.

A pair of thumps from inside—a stick against the roof—and he shook the reins. With a final snort of protest, the team started forward, muscles undulating in the rear pair's rumps, as effortlessly as if they were pulling nothing at all, instead of the hope and future of a nation.

3

Moments behind the departure of the coach carrying Bonaparte and his aides, his wife Josephine, accompanied by her seventeen-year-old daughter, Hortense, and sister-in-law Caroline Murat, the last heavily pregnant with her warrior husband's child, boarded the second coach. It had scarcely pulled away from the portico when Josephine signaled for the driver to stop.

"I'm sorry, dears," she told her companions. "This scarf won't do. The color is all wrong."

"How can you tell, in this wretched light?" asked her daughter.

"I've felt it all along, but now that we're underway I *know* it. I wish you would trust me in these things at least."

Caroline fanned herself. The chill of a Paris Nivose made no headway against the changes in the body of an expectant woman. "How you carry on! As if the fate of the world turned upon a scrap of silk."

Josephine had long since declared herself *hors de combat* with her in-laws, who hated her to the ground, as much for her social polish as for her infidelities; there was no court of appeal for the damned. She lowered the window and thrust her head out. "I *am* sorry," she told the driver, tilting that head toward the palace with a toss of auburn curls, her irresistible little-girl pout in place.

The driver complied—how could any man not, regardless of his social position?—backing the horses to the mounting-block to spare the Madame from spoiling her slippers in the mud. She alighted and re-entered the palace.

"How many hours have we spent waiting for her?" said Caroline, with a sigh.

"I'm used to it. But sometimes I think my stepfather is right not to put up with it." Hortense nestled her face into her fur rugs and awaited her mother's return.

From somewhere up ahead came a shrill whistle.

"Heavens!" Caroline's fan climbed to a blur. "What prey can a hawk hope for at this hour?"

Limoëlan's signal was short and piercing, accomplished as before by placing two fingers in his mouth and whistling through his teeth, a talent Pierre Robinault de Saint-Réjant reflected upon with boyish envy.

And entirely unnecessary.

A tyrant and his escort make as much noise as a battalion. Clank of spurs, jingle of chains, rattle of swords in their scabbards, and the heavy exhalations of tall horses prancing fore and aft between the traces, had Saint-Réjant on the balls of his frozen feet well before the signal, which in truth was nearly drowned out by the din. The damned incessant rain brought it to his ears as across the surface of a lake. He might have been riding in the coach right beside the upstart.

Indeed, the entire street was aware of the approach of the First Consul and his entourage: Shops which moments before had been dark and shuttered were suddenly alight with lanterns and candles, their doors and windows flung open and merchants framed inside, straining to witness the spectacle and cheer as it passed. Even the little girl whom Saint-Réjant had engaged to hold the horse stood on tiptoe, leaning forward, head turned toward the Tuileries, one hand gripping the frayed halter, the other the precious coins Saint-Réjant had given her, her basket of coal slung by its handle in the crook of one arm.

"Thank you, Citizen," she'd said when the pittance changed hands.

The hated Republican address made him wish to strike her. But rain and darkness hid the fury on his face.

She had an upturned nose and a large forehead, like an infant's. Her one visible eye in profile was open wide, the lashes long enough to cast a shadow on her prominent cheekbones. Had such innocence really survived the Terror?

Despite his mounting excitement, the Royalist general spat bitterly into the gutter. Since the defeat of the Austrians in Italy—no, before that; since the English were routed from Toulon by a raw major of artillery, Bonaparte had been the country's big attraction. His gaunt likeness decorated cheap snuffboxes and tins of candy in shop windows throughout the ghastly Republic. An entire industry existed to sell him, as much as the trinkets themselves: *Advertisement,* they were calling it now; whoring made respectable by open commerce. People were sheep, and Bonaparte swung the crook.

When he hired the team, Cadoudal had given orders merely to kidnap him and force him to surrender the country to its rightful heirs; but Limoëlan had ruled that out.

"What is the good of that?" he'd told the others. "His gullible flock would demand his reinstatement, and the government would swoon once again before the mob. But death is an argument without a rejoinder. There is no line of succession, and another generation at least must pass before a man of his diabolical talents appears. Meanwhile we take measures to ensure that history does not repeat itself."

Carbon had been reluctant. "But would that not make us no better than the rabble who murdered the King?"

Saint-Réjant, who was easily swayed by rhetoric if not Jacobin bullets, had thought this a good point. But Limoëlan had offered an argument as sound.

"*Petit* François! Can't you see the difference between assassinating a man placed in his position by God, and slaying a peasant from a slum of an island in the Mediterranean? The flaw inherent—the fatal flaw—in electing a man dictator for life is you leave the people with but one way to vote him out of office."

"We should discuss this with Georges," Saint-Réjant had suggested.

The major general shook his head.

"He is on the other side of the Channel, and that pig Fouché has spies at every port. We risk interception and execution after a sham trial. The lives of four men are nothing compared to our cause, but discovery would mean a delay of months—years!—while that monster in the palace gathers power."

Fouché. For Saint-Réjant, the mere mention of the name ended the discussion. The shadowy chief of Bonaparte's Ministry of Police was bathed in the blood of Royalists and the clergy. Mothers sent their children to bed with the threat that Joseph Fouché would get them if they disobeyed.

Carbon shuddered; he who had faced tempests at sea, and jeered at Neptune himself. He protested further, but any idiot could see Bonaparte must be destroyed. And when a plan was agreed upon—a ridiculously simple one, but it was the clever conspiracies that came most frequently to grief—Carbon was the one who volunteered to secure the gunpowder.

The first pair of grenadiers was in sight, their mounts reflecting shoplight off their splendid white coats, raiments glittering. Saint-Réjant snuffled up snot, drew away the oilcloth placed atop the cart to protect its contents from the rain, and struck flint against steel.

The first sparks fizzled. Rain had penetrated the cover, extinguishing the glowing points where they landed. He felt a stab of panic. Then a spot of red flared, faded—held. He blew on it, coaxing forth smoke. At length the straw caught with a sweet smell of scorched grain and carried the flame to the fuse. It sputtered and sparked. More smoke stole upward, a thread and then a column, accompanied by the spoiled-egg stench of sulfur.

Marguerite, the half-blind mare, smelled it and lurched, but the little girl had a firm grasp on the halter and the old mare was too spent to resist.

A reliable child, Saint-Réjant considered. What a shame she was a Republican. He parted company from her in three long strides, then broke into a run.

César frowned at the sight ahead. Some fool peddler had failed to pull his horse and cart off the right-of-way, leaving what looked like a slip of a girl to hold the animal. In a sober condition, he might have slowed down and maneuvered the coach cautiously round the obstacle. But the escort riding up front had kept its pace, and he was drunk, and damned if he'd be called timid by popinjays in plumes.

He unfurled his fine calfskin whip, cracking apart the air alongside Mameluk's ear. The princely beast responded with a virile whinny and a fresh clatter of hooves. César felt the wheels turn faster as if lifting away from the mud. Folly, under most circumstances. In this case, prudence would have led to tragedy.

The blast rang clear to the suburbs, a thump that flattened the air and sounded like near thunder. It shook windows as far away as the Marne, three miles from the city. At close range it burst eardrums. A gigantic ball of orange flame rolled forth like a cannon barrage, followed by a dense volume of black smoke and sawdust from the obliterated cask and cart, along with a spray of blood.

The concussion gutted buildings on both sides of the Rue Saint-Nicaise, killing some residents in their beds, hurled grenadiers off screaming mounts lacerated by pieces of sharp rock, and turned one of the master cooper's iron hoops into a spinning buzzsaw blade. It tore away the breasts of a woman standing in the open door of her establishment, the *Café d'Apollon* ("If the First Consul sees me as he passes, I'll simply swoon!"). Bodies rose on a wave of superheated air and fell to the street with a wet slap like bundles of laundry striking, followed by a pattering noise: pieces of an old mare named Marguerite and of a fourteen-year-old girl named Pensol, pelting the earth from rooftop height. Some thought it was hail.

The coach carrying the First Consul's wife and her party caught the outer edge of the explosion, throwing the team into a rearing, neighing frenzy, the coachman hauling back on the reins as the terrified horses pawed the air and tried to twist free of their harnesses. The windows fell apart. A shard of glass sliced across the back of Hortense's hand, releasing a gout of blood that sent Josephine, her mother, into a faint; or as close to one as her training had brought her. Caroline, Bonaparte's sister and the wife of one of the grandest generals of the Republic—certainly one of the most expensively tailored—slammed into the side of the coach, fetching a blow to the head of the fetus in her womb. The boy would be born an epileptic.

Had it been a hundred feet back of its position at the moment of detonation, the lead coach would have been blown to bits as surely as the shop fronts flanking the street. Had the second coach been a hundred feet *ahead* of its position, it would have suffered the same fate.

History often hangs upon such trifles as a scarf and a bottle of wine.

César brought his master's coach to a halt with the aid of all his muscles and his complete vocabulary of curses. It was still swaying on its leather braces when Bonaparte sprang to the ground, followed closely by Generals Lannes, Bessiers, and Lauriston, experienced soldiers seasoned by the atrocities of war but shaken nonetheless by this cataclysm in the heart of a civilized city. Lannes, like Bessiers and Bonaparte a veteran of the Italian Campaign, noted with annoyance that his brand-new lorgnette, purchased especially for tonight's opera, had a cracked lens.

"Can you see my wife's coach?" Bonaparte's voice shook—with rage, possibly; with trepidation, perhaps. The great man was known to be uncharacteristically illogical on the subject of his legitimate mate. Most Frenchmen of note reserved such sentiments for their mistresses.

Bessiers, whose eyes had correctly foreseen fierce resistance on the Arcole bridge, peered through the gloom and smoke. Flames lapped at frame buildings, illuminating the length of the street as brightly as during a victory parade.

"It stands, sir. The driver appears to be helping one of the ladies down from the coach."

"Idiot! There may be snipers."

"I think not, sir." This from Lauriston, who affected the nasal speech of a member of the aristocracy; either a suicidal fool, thought Lannes, or a man destined for a title. Was the hunting season still in force on the gentry, or not? Confusing times, these. "A charge of that magnitude indicates confidence of its success."

Bonaparte folded his hands behind his back and stared at the mud creeping round his pumps. His feet looked impossibly small when not sheathed in boots. At length he lifted his chin and nodded, a brittle movement. "Very well."

The four reboarded the coach. The First Consul leaned out the open door. "Proceed."

"*Oui*, General." César pulled at his moustaches, burped pure red wine, and cocked his whip. He wasn't precisely aware of what had taken place; in his state of mild befuddlement he suspected a spectacle of holiday fireworks gone wrong. Bastille Day in particular was notorious for claiming eyes and limbs in the orgy of celebration.

Years later, dangerously obese and crippled with gout, the coachman would grumble that he should have received a citation of valor for saving the life of the First Consul. Instead, he was docked a month's pay for being drunk on duty.

With the exception of the epileptic child, neither the prime target of the Christmas Eve Plot nor anyone connected with him, personally or professionally, was seriously injured by the attempt. Bonaparte himself—for the time being—was only mildly perturbed. Rage would follow; but no blood pact was ever struck with only the object of angering the intended victim. The affair was regarded throughout Europe as a horrendous failure, and a serious setback, politically speaking, to the forces in legion against the French Experiment.

Georges Cadoudal was warming his soles before the fire of his English host when word reached him. He expressed shock, and blamed the rabid Jacobins: "Revolutionists take cold-blooded murder with their morning milk."

The night of the explosion, Bonaparte sank back into the velvet-upholstered seat of his coach with his arms crossed. This was not the time to spin theories. He was late for *Creation*, and there was no telling if the curtain would be held. Theater directors were tyrants of punctuality.

He needn't have worried. The performance was delayed until his arrival, and when he entered his box, all those seated in the orchestra rose to acclaim the Savior of the Republic. He bowed, then gestured toward the red-white-and-blue bunting of the Republic framing the stage and placed his right hand to his heart.

Josephine, meanwhile, was hysterical. Her coach returned to

the palace, where doctors were summoned to examine her sister-in-law and bandage her daughter's hand. Her own personal physician, a quack in a powdered wig left over from the Royal court, prescribed tincture of opium to help her rest.

As the drug clouded her senses, she asked for her husband. She lost consciousness without hearing the answer.

Which was just as well. The First Couple of France were both hot-blooded islanders, sharing the same fierce temper.

4

In his office on the Quai Voltaire, not far from the Rue Saint-Nicaise, Joseph Fouché heard something that might have been a door slamming somewhere in the building. He paid it little attention; there was always some officious government supernumerary in residence who assumed that a show of haste was evidence of efficiency. In any case the shelves of books that surrounded Bonaparte's police chief, exquisitely bound in leather, gold, and watered silk, absorbed much of the noise.

He went about his present task with the measured precision he brought to all things.

Fouché had every lamp burning, along with a stump of candle on his desk, making the room as bright as day. It was a necessary expenditure in a time of austerity. He was staring through a heavy convex glass at the top of a wine cork sealed with vermilion wax, looking for the tiniest of holes.

He resembled the ecclesiastic he'd once set out to be: cadaverous, stoop-shouldered, and hollow-chested, with a habit when deep in thought of dry-washing his long yellow hands, like a minister presiding over a funerary service. The simple black tailcoat and gray knee-breeches he wore when the occasion did not call for the blue-and-silver velour of his office spoke of the pulpit; but he was no priest. He'd been spared that obsolete profession by Providence and the Revolution. He was France's judge, jury, and executioner, and clerics came under his jurisdiction as enemies of the state.

The Church had lost a fire-and-brimstone servant when Joseph

Fouché threw aside the cassock for a seat on the National Convention in 1792. In that post he had voted to kill the King.

Later, directed by the Committee of Public Safety to root out disloyal factors in the provinces, he'd ordered the infamous Massacre of Lyons, slaying seventeen hundred citizens for the crime of disloyalty.

He'd stood the first lot between trenches and blasted them with cannon. Sabers dispatched the survivors, matchlock muskets and the guillotine saw to the rest. Some were accommodating, falling directly into the trenches; others had to be kicked. A number of them were his former fellow divinity students. *De-Christianization*, the Revolutionary government called it. The Committee hadn't the ironic sense to recognize the truth in the term.

That had been under the Committee of Public Safety. After that body fell, much of it into other trenches, the Directorate followed. Immediately after taking power, the First Consul himself had appointed Fouché to the Ministry of Police. Reminded that the man was nothing more than an assassin, Bonaparte shrugged. "He is the sort of man we need in an affair like this."

Like Bonaparte, Fouché appeared to subsist mainly on oxygen, sleeping only a few hours out of twenty-four and, when his belly demanded, snatching an unbuttered roll and a draught of water on his way out to attend to the duties of his office. He was no *gourmand*. His taste buds, like his faculties of mercy, were underdeveloped. He could eat lamb in champagne sauce followed by a rotten egg and not notice the difference.

He spared his appreciation for things less ephemeral.

At length he found what he was looking for through the thick glass: a hole the size of a pinprick in the sealed cork.

That wouldn't do. The fellow was a fool as well as a thief, but his eyes were younger than those of the police chief.

He applied the flame of the stubby candle—vermilion also—to the wax, softening it, then smoothed over the blemish with the ball of his thumb. He set aside the bottle and passed time reading one of the police reports heaped on his desk, a fantastical mass of solid mahogany carved into gryphons and other mythical creatures. It had belonged to an aristocrat, since deceased.

It was a surveillance report, compiled over a forty-eight hour period in the case of one Felix Desmoulins, an army quartermaster suspected of stealing supplies and selling them on the black market. The operatives had dined where he dined, whored where he whored, and kept tabs on everyone with whom he came into contact, providing descriptions when the names were unknown. The pages would fill a substantial pamphlet.

The outlook for Citizen Sergeant Desmoulins was grim.

Humming to himself, Fouché selected another sheet and filled out a warrant for the man's arrest. Small enough fry, but he would name his co-conspirators before a musketeer's ball released him from the cares of this world.

The wax on the cork had hardened by the time he sealed the document and slid it inside his dispatch case. He examined the wax again through the glass, pronounced the result satisfactory, and returned the bottle of wine to its rosewood cabinet where he could be sure his servant would find it. He took the precaution to identify it for his own safety with an infinitesimal scratch at the base of the neck from the diamond ring on the small finger of his right hand. It wouldn't look well for a highly placed official to drink his own poison by mistake.

The rest of the evidence—a metal tube with a plunger at one end—he disposed of by stopping the hollow point on the other end with a cork and placing it in his safe, locking it securely with the only existing key, a small gold one attached to his watch chain. He was grateful to Monsieur Jenner for the invention of the hypodermic syringe, a development but two years old, designed to introduce his smallpox vaccine into the bloodstreams of willing subjects. Fouché admired it not for its humanitarian use, but for its part in his own contribution: the means by which a man could lace wine with deadly arsenic, the victim unaware that the bottle had been tampered with.

It was an experiment in a more effective type of execution than either the noisome firing squad or the unwieldy guillotine, but he could not be certain of its success until he put it in practice. The servant was a contemptible sneak who thought he could sample the product of his master's excellent wine-cellar undetected, merely because he assumed no account was kept of the number of bottles in his cabinet. Fouché despised small thieves: Why filch a bottle of wine, when there were countries to be stolen? As well pilfer needles and buttons like that imbecile quartermaster. How much better to align oneself with a Bonaparte, for as long as he lasted. The Minister himself hadn't paid a sou for his books and statuary, the extravagant fixtures that had transformed his policeman's office into a museum.

Arsenic poisoning was a hideous way to die, with excruciating cramps and vomiting, and the coma near the end its only respite; but what the compound lacked in mercy it more than made up for in effectiveness, and Fouché was not a fellow who trusted to chance. He would, of course, attend the man's burial ceremony out of respect for his months of service, and cluck over the sudden tragic attack of some mysterious malady in the prime of life. Medical science had still much to learn so early in a new century.

The pettiness of the offense was immaterial. A man who would steal from his master would betray his country. Had Louis Capet acted to snuff out all intrigues at the beginning, he would still have his crown, and a head to wear it.

Mostly, the chief was curious to see if the trick worked.

He sighed. His method really was an ingenious device, almost on a par with Jenner's great discovery, and it was a pity he couldn't claim credit. But he was a realist, a true child of the Age of Reason, and resigned himself to anonymity. Somewhere, sometime, someone would receive the credit; most probably the fellow would not seek it, and pay the price.

He inspected his watch: quarter to nine *post meridian,* allowing for the five minutes he set it ahead, to maintain his reputation for punctuality. Early to bed, for once, that the Republic should receive full measure of his devotion beginning before dawn.

He was blowing out the last lamp when a loud knock came to his door, the reports so close together they sounded like a fusillade.

Fouché frowned. Plainly this was not the unctuous knock of his dishonest servant. It was the one employed by his own officers when the matter was pressing.

Groping in the dark, he drew a tinder box from his desk and reignited the lamp. He thought back to that earlier noise and wondered if perhaps it had not been a door slamming after all.

5

"Jacobins! Cowards with cunts instead of cocks! They would blow up a convent, burn down an orphanage, just to get me! The firing squad is too good for this human shit. That's a death reserved for military officers. The guillotine is too swift. They should be tied up in sacks and drowned in the Seine like common curs! The fish can feed on their balls, small sustenance that it is!"

The Tuileries had rarely, if ever, borne witness to so raw a display of barracks language. Even the sallow Fouché—who it was said was the one man Bonaparte feared—blanched further in the presence of his superior's volcanic rage.

Face red as claret, gold-laurel collar sprung, the First Consul pounded the desk in his private study with both fists; the tantrum of a spoiled toddler, grotesque in a grown man. One grew sick in its presence. Was it genuine? Was he acting? Could even he tell? That was the crux of his singular position on the world's stage. The theatre had lost another Talma when the Corsican had chosen the military.

"Drowning would be an interesting change," Fouché said, "but time-consuming, and we need the sacking material for uniforms. What makes you so certain this was the work of Jacobins?"

That sect, the first to have called for the death of Louis XVI, was hell-bent upon eternal revolution. They'd have made the Terror a permanent fixture of government had not Robespierre, its architect, himself followed his thousands of victims to the scaffold.

"Who, if not them?" But the unexpected question had halted Bonaparte's wrath.

"There are others just as eager to see the government fall. Foreign powers, for example."

"Unlikely. I gave them reason last time to think twice before they pinch the eagle."

Fouché's tone was silken. "Of course, kings and princes never act against their countries' best interests."

"You're trespassing in Talleyrand's yard. He won't thank you for it."

"The Foreign Minister confides in me when our yards overlap, as do I in him." That smooth fellow was as easy to admire as he was to despise.

"No. Who else?"

He'd saved his favorite for last. "Royalists."

"Those powder puffs? You're mad."

"Perhaps they've changed the color of their powder."

The First Consul scowled at his reflection on the desk's glossy top. It was seldom so bare, even at this early hour. Every evening, some trusted adjutant cleared it of its burden, and every morning it was heaped once again with books splayed open and maps the size of bedsheets, sticky from handling by fingers stained with peppermint. There was, of course, the inevitable sack of striped sweets, intended to settle the nervous stomach of the head of state. They had their work cut out for them this day.

The fact that the First Consul had chosen to stay in the Tuileries, when he preferred to spend Christmas at Malmaison, Josephine's charming house in the country, underscored the meeting's dire purpose. Every member of the government, and all of the military, had been recalled to duty pending a definite plan of action. Fouché longed for the local peppermint concession. A plague of dyspepsia was in store.

"Bah!" Bonaparte turned his back, locking his hands behind him in a characteristic pose. "Those perfumed rascals haven't the stomach for murder."

"I suggest they've developed one since the head of their king rolled into a basket."

"It's too direct for them. They started the rumor that I was dead on the Nile. They invent vacuums, which they hope to fill just by existing. They don't actually bring them about. Instead they play croquet on lawns borrowed from the nobility and depend on others to do the dirty work, like the English who shelter them."

The Minister of Police patted back a yawn. Bonaparte turned just in time to see it.

"Am I boring you? Is the near prospect of my own destruction—and three of the women in my family—not enough to keep you alert?"

"No, Citizen. It's just that I've been up all night."

"You think I have not?"

Not all of us have managed to turn insomnia into an asset; but the thought remained unspoken. Fouché was determined to reintroduce calm. Such meetings were fire and ice, with the police chief obliged to supply the latter.

"I merely ask that you consider my suggestion. This government has too many enemies to discount any of them at this point."

"Perhaps you've forgotten the Jacobins tried to carve me up like a Christmas goose in the opera house earlier this year? They're so keen on mayhem for mayhem's sake they lack even the imagination to change their venue."

"I have hardly forgotten. Perhaps it has slipped *your* mind that I heard them spilling their plans—by listening for just that, not by happenstance—and spared you that fate."

"Water under the bridge!" The Strong Man of France was working himself into a fine new lather, and it was no metaphor; spittle actually bubbled in the corners of his classically shaped mouth. "For the love of Christ, Fouché, these jackals poisoned my snuff!"

"*That* showed imagination, you must admit."

"As if a man who kept the positions and numbers of scores of regiments in his head—in his head!—in the course of a campaign would not notice the difference between the box he carries every day, a gift from the Emperor of Austria, and a cheap imitation. These ragged rebels seek to make war on a pauper's budget. What is the current market rate of a charge of gunpowder?"

Much less, thought the other, than the price of the scarf Josephine had returned to the palace to retrieve.

"Still, Citizen, I'd like to make inquiries abroad. All these Royalist plots originate in England, as you pointed out. Allow me at least to brief the spies I've placed in their circles. They could do with some exercise. They've grown fat on black market caviar."

Again Bonaparte's fist came down. The desk, more splendid even than Fouché's, was made of some African wood liberated from Egypt, and boomed like a regimental drum.

"You will confine your investigation to France! These rats burrow into holes throughout the countryside. You will make arrests! I will prepare a list to get you started."

"That won't be necessary. The Ministry has files."

At this, the First Consul abruptly changed tactics. Fouché's files were infamous, but what they contained was known only to him. Was this a logistical retreat? Impossible to say. The man changed moods the way his lady changed ensembles.

He popped a peppermint into his mouth and crunched. He had the jaws of a mastiff. "What is Dubois up to?"

The Minister scratched his long thin nose, dissembling his distaste for Dubois. The Prefect of the Paris Police was altogether too capable a man for the comfort of one placed just above his station, and without apparent ambition. That alone was sufficient to inspire distrust. Who in these turbulent times did not hope to capitalize upon them to his benefit? But here was an opportunity to gain a march upon the fellow.

"When I left him, an hour ago, he was inquiring around for an experienced veterinarian to reassemble the remains of the horse that was attached to the"—what was the city press calling it, in those remarkable broadsides that miraculously managed to appear moments after the police themselves arrived at the scene of an atrocity?—"infernal machine."

Thus—*le Machine Infernale*—was the name the journals had colluded upon, to exalt a simple charge of gunpowder placed in a hay cart into screaming headlines.

The gambit backfired. Bonaparte was a native of an agricultural island, who would know about such things as livestock. He appeared interested.

"Reconstruct the carcass? To what end?"

"It is his conviction that by this means the animal can be identified, and the man or men who hired it identified also."

Had he scored? Impossible to tell. One moment the man was as transparent as cheapest muslin, the next his thoughts were enclosed within a square of armed infantry. A dedicated bureaucrat could spend a lifetime attempting to collate and codify the structure of a Bonaparte and end up filing him under *miscellaneous*.

The First Consul straightened and buttoned his collar.

"I want reports, Minister. On the hour, unless you uncover something useful in the interim. I want the Jacobins responsible in irons or dead, and the rest nullified. By Easter!"

Fouché thought it impolitic to point out that Easter was just another day in the Republican calendar. He inclined his head and left.

6

"Is this all?"

The veterinarian shrugged; a Gallic specialty that made Dubois feel shame for the French.

"One cannot say for certain, *Monsieur le Prefect*. Under these conditions, parts of people and parts of animals are a challenge to sort out. Fortunately, people don't have hooves."

Louis Nicolas Pierre Joseph Dubois—he had been christened in 1758 for the King, but had judiciously dropped the first name after the Bastille fell—pursed his lips at the man, whose leather apron was stained with blood and gore. Between them, arranged in no particular pattern on a large sheet of butcher's wrap, lay the torn and reeking parts of what had arguably been a horse, if the one hoof that Dubois' officers had scooped up along with the remains of humans sundered by the blast was any indication. Dubois himself reserved judgment. He had not been Prefect nine months, and assistant to the lieutenant-general of police for two years before that, to form conclusions based on evidence so flimsy.

Paris' first Prefect of Police—the post had been established the previous March (19 Ventose by current authority), and its occupant appointed personally by Bonaparte—was not a tall man; he was exactly the height of the First Consul (not that that made him small; his superior was of average height, despite the runt cartoonists made of him in the British press), and wore the simple uniform of an ordinary patrolman without insignia of rank, decorated only with a single row of brass buttons and a broad leather belt, convenient for tucking one's gloves under or one's thumbs, as he was doing now. He'd been offered a white monstrosity with frogs and ropes of gold braid, but had declined it as too grand for a humble public servant, and the devil's trouble to keep clean. Privately he thought it better suited to an organ grinder's monkey.

A plain oilcloth cloaked his shoulders against the rain that had regressed from a drizzle to an icy weep. The hat, a bicorne worn fore and aft like an admiral's in a comic opera, marred the egalitarian effect; but as he was a stickler for regulations he never appeared in public without it. Once behind closed doors it vanished.

When he was bareheaded, he admitted to himself, he lost a great deal of his authority. So, in deference to both duty and presence, he wore it now.

At forty-two his face retained much of its baby fat, and his moustache resembled a caterpillar. Comb and oil was no remedy for his lank brown hair, which hung like crepe on either side of his forehead. Soon after his appointment, his caricature, a swollen infantile head on a puny body, had become a fixture on the wall of every sporting club he had cited previously for its criminal clientele. He would shut them all down and have the offensive illustrations burned, but it would be like kicking apart an ant heap. By the end of the ten-day Republican week, a dozen more would rise in its place. He had no time for it with murderers about.

He sniffled. The city's premier peace officer had caught cold; a bright red nose lent no dignity to his aspect.

"They say you are the best in your field in France," he told the veterinarian.

The man shrugged again. Some men were immune to flattery, which was one of Dubois' most effective methods of persuasion.

"Had I not been as good, you would not have asked for me. Had I been better, I should not have come."

"It's my opinion there's enough material here for someone who remembered the horse to place it. It's only a matter of arranging the pieces in the proper order."

"If it is so easy, put your men to it. My business is with pre-serving life."

"My men are more familiar with human offal than the animal kind. In any case, they are all busy pounding on doors looking for witnesses."

"Monsieur, I am not trained in assembling puzzles."

Dubois regarded the others at work in the courtyard of the Prefecture near the Quai Desaix. One, a cartwright, was at-tempting to match two pieces of a wheel belonging to the vehicle that had been blown apart by the charge in its bed; near it lay both the shafts, which had survived nearly intact while the ani-mal that had stood between them had been reduced to the bloody mess at the Prefect's feet. Another, a seamstress, sorted heaps of charred clothing into piles, pausing only to place a pinch of snuff in one nostril or the other, blackening her nose with her fingers. Near the rear entrance to the building a cobbler stared with arms akimbo at a mountain of shoes, seeking a starting place to look for his work or the work of a competitor. Those who had belonged to all these articles of apparel were either being treated for shattered bones and severe burns or would never have need for them again.

Dubois thought it unlikely any of those responsible for the car-nage were among the casualties; but victims must have names, survivors must be informed.

Puzzles, yes.

"Neither are these others so trained, Doctor," he said. "Yet you see they are doing what they can, as experts in their own fields. I needn't add that the government will be grateful. I answer di-rectly to the First Consul and the Minister of Police."

Double inducement, this choice of titles: first the lump of sugar, then the cudgel.

If the fellow only knew that Fouché was hoping for Dubois' unconventional plan to fall on its face in full view of the chief of state! The Minister had recommended him for this post, but the

Prefect had proven disconcertingly efficient in a political climate that turned topsy-turvy whenever the wind changed, forcing superiors and subordinates to switch places without warning.

Dubois could not so much as feign incompetence, however wise it was to conceal one's light beneath a bushel in parlous times. His fortunes hung upon his favor with the First Consul: Night after night found him at the palace, entertaining his host with salacious gossip uncovered during investigations, seasoned heavily with salty asides best reserved for career soldiers and fellow policemen. The master of France's fate remained outwardly an infantryman at heart. Whether this was by inclination or design could not be determined. The man was a Chinese box.

A jester's role, Dubois', degrading in the extreme; but the colorless Fouché could not compete with it. In any event the Prefect's position was precarious. The slightest indication that he thirsted for advancement would spell disaster. And so he must continue to play the fool, but without precisely committing a foolish act.

Politics, *phui!* He wanted nothing other than to be let alone to do his job.

Put a name to the horse, connect it and the cart to their original owner or owners, and the men who brought it here were as good as in the hands of justice. That was police work.

Fouché, on the other hand, went about his like a hyena, searching for weakness in his rivals and pouncing upon it, securing his own position through fear. A man like that would never understand the basic principles of investigation, the endless sweeping and accumulating, the simultaneous picking through and piecing together of scraps—most of them meaningless, but at the start there was no telling which—all by a drab army that labored day and night, without hope of honors or simple recognition, moving backward and backward until they arrived at the place where the thing had begun.

No one feared Nicolas Dubois. At worst he was a minor annoyance.

Which was where his enemies went wrong. He was as ruthless as any Septembrist once he caught the scent.

In this minor engagement with the veterinarian, he'd succeeded in cowing the opposition. The fellow ran a hand through his rumpled gray hair, streaking it with blood, and knelt to his task.

Dubois left him for his own, a desk heaped with anonymous letters directing the attention of the police to the culprits who were certainly responsible for the massacre. They had been streaming in ever since the first broadside had gone out announcing the cowardly attempt on Citizen Bonaparte and his immediate family.

Merde.

It was the Terror all over again, neighbors denouncing neighbors to settle old grudges, brothers and sisters hoping to snatch away the family inheritance with the help of the authorities, to whom fell the chore of separating the wheat from the chaff, the shit from the silver.

Not, perhaps, as filthy a task as handling burned shoes and blasted vital organs, but every bit as disillusioning.

It was a good job Christmas was outlawed. He should hate to have to spend it this way. Inside the narrow corridor leading to his office he thrust his cloak and the ridiculous hat into the arms of a secretary and marched to his door.

7

The Lord—make that the State—deliver a man from amateurs; this was Dubois' prayer.

Discounting those accusations that were patently the inventions of invidious Parisians, and discarding outright those that were unsigned, the clerical workers Dubois had pressed into service to free his men for other duties spent hundreds of hours matching names to official files. They reported their findings to the Prefect, who dispatched forty-eight teams of officers, each commanded by a police commissioner, to question witnesses and suspects who might shine light on the Christmas Eve affair. Based on their reports, one hundred thirty known Jacobins were questioned, then forcibly expelled from Paris and warned—in some cases with physical encouragement (Officer Junot was particularly suited to this activity, having trained after hours in the brickyards) not to return on pain of imprisonment or death. A shattered rib cage and the loss of a kneecap were persuasive arguments in favor of exile.

Bonaparte himself contributed names to the list on hastily scribbled sheets of foolscap stuck together with peppermint, which were brought by messengers to the Police Ministry and Fouché's private quarters in the Rue de Bac, many in the middle of the night when inspiration struck and old insults recalled, with orders to act immediately. *À la carte* retribution was a meal best served cold.

Fouché deeply resented these incursions into his private life. He was genuinely fond of his wife and children, and the experience of the past dozen years had taught him to insert a wide distance between his domestic arrangements and the affairs of state. But off would go his dressing gown, on with his tailcoat, and away messages to his office staff to rouse them from their beds.

Dubois, who frequently attended these midnight confabulations, twitched his smear of moustache and went off to alert the Paris police force. He offered no opinion in the Minister's presence or anyone else's, but privately he regarded these addenda on the part of the First Consul as no improvement over the baseless calumnies that continued to pour into the Prefecture from every quarter. The only difference was that these were signed, by that angry slashing hand in which only the letter *B* was legible.

It had all led to a great show of energy on the part of the Myrmidons, and screaming broadsides, but nothing of account; unless one regarded removing notorious rabble-rousers from under official scrutiny and releasing them abroad as progressive action. The enemies of the Republic were only too eager to harbor French subversives. The First Consul was as adept at raising armies for the jackals as he was for France.

Dubois fumed at such an uncharacteristic lack of vision on the part of his master; but not being a political creature, he lamented only the waste of industry.

Jules Limodin, his chief inspector—a more outspoken type—viewed each new list with mounting distaste.

"If these swine continue to provide names without leaving their own, no one in France is safe. Something must be done."

"I concur," the Prefect replied. "That is, in the case of the *anonymous* denunciations. This one, as you see, bears the seal of the Consulate. You have your instructions."

Limodin saluted, palm forward, and turned on his heel to carry them out.

Good man, Dubois reflected; but so many good men had perished on the altar of the Revolution. The Prefect, for his part, wished only for things to settle down.

But such was not the case. More iron-reinforced wagons rattled away from the extinct monastery of Les Carmes, the political prison that had replaced the Bastille, and another score of accused conspirators were dragged out into the cold, barefoot and in their nightshirts, for a session with the formidable Officer Junot.

Dubois finally confided his doubts to Fouché, who was wearing a black band of mourning for the recent loss of his exceptionally talented personal manservant to an undocumented disease.

"We have nothing to connect these individuals to the incident of the fourth Nivose." The Prefect's language was always correct in these official meetings: *Christmas Eve* would have been inappropriate in the book-lined office on the Quai Voltaire. *Impolitic*, he thought, with bitter irony.

Fouché was admiring the illustrations in some ancient tome plundered from Italy. He gave no indication he'd been listening.

Dubois cleared his throat. "I fear we're wasting all our time and resources inventing a reason to hold on to the people we already have in custody, instead of looking for the ones responsible."

With apparent reluctance, the man behind the desk closed the book, marking his place with a worthless assignat left over from the first Revolutionary government.

"Precisely right, *Monsieur le Prefect*. We could exile or execute every Jacobin in the Republic—in Europe, for that matter—and not touch the true villains. This is a Royalist plot. I feel it in my bones."

Dubois did as well, although his bones were considerably less obvious beneath his healthy quilting of flesh. One could see the very workings of the jointed tubes beneath the sallow skin of the Minister's hands.

"Then why are we not questioning Royalists, may I ask?"

"Because the First Consul has decided it is Jacobins, and as you know, Bonaparte is never wrong."

"Nevertheless I should like to investigate the other possibility, if the Minister has no objections."

Fouché's brows lifted. "Something?"

"Possibly so. More probably not. But we have a description from one of the National Guardsmen on duty that night, of a man standing near a cart who asked him for flint and steel to light his pipe."

"Why have I been told nothing of this?"

"The fellow just came forward. Quite likely it slipped his mind in the excitement that followed, as he claims."

"Likelier still, he was drunk on duty and took the time to sober up."

"I think we can leave that to his commander. In any case it is no crime to happen to be standing near a cart and request a light, even if it's the same cart; it is not even suspicious. No less than a dozen people passed it in the course of the evening, not counting twenty-seven of the National Guard. It's also doubtful a guilty man would risk calling attention to himself in that way. He must have come there with means to ignite the fuse! But the description is specific enough to act upon."

"What is it?"

Dubois read in a monotone from his greasy notebook. "'A stocky man with a scar above his left eye.'"

"Do we know of such a person?"

Dubois shook his head. "That is to say, we do not want for stocky builds and facial disfigurations; since the Revolution we have rather more of both than not. As well separate one crow from a flock."

"Circulate the description regardless. Perhaps our culprit has a mistress with an axe to grind."

"I've taken that liberty. I'm reporting it to you now so you can inform all your . . . people."

"Spies, you mean. I'm not offended by the term." Fouché sat

back with a quizzical smile on his pale features. "What news of your experiment in equine reconstruction?"

"The veterinarian was able to provide us with a description based on the remains. My men are knocking on doors. I have hopes for the cart as well. No two are alike, despite all appearances."

But the Minister was scarcely listening. He thought of the first trip he would make to the Tuileries, should anything come of the man with the scar, and his opening address:

"Your excellency, the Ministry has uncovered something which I feel important enough to report. . . ."

"Citizen?"

He'd almost forgotten the ridiculous little man was there. He looked so much like the officious policemen one saw directing traffic at the Place du Carrousel that one wondered why he was worth so much concern; but what was Bonaparte before Toulon? A shabby lieutenant who spoke French with the accent of a Dago rag peddler. One could no longer count on appearances. As if one ever could.

"Yes, Dubois. Follow up on those descriptions. If we can convince the Strong Man of France that this business is Royalist in origin, we can convince any court."

Not that the courts meant so much as a pile of dogshit under so impatient a governor.

Beginning Christmas Day (5 Nivose, in the official record), Parisians and visitors from the suburbs filed through the Prefecture courtyard round the clock, as if the remains of the cart horse belonged to a great leader lying in state. Some came in response to a broadside asking for assistance from the public, others merely out of curiosity. The officers Dubois assigned to conduct the tour quickly developed a line of questioning that separated the gawkers from those who sincerely wished to contribute to the investigation. The former were turned away at the gate.

The remaining parties entered, examined the splintered boards of the cart, stared at the carcass, which had begun to turn with the weather; they pressed wadded handkerchiefs to their nostrils, scented if they could afford it, and shook their heads. Some appeared relieved that relatives and close acquaintances were not involved. Others seemed disappointed; their opportunity to shine, however briefly, had vanished.

Then three things happened in rapid succession.

Ironically, it was a police inspector who provided the first item of real intelligence based on the display; the investigators had been so intent upon recruiting civilians for the case they had neglected to invite their fellow officers to view the evidence. The man had simply wandered in for a look. The horse meant nothing to him, but the cart resembled one he had passed four days running in the Faubourge du Temple.

Next, a farrier from that neighborhood happened to drop by the courtyard out of curiosity; on his way he actually had to hurry aside to avoid being run down by the commissioner and his team hastening to Faubourge. He inspected the shoe on the mare's one surviving hoof and recognized it as the product of his forge.

"You are certain of this, monsieur?" asked the officer on courtyard duty.

"I should say so. I kept this poor beast shod for four years."

"You know the horse?"

"Naturally. I don't just look at hooves all day."

"To whom did she belong?"

"Lambel, the grain seller in the Rue Meslée."

A messenger was sent to the police team in Faubourge. Lambel was located on the street the farrier had named, and brought.

Chief Inspector Limodin himself accompanied the grain seller personally.

He spent several minutes scrutinizing the horse's head in particular and the bits of bridle that had been reassembled and placed where it had been worn in life. Straightening, he shook his head, as had so many.

Limodin, muttering to himself about cocksure farriers, turned in discouragement to show him the cart.

"Poor Marguerite," said Lambel then.

"Marguerite?"

"She was not worth much, but she did not work hard all her life to die in such a way."

Limodin seized his arm. "You know this horse?"

"I used to own it."

The inspector hauled him to the shattered vehicle. The grain seller recognized it as the one he'd sold along with the mare on the 17th Frimaire, the month of frost, to a man claiming to be a cloth merchant.

"Can you describe this man?"

"A roughneck, Citizen, with a sailor's roll and an evil scar. I would not have bought a bolt from him for fear of attempting to resell it to its proper owner."

"Where was this scar?"

"Above his eye. The left, I think."

Chief Inspector Limodin drew a deep breath—and nearly retched from the stench. The National Guardsman who had refused to give the man in the Rue Saint-Nicaise a light had been quite emphatic about the fellow's scar. "Come with me."

With Limodin present, Prefect Dubois questioned Lambel personally in his Spartan office overlooking the courtyard and its contents, which by then had emphatically outstayed their welcome in all five senses, including the din of buzzing flies. In the interval, the grain seller had remembered more. Standing before the desk, circling his tattered hat brim between his fingers, the man hesitated.

"Come, come, Citizen." The little man with the great responsibility of keeping Paris safe could be unctuous when required. He suspected Lambel was holding back something that was uncomplimentary to his character: Scratch a man in trade, there was always larceny to be found. "We're concerned with murder and nothing else."

The merchant had been holding his breath. Now he let it out with a whoosh redolent of onion.

"He offered two hundred francs. The horse and cart weren't worth it, but the times, monsieur, so many changes in government, licensing regulations, the wholesale grain market—" He shrugged in a way entirely Gallic.

"You made a good bargain. It isn't a crime." Dubois kept his patience. If only the guilty intimidated as easily as the innocent.

"That isn't all. When the other man came and paid—"

"Other man?"

"He was so happy with his friend's purchase he gave me an additional six francs."

Now he pounced.

"*What* other man?"

"He said his name was Brunet. He came with the first man to pay me three days later, and I invited them for a drink in the Rue du Temple. He accepted."

"You must have gotten a good look at this man Brunet"—surely an alias—"in the course of your celebration."

Lambel furnished details, but Brunet's description offered nothing so easily spotted on the street as his companion's scar; that fellow had not troubled to give even an invented name.

Limodin took him to another room, where in response to questions the grain seller repeated the information to a secretary. The inspector was much more imposing physically than his superior, and barked his inquiries like a prosecutor cross-examining a prisoner in the dock. But the Rue Meslée merchant gave him the same answers he'd given the Prefect. As the secretary sprinkled sand on the document, the inspector asked Lambel if he could read.

"No, monsieur."

The secretary read aloud from the paper and Lambel made his mark, with Limodin writing the name beside it and adding his own as witness. Told he was free to go, the man stood, but did not put on his hat or move to the door.

"May I keep the two hundred francs, monsieur?"

"I don't see why not. It was a lawful transaction upon your part."

The man's face relaxed for the first time.

"Thank you, thank you. You see, the last time I was asked about my business, I had to pay ten francs for the privilege of answering."

"When was this?"

"Two years ago."

Limodin nodded.

"Under the Directorate. Well, you needn't worry about such things now." Thanks to Bonaparte, the graft was spread more evenly.

Lambel said "Thank you" twice more and put on his hat. Then he took it off again. "Poor Marguerite."

"Not so poor, Citizen. Had I my way, I would recommend her to the First Consul for a posthumous decoration."

8

"Good night, monsieur."

Without responding, François Carbon, France's most notorious fugitive, took leave of the sisters Saint-Michel and climbed the stairs to his garret, swaying on his sea legs, also from inebriation.

His intimates did not call him "*Petit* François" out of irony. He was no larger than Bonaparte himself, which was not unusual in his former profession. Beefy, brawny sailors existed mainly in popular novels; maritime men were frequently compact of build, to suit the cramped quarters belowdecks. The narrow steps accommodated his small feet, unsteady as they were.

They were steep, nearly as much so as a ladder. They brought memories of the wretches' climb to the guillotine when the Terror was in full swing.

At the top, he crossed himself. He had a sailor's superstition, and to think of such things just before retiring did not promise a good night's sleep.

The sisters shook their heads at his retreating back. As usual, their guest had neither bowed nor offered thanks for the superb meal their girl had served that evening.

In that house, every repast was a seven-course ritual, the table laden with out-of-season delicacies and joints roasted to a golden turn, the desserts worthy of state dinners. The sisters, former nuns done out of a job by the atheistic Republic, forgave the gruff

Breton his bad manners, according to their religious training, and because such men were useful in the struggle to restore the monarchy and the Holy Church. With patience and proper training they would make reliable servants.

Their vows of poverty aside, the Saint-Michels were of good family and lived in a house in the Rue Notre-Dame-des-Champs, a former rectory now carpeted in silk and sparkling with precious metals. Their front windows provided an excellent view of the venerable cathedral they still considered their place of work.

They had been asked by their aristocratic acquaintances to board Carbon indefinitely. They were not told why, but the prospect of intrigue seasoned a life of waiting, waiting—waiting—for the grand event that would return the world to sanity. They took the man in, and resisted the compulsion to glare when he ate truffles off one of their gold-chased knives and guzzled wine their great-grandfather had placed in the cellar during the Sun King's reign as if it were English grog, intended solely for inebriation.

It had been exciting at first, having such a creature living under their roof: the stuff of high adventure, and swashbuckling tales of pirates and smugglers from the coast. But that had been at Christmas, at the height of the excitement over the explosion in the Rue Saint-Nicaise, which had come so near to ridding the world of the appalling Bonaparte. Now it was two weeks into the new year—the new century!—and their boarder's ill manners and assumption of entitlement had tarnished the glitter of adventure.

Carbon, for his part, was bored.

He'd been cooped up in the house so long his sunburn had faded for the first time in his adult life, and he found the sisters' company no more diverting than they had his. When they'd given up trying to draw him into any sort of genteel discourse, they'd fallen to gossiping about neighbors and highborn families who meant nothing to him—indeed, he suspected some of them had either been beheaded or had perished in prison, their names so obviously marinated in the *Ancien Regime* they could not possibly have survived the first frenzy; the sisters' world was inexorably buried in an idealized past.

They were jackdaws cawing nonsensically outside his window, and without cease. It had never been his ambition to be privy to aristocratic tittle-tattle. His sacrifices on behalf of Restoration were purely mercenary in intention; Cadoudal himself had promised him a high commission at journey's end, with a pension and a grant of land in the wine country, where he could live out his days in leisure while others of his class tended the vines and he drank up the profits.

He'd hoped by now to be in close conference with Cadoudal, circulating the word among Royalist troops to strike into the heart of Paris and wrest the Tuileries from the dead hands of the monster. But that fool Saint-Réjant had touched off the fuse too late, and God alone knew where he and Limoëlan had gone after the debacle.

Now Carbon was stuck in this rose-scented prison, waiting for the police to shift their activities away from the city and the ports and out into the countryside, where the Jacobins cowered. Then it would be safe for him to leave the country.

He took some comfort from the fact that the very Revolutionaries who had made a Bonaparte possible should be accused of attempting to end his existence; Police Minister Fouché rarely made such a blunder, aiding the Royalist cause by eliminating its traditional enemy. Surely it was only a matter of time before the two anti-Bourbon factions slaughtered each other.

Meanwhile he fought *ennui* the only way a sailor knew how: stuffing himself with rich foods and sucking up grape.

This night, dizzy and flatulent, he hurled himself fully clothed onto his cot and clutched the rails tight, riding out the storm in his muddled head. At length the inner sea grew flat and he sank into sleep.

The stairs below thundered, gaffing and jerking him back to the surface.

He threw his legs over the side of the cot, but his reflexes were boggy with sleep and spirits. He got to his feet just as the floor hatch crashed open and what seemed a battalion of heavily armed men in uniform collided with him and bore him to the floor.

He tried to speak—*Gentlemen, a terrible mistake has been made!*— but his chest was constricted. The point of a bayonet pierced the skin of his throat, releasing a warm trickle inside his collar. François Carbon knew himself as good as dead.

How the Republic of France found Georges Cadoudal's most trusted menial was this:

After canvassing the neighborhood around the Rue Meslée, where the grain merchant Lambel had sold his horse and cart, police learned that there were at least three men involved. Early eyewitness accounts had prepared them for four, but then the fourth man was located and identified as Philippe Jardin, the cooper who had been paid to reinforce a barrel, a job like all the rest; "Sirs, I assure you I supported the plebiscite in favor of the Consulate." Chief Inspector Limodin was inclined to believe him. He was tortured but mildly.

When the screw was removed, the man confirmed that there had been a horse and cart on the premises at 23 Rue du Paradis.

"Did you see any bolts of cloth?" Limodin asked.

"No. Only the cask."

"Sacks of brown sugar?"

"The cask, that was all."

The chief inspector interviewed others, including Rue du Paradis neighbors and Auguste Marmont, a half-pay general of the Republican Army: a figure above reproach, and therefore not to be tortured.

"Citizen General, I understand you own the shed where the horse and cart were quartered."

"Times are hard, monsieur. The rent is a necessary supplement." He agreed with Jardin's description, in particular of the man with the scar, who had paid cash.

"Did he give you a name?"

"No. But one of the others addressed him as *Le Petit* François." Further, Marmont identified the man's accent as coastal.

At the Prefecture, officers gathered to hear the information.

"I think I know this man," said one, who patrolled the area between the Portes St.-Denis and St.-Martin. "His sister runs a rooming house."

Madame Valon was a self-proclaimed widow who boarded sailors when they were between assignments. She filled in the craters in her face with lead-based powder, and dirty brown strands of hair strayed out from under an ancient white wig tipped with brown, inviting an instant comparison to bird shit.

The house, like its mistress, was in an advanced state of dilapidation, the atmosphere inside sordid. It reeked of cabbage and unemptied chamber pots, a situation that Prefect Dubois found nearly as offensive as assembling parts of a rotting horse.

Dubois, who conducted the interview personally, compared the harridan to a parrot in a seaside inn: The blasphemies that laced her speech appeared to have no meaning to her.

"You have a brother you call *Le Petit* François, Citizeness?"

"I do."

"What is your maiden name?"

"Carbon."

"Your brother, then, is named François Carbon?"

"It would stand to reason."

"When did you see him last?"

"Not in ages."

"Can you be more specific?"

"Certainly not since before Christmas."

Valon and her two adolescent daughters—coarse creatures, after the maternal example—were placed in custody and removed to a place of questioning not mentioned in the city broadsides (or anywhere else), while bulletins issued from the Prefecture bearing the name and description of the fugitive sought in connection with the incident on the Rue Saint-Nicaise. His companions were described also, with the putative *nom de guerre* Brunet—he of grain merchant Lambel's windfall six francs—appended to one.

Relentless, round-the-clock interrogation followed, with the woman and her daughters shaken awake whenever they dropped off to sleep. Dubois, who clung to such scraps of chivalry as a man in his position could support, was discreetly absent during much of this time, and when he stepped in to observe and participate, did not remark upon swellings and bruises. They might have been obtained, after all, when the person under scrutiny fell off her chair from fatigue.

The daughters were the first to break the chain of lies. First one revealed, then the other confirmed, that Uncle François had stayed in the rooming house for a time after Christmas Eve. No, he had not mentioned what he'd been about, or why he preferred not to venture outside during his residence there. No, they had suspected nothing.

Dubois ignored this obvious untruth when they added that he had left the house to stay with friends.

"What friends?" He asked this of each separately. Both claimed ignorance.

"Madame?" he inquired of the mother.

"You must not pay attention to whatever those girls say. They're filthy little liars."

Dubois spoke again to the younger sister. A homely child with a bulbous forehead, she looked more like a stubborn and unpleasant infant than the sullen courtesan she attempted to resemble in her mended petticoats and bead necklace.

"Come, come, little one. Time is not on your side. If your sister speaks first, it will be good for her and bad for you. The workhouse needs healthy hands." He leaned in close, in the attitude of confiding a secret. "Do you know what work is done in a workhouse?"

"No, monsieur." It was barely a murmur, with her gaze on the floor.

"It has the laundry contract from the prisons. Maggots and worse on the stained sheets, and lye soap to spoil your lovely hands for life." In fact her nails were dirty and appeared to have been gnawed by vermin.

The Prefect had counted upon the younger girl to fold like a standard shorn from its lashings; but in this he was wrong. She kicked her feet and sucked in her lips, as if to prevent anything from issuing from them.

Came a knock: Limodin, who had been interviewing the older girl in a separate room. Dubois stepped out into the narrow hallway, impatient with the interruption.

The chief inspector's eyes were bright. His superior forgot his vexation. The older daughter had broken: The maggots had worked the trick.

François Carbon was in custody within the hour.

9

"What I cannot understand is why this man Carbon isn't in the Quai Desaix files," said Nicolas Dubois.

Police Minister Fouché spread his long yellow palms.

"There is no reason he would be. Threats to the government are outside your bailiwick as a Paris police officer. It took an infernal machine to cross you over. Had the attempt been made at Malmaison or Saint-Cloud, you'd have been out of the thing entirely."

In saying this, Fouché neither confirmed nor denied that the man was known to his people. He would hardly confide to a subordinate that his system contained holes; but Dubois himself could scarcely imagine such a thing. The popular phrase "The walls have ears" had originated during the Minister's first year in the post, and in the interim it had become a maxim.

In any event, the cadaverous man with the jaundiced complexion could not be shaken from a deep sense of satisfaction. The reason? After days of relentless questioning under the supervision of Chief Inspector Limodin, Carbon had broken, and broken big. He'd confessed to his part in the assassination attempt on behalf of the Royalist commander, Georges Cadoudal. Neither had any connection with the Jacobins. The fanatic Republicans had not had even so much to do with the plot as the hapless Marguerite.

The First Consul would not care for that. His favorite goat had come away clean.

Fouché bore on his lap, in a worn leather portfolio tied with a cord, that evening's edition of the *Bulletin de la Police,* a newspaper with the most exclusive subscription in France. Only two copies were ever printed, one intended for the Minister himself, the other for the First Consul. It kept both men abreast of what Fouché's truffle-dogs had dug up in Paris and the provinces and was shared with no one, not even Dubois—especially not him. The printing plates were broken apart while the ink was still wet, and the compositor sworn to secrecy or face a firing squad; that position changed hands on a regular basis, lest the lesson be lost through tedium, and the fellow transferred to some bailiwick far beyond communication with Paris. This particular number contained a summary of Carbon's confession, along with other bits of business of no useful interest to the Prefecture. (The decision as to what was or was not of such interest lay, of course, with Fouché himself.)

The two policemen were riding in the Minister's fine carriage to Malmaison, where the First Consul could be found most evenings and *decadi,* or days of rest at the end of each ten-day week in the Republican calendar. It was a ten-mile journey along the Seine. The conveyance was open, not a coach, but the evening was mild for the month of snow and they were not greatly chilled in their cloaks and scarves. Their breath curled slightly in the air sweeping over the windscreen. The ancient chestnut trees flanking the road resembled the buttresses of a cathedral, with the moon a chandelier.

Dubois knew nothing of the *Bulletin* beyond rumors of its existence; but he knew well enough what information the portfolio contained. He hoped he would be invited into this important meeting with Citizen Bonaparte. He should like to see how a truly gifted flatterer managed to convince his master that his humble servant had been right all along concerning the true identity of the conspirators, while creating the impression it was the master's idea from the start.

The Prefect was an investigating machine. His talents were

crude compared to those of a courtier, experienced in the delicate art of feathering one's nest with platitudes. Oh, Dubois
could cosset a reluctant witness until the truth flowed like the
fountains in Citizeness Bonaparte's fabled gardens. But stroking a
civilian and currying a head of state were very different things in
the eyes of one born to the lower classes.

If allowed, he would observe this curious creature Joseph Fouché
at work, not hoping to learn anything of value but marveling at the
spectacle. It would be like looking at a camel or some other strange
beast on display: One could not resist straining closer for a better
look, knowing all the time that at any moment the attraction might
turn its misshapen head and spit something vile into one's face.

"What of this fellow Brunet?" Dubois said. "Carbon would
not go so far as to mention his true name." Hidebound policeman
that he was, he shuddered at the prisoner's refusal to cooperate.
Nose and jaw broken, bleeding from his ears, still he had declined
to give up his accomplices beyond what was already known. The
firing squad when it came would be anticlimactic.

"That one was easy, once we knew Carbon was involved. Pierre
Robinault de Saint-Réjant. He did not scruple to make himself
invisible during skirmishes with the heroes of the Republic, but
his appearance was not sufficiently beyond the ordinary to point
him out without a connection. He commanded a division under
the cream puffs." Broken to the traces though he was by fine living, the Minister remained a Revolutionary through and through,
and liked to employ the derisive popular phrase whenever the
subject of Royalists came up. His instincts aside (and he relied
upon them far more than upon his personal predilections), he'd
hoped for this outcome. His sympathies were Jacobin. His official
responsibilities, and his personal well-being, lay elsewhere.

Certainly, his moral convictions had not prevented him from
placing spies in the inns and taverns where the Revolutionaries
gathered, snuffing out their plots as close to the source as possible.

He profited from his job without shame, but he took his responsibilities seriously.

"What of the third man, Beaumont?"

This was the only name Carbon would give to the conspirator who gave the signal to light the fuse. Clearly it was as much an invention as Brunet's.

Fouché smiled his grim pastor's smile.

"You must allow a magician his little tricks. All will be revealed before the proper audience."

Meaning his superior would snatch all the glory. Dubois crossed his arms under his cloak and sank back into the cushions, settling in for the ride.

10

Bad house; how like Josephine not to change the derisive name given the estate by a disenchanted former owner, while transforming it into its precise opposite. She was as ironic as her husband was sincere. Sincerity was a quality common to all the great pirates, irony to the women who put up with them.

Malmaison's extensive gardens slumbered under frost, but the effect was anything but dismal. Moonlight reflected off the silvery surface, gleaming calm and pale on the walls and slate roofs of the rambling chateau.

The carriage rattled through the open gates and came to rest before the front door. As his passengers alighted, the driver doffed his hat, set a tinder pistol to his pipe, and huddled into his fur blanket to await their return.

Inside, marbles and porcelains stood at every turn in the corridors, paintings on every wall. Dubois paused to admire a portrait by a sixteenth-century Florentine of a titled lady with an enigmatic smile.

The gardens were the talk of Paris. Three hundred francs were said to have changed hands over a single tulip bulb. The Prefect of Police regretted visiting in winter. He should like to see this magnificent blossom, whose price would feed a family in Chartres for a year.

"Get a move on, Dubois. We're not here for the tour."

Fouché was already at the end of the corridor leading to the library. The Prefect trotted to catch up.

First Consul Bonaparte was expecting them. He met them

at the door, wearing a swansdown dressing gown over a linen nightshirt, silken slippers on his feet. Dubois, who missed nothing, observed patches of high color on that alabaster face. Every day, it seemed, the man resembled more and more one of Josephine's stone pagan gods. He wrung Dubois' hand while Fouché stood awaiting a greeting.

Born barracks-mates, this pair, Fouché thought. The Minister envied their easy companionship. He himself was incapable of such intimacy outside his own family.

Plainly, abolishing the Prefect's office would require something less overt than driving a wedge between him and Bonaparte. The mission called for nuance, patience, and possibly years of undermining; arduous work.

Unless—stimulating thought—the Christmas Eve Plot could be turned to advantage.

Yes. Fouché would modernize intrigue the way Bonaparte had thrown away the traditional rules of war and brought Europe to its knees.

The First Consul clasped Fouché's hand briefly.

"Punctual as always. Madame Bonaparte regrets her absence. She has a headache."

A quarrel, no doubt. Aloud, the Minister said: "Believe me when I say we find it more regrettable than she."

They entered the library; curtained, papered, and carpeted Corsican green. Large-scale military maps draped scattered tables and desks like tablecloths.

The maps were not intended for decoration. Clearly the First Consul was preparing a new campaign; to spread the ideals of the Rights of Man farther across the Old World.

But where? Fouché wondered. Someplace with a treasure chamber, that much was assured.

On every surface, the carpet included, lay sheets of foolscap scribbled with Bonaparte's jagged, impatient script, mutilated into indecipherable shorthand by a brain racing perpetually beyond the physical: the proposed new Civil Code that would revolutionize law the way its author had revolutionized warfare. The project had occupied his every waking moment for months. War was his profession, but at present it amused him to toy with the law of the land.

War, plots, law, marriage. Dubois, a man wedded to his own work, feared the First Consul would explode under the pressure from so many fronts.

But then the Prefect had been obsessed lately with explosions.

Bonaparte dropped into a chair behind the largest desk and folded his well-kept hands across his middle. (Not so spare as in the heroic engravings from the battlefield, Dubois considered; seven courses eaten in twenty minutes were still seven courses.)

"Report."

Fouché untied the portfolio and placed that evening's edition of the *Bulletin* on the border of Luxembourg. The First Consul read swiftly, then sailed it across the Zuyder Zee. The Netherlands? Fouché thought. More tulips for the first lady's gardens?

"Satisfactory, *Monsieur le Ministre*. So far as it goes."

"I was certain your excellency would notice something was left out. The *Bulletin* is no place for speculation, only facts."

"Speculate."

"Undoubtedly Brunet is Pierre Saint-Réjant."

"Arguably. What else?"

"This man Beaumont. The name appears again and again in Ministry files. Major General Limoëlan uses it whenever he's in the country. It's a badge of honor, as he sees it; a signature. He never departs from it."

The First Consul's eyes, smoky gray under most circumstances, became gray steel.

"Limoëlan is no more a general than the underground army is an army. Where are their regiments, their colors?"

"Hidden beneath haystacks and in country houses in England. When we unearth Limoëlan, can Georges Cadoudal be far behind?"

This, Dubois noted, was the morsel the Minister had kept from the Paris Prefect. He wouldn't trust an underling not to run to the Tuileries with it and upstage the master magician. How tiring, these intrigues; yet they seemed to energize his superior.

"Cadoudal! *Incroyable!*" Bonaparte sprang to his feet and began to pace. He stopped and spun on his heel, facing Dubois. "Are you in agreement, *Monsieur le Prefect*?"

"All the evidence points to the fact, Citizen." How else to respond, not having known of the business until this moment? In any event, one did not contradict a brother officer before the brass.

Fouché played his courtier's card. "Your excellency will remember that we discussed the prospect that the affair of the fourth Nivose may as well have been the work of Royalists as Jacobins."

"Cadoudal must be arrested."

"First he must be found."

"Start in Brittany. He is a Breton, is he not?"

"As am I, but I am here as you see."

"When last I checked, Brittany still belonged to the Republic. Send a battalion if necessary, but fetch him back. He'll have a fair trial and the dignity of a squad of able marksmen. Some of them served under him, and will be sure to aim for the heart."

Fouché maintained his repose. "Forgive me, but I don't consider the plan practical."

"Make your case."

"Our latest intelligence places Cadoudal in England, enjoying the hospitality of Lord Rexborough in the country. My people there have orders to report to me immediately should he leave the estate."

Bonaparte looked down at the map on the desk, his gaze straying across the Channel.

"Always meddling over their mutton, these fellows," he said. "God save the king from Republicans in their precious empire. And so narrow a strip of water." Making laws and meeting treason could not distract him from his favorite pursuit.

"Short of an invasion, your excellency, I suggest we bottle up Cadoudal's remaining two associates, obtain additional evidence from them, and file it away until their commander makes the blunder of returning to France. Then we shall reunite them all in Traitors' Field."

"What makes you certain they're still here?"

Here the Minister was on firm ground.

"Carbon went into hiding, hoping to outlast our patience. We must assume the others did the same. We will continue to hold Carbon's sister and nieces, to prevent them from communicating the information of his arrest. Meanwhile we will announce that Jacobins were responsible for the fourth Nivose beyond doubt, as you were so wise to suggest from the beginning. They will think themselves safe, and when they resurface, my spies will report."

Was the Great Man flattered by so palpable a shift away from his own impulsive assumption? Could he be, at all? Dubois had never known a man who could not. But who had ever known a man such as this?

"You place great faith in your spies."

"I trained those who trained the rest."

"You place even greater faith in your abilities."

"A brilliant man once said the principal object of a general is to secure the flanks of his army. I remind myself of it every day."

"Sound tactics."

"Thank you, your excellency."

A touch! The Great Man could be flattered. Shakespeare was right.

Bonaparte looked at a framed engraving of Frederick II at Breslau, at the bust of Alexander: his cabinet.

"Refresh my memory, Fouché. Who is next in line to the Bourbon throne, were it still to exist?"

The Minister was caught off guard for once. "I—can't say. It isn't my province."

"Dubois?"

"Nor mine, Citizen." What was he getting at? Deciphering the complex business of royal succession had stumped men far more learned in such things.

"Find out. You're policemen, are you not?"

"I shall look into it." Fouché bowed. The man knew how to retreat without surrendering.

"Tactics are worthless without a solid strategy in place." Bonaparte might have been delivering one of his famous addresses to the troops. "The head of a Republic, elected by a majority of the people, can be removed from office by a single ball of lead. These cream puffs seek to replace me with a man who is guaranteed a line of succession."

Fouché acknowledged this to be true.

"Well, we cannot have that under a Republic."

He smiled then, showing the polished teeth that never appeared in official portraits. "And you, Dubois. What news from the brothels?" He rubbed his hands.

The Prefect concealed his discomfort; he could feel the Minister's envy. Prodigious as they were, his political skills lacked the spice of gossip from the slums of Paris, and that was a sore point that would never heal. Whatever one gained in the estimation of a Bonaparte, he lost in the eyes of a Fouché. The man of strength, and the man of intrigue: Which was more dangerous?

11

One week later—30 Nivose, the last day of the month of snow—a combined force of officers from the Paris Prefecture, the Ministry of Police, and the National Guard surrounded a country house outside Orleans and arrested Pierre Robinault Saint-Réjant, the plotter who had paid for the unfortunate mare Marguerite. He offered no resistance.

A wretch who was regularly thrown down the steps of a café on the nearest corner had recognized him from a rude police sketch, dining near the hearth, and had followed him when he left. A grateful Fouché had signed a voucher freeing one hundred francs from the Ministry budget, supplementing the vagabond's monthly stipend as a spy in good standing. The Minister's tentacles wound into the press, the arts, wayside inns, the military, and even the First Consul's own Republican guard; he could hardly have been expected to overlook the gutters.

The owner of the house, a friend of the prisoner's and a Royalist sympathizer, was taken as well and put to the Question, then released when Saint-Réjant gave up the identities of Carbon and Limoëlan but refused to name his host as a conspirator.

Early in Pluviose, the month of rain, Carbon and Saint-Réjant were taken from their place of confinement and stood before a firing squad under a drizzle not unlike the one that had drenched the Rue Saint Nicaise on the notorious 4 Nivose.

"Last words, Citizen?" the sergeant of the squad asked Saint-Réjant.

"Vive le Roi." He mumbled through lips torn and swollen. "Just so. Fire!"

"And Carbon?" asked Bonaparte.

"He said nothing, your excellency," Fouché reported.

"Precisely what he believed in. I can respect an adversary and loathe a traitor. Mercenaries leave me cold."

Days later, without fanfare, some 223 Jacobins and Jacobin sympathizers were turned loose by Consular order, dumped like refuse beyond the frontiers of France. Some of the same carts which during the Terror had trundled the condemned to the *Place de la Revolution* were pressed into this service. Stories went round of trees denuded to make crutches for those who could walk, litters for those who could not, provided they had comrades willing to drag them. Others crawled into the backs of passing wagons; those whose drivers would have them. The remains of still others were found in Germinal, the month of budding, when the snows receded.

Joseph Pierre Picot de Limoëlan, who had rejected Cadoudal's kidnap plan in favor of assassinating Napoleon Bonaparte; the man who had whistled the signal to touch off the gunpowder, killing many and maiming more, vanished from France.

Months later, a man answering his description surfaced in America and entered the priesthood.

"May the red Indians have him." Dubois crossed himself, remembering the wretched remains of the girl Pensol.

Broadsides and public bulletins announced that with the deaths of two of the major conspirators the affair was at an end.

Joseph Fouché, meanwhile, read reports and filed them. He still wore a black armband for the servant who had come face-to-face so early in life with the Great Mystery. His successor, the Minister was pleased to note, had no taste for wine.

———

On the third day of Germinal, Year VIII (March 23, 1801), a man took a room for the night at an inn in Doudeville, a port on the English Channel. A storm raged without; the guest stood in a puddle as he signed the registry.

The proprietor read the name upside-down. "What brings you to France, Monsieur Chaucer?"

"I'm visiting friends."

The stranger spoke French with a peculiar accent, possibly an English dialect with which the innkeeper was unfamiliar.

"A terrible time to cross over, just to be social."

The Englishman—if that's what he was—made no response.

"Christine will carry your bag."

"Thank you. I'll manage." He hoisted the valise, a fine one although worn.

Christine, the girl who made up the room, was a spy in the employ of the Ministry of Police. She waited until the man went down for supper, then went through the items in the valise: shirts, breeches inexpertly darned at the knees, stockings, underdrawers, some books in English, which meant nothing to her as she couldn't read in any language. There were paraphernalia for the mainte-nance of a pistol, excluding powder and balls; these she did not touch, as she had a fear of things that were designed to blow up. The Christmas Eve affair had kept her awake for several nights.

She assumed the weapon itself had remained on its owner's person. Although it was not a crime (nor, for that matter, a rarity) in France to travel armed, she thought the absence of loads worth noting, in case she was asked. (Surely a man did not venture out in these unpredictable times with only the single charge in his pistol.) She found nothing worth the formality of a report.

She was not a professional. She overlooked the false bottom.

II

GERMINAL

(Month of Budding)

12

His features had been reported as handsome and ordinary. He had been described as tall and of medium height, slight and muscular. Yet his suits had been made to the same measurements for years, and he certainly had neither shrunk nor grown.

There was artifice in the thing; but a magician didn't share secrets.

He was fluent in six languages, but could make himself understood in rather more, with no discernible foreign accent—when he chose not to display one. For the present, a twist of Boston gentry served his purpose.

His name was not Chaucer. Even Georges Cadoudal didn't know what it was. Then again, the Royalist leader had been only vaguely aware of his existence until one foul English night. . . .

Cadoudal had little respect for Geoffrey Randle, fourth Earl of Rexborough; his host.

The man had spent his first twenty years with no expectation of assuming his father's title, and so had squandered his youth hunting by day and gambling at night. By the time his eldest brother died of smallpox and the brother next in line lost his life on the field of honor, the family hopes for Geoffrey had run their course, ending in a fatal apoplectic stroke for his father, the third earl, when his only remaining heir was named as co-respondent in a public divorce case.

The brother had died because Geoffrey had not made good on

a gambling debt; Geoffrey himself could not be bothered, and so the formality of a duel had fallen to his sibling, along with its tragic outcome. The new earl had been ejected from all but one of the gentlemen's clubs in London and had established a reputation for philandering that was nearly as notorious as his wife's.

Privately, Cadoudal suspected Lord Rexborough's romantic relationships ended in disappointment for his partners.

He was simply too good-looking, with his thick coppery hair shorn short against current fashion, his face shaven close by a barber, and his waist and hips narrowing to well-shaped legs in skin-tight breeches. He was either impotent or a *pouf.* Lady Rexborough's escapades were likely the result of frustration at home rather than public humiliation.

Now nearer forty than thirty, the peer was losing those good looks. His appetite for brandy and port had consigned his storied waist to a corset, and as for his hair, his guest, who remembered the glory days of the French court, knew a henna treatment when he saw one. His face was ruddy, certainly not from the watery English sun, and there were burst blood vessels in his cheeks. He was one of those men who resembled boys well into middle-age, then became old overnight. Daily, it seemed, the ten-year age difference between Randle and his radiant blond wife became more marked.

The leader of the French Royalists despised the man, but took pains not to show it; Rexborough was his benefactor, after all.

Randle's wasn't the only house in England that would harbor a man condemned to death at home, but it was the only one Cadoudal trusted not to be riddled with paid informants.

Although he knew it was no secret where he was living—Joseph Fouché's system for gathering intelligence was the envy of all the nervous crowned heads of Europe—he slept soundly in his borrowed bed, secure in the belief that no greedy footman or chambermaid would conveniently leave a door unbarred to an assassin in the dead of night; for Lord Rexborough, who had never had reason to learn the value of money, overpaid his staff ludicrously. No one-time bribe was worth the loss of a position whose benefits could not be duplicated. It would take a troupe of French cavalry to remove Cadoudal from that rambling country manor, and even Bonaparte wasn't so reckless as to risk war with Great Britain merely to bring one man to justice.

It would be rash, however, to count upon the Corsican's restraint for long. The affair of Christmas Eve had placed everything in a state of uncertainty.

The fools. He had intended merely to humiliate the upstart, not make him a martyr.

The one club to which the earl still belonged had no official name and no fixed place of residence. It was not registered like the others. Its rolls included a former prime minister, the current home office secretary, former and sitting members of the House of Lords, and the owners of a half-dozen firms that conducted business with the British military and the royal family. (Rumor held that at least one member of that family belonged also.) They met infrequently and never twice in the same place in succession, not to play cards or socialize, but to plot the destruction of the French Republic.

Those who whispered of the association's existence referred to it as the Cutthroat Club.

Some of these men detested Rexborough. Others, remembering their own checkered histories, refused to judge him. They all tolerated him because he could finance the lion's share of any plan that would hasten the fall of the current government across the Channel, return a Bourbon to the throne, and spare England from the same ghastly egalitarian fate that had snatched America from its grasp. The mere thought of a commoner determining the course of a nation chilled their already icy blood.

Rexborough was neither political nor a patriot. He was just bored. With the doors of all the gambling houses closed to him, intrigue was the only game in town. It amused him to bankroll the destruction of foreign states the same way he'd laid bets against the house.

Cadoudal had no use for any of them; beyond, of course, their assistance. He was a Breton himself, like the late François Carbon (may he rot in hell for an imbecile), and knew too well the ways of the English to trust them to act upon any motive other than their own best interests.

They were quick to move against any country that threatened their colonial investments in Europe and Africa, but rarely exposed themselves to fire, paying others to fight in their stead. The dunes of the Sahara drifted over the carcasses of thousands of Mameluks who had died for the British cotton trade; the Austrian Empire had paid for its Anglo alliance with the slaughter of its troops in Italy.

But their purses were deep, these English, and if history had taught him nothing else, it was that in the end, gold trumped iron. Bonaparte's army was no match for the Bank of England.

Cadoudal at forty-five was ugly by any standard: toadish, with a broken nose like a torn iron coupling and one watery eye larger than its mate, a deformity of birth; a Royalist general who resembled a rank sergeant. Brute strength had earned him respect. He was heavily muscled but fat. His belly had swollen on an English diet of boiled beef, suety puddings, and fruit so thoroughly stewed he suspected Rexborough's cook had set out deliberately to constipate him. He consoled himself with the advantage gained: A man sitting waiting to make stool found time to hatch plots.

It had been during one of those sessions, distracting himself from his misery with a week-old copy of the *Times* of London, that he'd learned of the "infernal machine" that had destroyed much of the Rue Saint-Nicaise while failing in its object, to destroy Bonaparte. The Jacobins were blamed. He'd shaken his head, both at the callous disregard for innocent life and at the crudity of the attempt. It was just like those Republican fanatics to attempt such a thing. They had learned nothing since the Terror. Plainly they'd acted exactly as they had in 1789, lashing out at the most obvious target without thought as to what should follow: no plan save chaos, and chaos the inevitable result.

And it had made things that much more difficult for his own strategy to succeed, of capturing Bonaparte alive and holding him hostage until Paris capitulated and welcomed back the *Ancien Regime*. That devil Fouché, who never missed an opportunity to tighten his hold on the citizenry, would use the incident as an excuse to isolate the First Consul even further from the people who had put him in power, and from those who would remove him.

Before now, the Strong Man of France had ridden at the head of victory parades astride a white horse, dressed in his famous cocked hat and gray greatcoat, within arm's length of the throngs lining the pavement for a glimpse. From now on he would cower in his coach, ringed on all sides by grenadiers.

The thought had not occurred to Cadoudal, even during the painful straining to void his bowels, that the very men he had entrusted with that plan were the ones who had touched off the gunpowder.

When Carbon and Saint-Réjant were taken and stood before muskets, having named him as the mastermind behind the slaughter, he had kicked in a panel of the tall mahogany cabinet Rexborough had lent him to hang his clothes, including his old field uniform. The white cockade of saner days looked at him like a sad wise old eye.

"What does this mean to us?"

The earl, who had brought him the news, seemed amused, as if this were a game of whist and his opponent had played the one hand he hadn't expected. A man for whom money sprouted from the ground, who knew no loyalties except to his appetites, had no concept of loss.

But Cadoudal, who like any good general grasped the situation well enough to begin thinking how to reverse it, was calm after his outburst.

"You are a gambler, my friend, and my English is faulty, mixed with Celtic and border French. What is the phrase, when one lays a wager and another matches it?"

"'Fold'?"

"No. When one does not wish to retire from play. There is a phrase, I know."

The earl grinned suddenly, like a pupil who'd stumbled on the answer despite himself. "'Raise the ante.'"

"Yes! My hand is forced. Now we raise the ante. Bonaparte must die!"

"Oh, jolly good!"

The idiot.

Carolyn Randle disapproved of her husband's guest; but since she disapproved of her husband, she found the imposition no less bearable than life in general.

One day there would be a term to describe Lady Rexborough: "Professional beauty." She had no skills worthy of public consumption, beyond the obligatory sketching in parlors and piano lessons, activities designed by the upper classes to pass a young matron's time while her husband was off killing small creatures or betting a banker's wages on the turn of a tile.

In town, she rode in open carriages under elaborate bonnets and parasols, lifting the spirits of the creatures who lined the streets hoping for a glimpse at perfection; in the country, she batted wooden balls about the lawn, discussed menus with the cook like a general planning a campaign, and smiled politely at the gray men who filed into the library to smoke cigars and stoke their gout with fortified wine. She was, as had been written about her, like a spray of fresh flowers brought suddenly into a winter room: breathtakingly fresh, indescribably lovely, and heartbreak-ingly fragile.

Not to mention utterly without shame.

There was, in truth, an ephemeral quality about her golden hair worn in a simple chignon (to keep the damn strands off her face), ceramic-blue eyes, and rose-stained cheeks, that seemed destined not to live out the day. The same had been said about her for a decade. She had reached her peak at eighteen, and had been holding that position like a grim and determined veteran soldier ever since. She had the athletic figure of a Diana, with just enough Aphrodite above the waist to sacrifice eye contact with every man she met, and was, as her husband had observed of her before his intimates, in a perpetual state of heat.

Well, what of it? Certainly there was no remedy for it in milord's bed. *Someone* in the arrangement ought to have needs.

Their guest, the Brittany Frenchman, was not one of them. That great belly, and the arrogance of his conduct, made it easy for her to assume the role of charming hostess only. She gathered that he was one of those émigrés from the Parisian court who had been polluting the English population with their pompous ways and impossible accents for a dozen years, but knew nothing about him except that he enjoyed the hospitality of the house without offering to contribute to its upkeep.

Her husband seemed fascinated with the fellow; he was his latest avocation. Geoffrey had given up racing horses and collect-ing Medieval armor, but hadn't troubled to sell the paddock or the breastplates, visors, gauntlets, pauldrons, and cuirasses that gathered dust in piles throughout the house. He would tire of the unpleasant foreigner as well. She just hoped that when the time came, he wouldn't forget to show him out. Like his other inter-ests, his forgotten guests had a habit of loitering about.

Someone put the great bronze front-door knocker to use. The noise thundered along ancient rafters.

She looked at one of the clocks that were always chiming out of step in that drafty barn. Another visitor, at that hour? She lifted her skirts and went toward the entrance hall.

"The general is expecting me." A pleasant light baritone, foreign but cultured, and strange to the house.

She got to the hall just as the butler took the man's hat and greatcoat. Both were dry; a fortnight of winter drizzle had given way to a sky aswirl with stars. The servant looked expectantly at the object standing on the floor at the visitor's feet.

The man shook his head. "Thank you, but I'll keep the valise."

13

The butler passed his mistress without seeing her in the shadows, carrying the visitor's outerwear. A not-unpleasant odor of horse and woodsmoke came in its wake.

The man carried his valise—good leather, well-traveled—to the stone hearth, set it down, and spread his palms before the fire. He wore a simple gray double-breasted waistcoat under a sporting jacket, gray also and plain, ankle-length trousers to match, and boots fastened with strings instead of buckles, the fashion in London that season. He was trim, fair, of middle height, and wore his hair to his collar. Lady Carolyn thought he looked like a wild Irish poet.

She placed his age at thirty, but he might have been older; firelight was kind to the tracks of time.

After warming himself front and back, he strolled about the hall, taking in the gloomy canvases on the walls. Coming to a stop before the newest, of the mistress of the house, he seemed to smile; again, perhaps, an illusion.

She approached him then. The rustle of her skirts and petticoats made him turn. No, he was not smiling; but neither was his expression stern.

"Welcome to our home, sir. I'm Carolyn Rexborough." She offered a hand weighted down with rings.

The visitor bowed over it, but did not take it. "Your ladyship is most kind. I'm here to see Lord Rexborough."

She could not place his accent. American, possibly; although the American industrialists she'd seen at court all spoke in brays, their cheeks stuffed like a squirrel's. She tolerated snuff, but found tobacco taken in such a way despicable. This man bore no trace of the practice.

His eyes were a smoky shade, not blue or brown; rather a greenish gray, with light webworks at the outer corners. He was older than thirty. She felt a frisson then, extending from the top of her spine to her loins. The old familiar tingle.

"And you are . . . ?"

"Here to see Lord Rexborough."

"You said that. I was asking your name."

Something tugged at the corners of his mouth. A well-shaped mouth, although the lips were somewhat thin. Not a drawback. Geoffrey had the lips of a voluptuary, meaty and moist when pursed, like boiled plums.

"If he hasn't told your ladyship, it isn't my place to supply the information."

"Is your name not your property?"

"With respect, madam, it isn't yours."

The frisson thawed abruptly. "You're insolent, sir!"

"Again, with respect, I'm not the one who persists in asking a question once an answer has been given."

"Not a satisfactory answer."

"I found the question unsatisfactory."

"I'll have you thrown out!"

"Not your decision. I shouldn't have to keep repeating I'm here to see your husband."

Her cheeks stung, but she had the breeding and the presence to curtsy briefly before turning and rustling away. As she left the room, she thought she heard a low chuckle behind her, but it may have been logs shifting on the grate.

Lady Carolyn did not share her husband's taste in houseguests.

The butler returned, bowed, and conducted the visitor to the library. Two men were seated in the enormous room, facing each other across a long refectory table, heavily carved from cherry and piled with books, sporting journals, and copies of the *Times* of London.

A youngish man in a tight figured waistcoat and lilac knee-breeches sat at the near end. His companion was grossly fat. He wore a coarse pullover appropriate to an English spring and woolen trousers.

A mismatched pair, these men, like the older one's eyes. Soft firelight glowed on gold-leaf bindings and glistened in the larger orb.

The visitor bowed in the direction of the man at the near end of the table. "Milord." Then, to the man in the pullover and trousers: "General Cadoudal."

The second man lifted his brows—rusty brown, like his badly shorn hair. "Have we met?"

"Never. But you were described to me."

"By whom?"

"A mutual acquaintance."

Rexborough scowled. "Who are you, sir, and what brings you here? My servant said you're expected, but I assure you he's wrong."

"Stop playing the imperious country squire, Geoffrey; it doesn't suit you." Cadoudal was still looking at the visitor. "I was told weeks ago a certain party was on his way, without being told his name or his business; only that it might coincide with mine."

"Preposterous. How do you know he's the one you're expecting?"

"Because I've expected no one else since before the new year."

"You're making free with my hospitality, inviting strangers into my house. With a bag, no less. Am I to be told how long he plans to stay?"

The stranger said, "I never go from London without it. Where I sleep tonight is of no consequence to me."

"Geoffrey. The business we have to discuss is political. It wouldn't interest you."

"I'll be the judge of that. Allow me my own mind at least."

The visitor set down his valise and came forward to whisper in Cadoudal's ear. The Breton hesitated, then nodded.

The man bowed to Rexborough. "Milord, you would not only find the conversation tedious, but dangerous. The Crown doesn't look kindly on British subjects who conspire against foreign governments."

"That addle-pated old fool can barely understand English, even had he his hearing. He's deaf as well as blind."

"*Lèse majesté.*" Cadoudal smiled. "It's pleasant to challenge authority in one's own library. To ignore Parliament policy is treason. My friend, events of the most far-reaching nature have come to your door. You'll learn of them in the fullness of time; but rude guest that I am, I won't be the one to place your household in danger. Please honor my wishes."

The fourth earl of Rexborough rose.

"Call on me when I'm of use."

After he left, seconds passed in silence. The stranger broke it. "He'll eavesdrop, of course."

"Nonsense. He'll have a servant do it."

"The trouble with the English is they've ruled the world so long they think everyone else's affairs are theirs as well."

"Are *you* not English?"

"Your friends didn't tell you?"

"They said someone was coming who would make up for Christmas Eve. I knew nothing about you beyond that. I'd thought from your speech you were a Cornishman or some such outlandish creature. Most of my travels take place between France and the Channel."

"That's encouraging; your ignorance, I mean. Nothing then has leaked. I'd hate to have come all this way only to spill my secrets to a spy."

A cramp gripped Cadoudal's stomach. He leaned forward until it passed, then sat back to mop his face with a silk handkerchief. "This wing was built under Charles I, when the Puritans lusted for noble heads; the Jacobins didn't invent the practice. The interior walls are two feet thick, and the door black oak banded with iron. It's entirely soundproof. I tested it."

"How?"

"Before I came, I salted the domestic staff with soldiers I commanded in France. I suppose you'd call them spies. I placed one outside, closed and barred the door, and sang a medley of fine old marches at the top of my lungs; which you would appreciate if you ever heard me bellowing orders in the field. Then we traded places. You could slaughter a pig in here and leave the household none the wiser."

The visitor spun on his heel, strode to the door, and tore it open, all in one motion. The hall outside was empty.

He turned back, withdrawing a hand from his waistcoat. Evidently the man was armed.

"It must be lonely to trust no one," said the general.

"Not a fatal condition." The other unwound the stock from his neck and stuffed a corner of it inside the keyhole. Then he turned back.

"Satisfied?"

"Never. But my work's never entirely without risk."

"What *is* your work?"

The stranger inclined his head toward the cut-crystal set on the table. "Refill it. It will make our talk more enjoyable."

"Will you join me?"

"I like to keep my wits when I'm working."

Cadoudal poured claret for himself. "Work. There's that word again."

His visitor drew out the chair Rexborough had been sitting in, dragged it the length of the table, and sat facing Cadoudal at an angle. The rest of their conversation was conducted in unassailable French.

"What are you called?" the houseguest asked.

"In France I use Chaucer. In England Molière. Among others as the situation suggests."

"A literary man."

"If you like. I rarely read fiction. But the names come easily when I'm forced to change without warning."

"How do I know you represent whom you say? Fouché has rats everywhere."

The room fell silent again. After a moment the man took something from a waistcoat pocket and placed it in Cadoudal's palm.

The ring was no larger than a centime, but heavier than a gold Louis. He judged it to be twenty-four karats. It was decorated with a white alabaster fleur-de-lis on a shield encircled by tiny sapphires. Blue stars leapt from them when he turned it in the firelight.

"You could have stolen it, of course."

"If it were stolen, you would have heard about it."

"A forgery, then."

"Have it assessed. I know an expert who can be trusted not to talk, but how could I prove he's not my creature? It's an endless process."

"May I?" Cadoudal closed his hand around it.

"By all means. It's death if I'm discovered with it."

"It's death if I'm discovered at all." He pocketed the ring. "An endless process, as you say. Very well. But I must know something about you."

The man's lips were thin, his smile thinner. "A trust for a trust?"

"You must agree it's a fair request. You know everything about me."

"I'll begin with my qualifications. I can handle a pistol, but I'm more comfortable with a cutting edge. I've taken lives with both."

"How do you stand with powder?"

"As far away as possible."

"I'm a humorless man, sir. I've no time for jests."

"It was no jest. I think you'll agree powder's lost its charm since Christmas Eve."

"Did you serve in the military?"

"I held a commission."

"In which army?"

"I fought in Paris and Egypt."

"I can count a half-dozen armies that did; most recently Bonaparte's."

The visitor made no response to that.

"You've killed Englishmen?"

"Yes."

"Frenchmen?"

"Austrians, too, and Russians. I've never killed an American, although I'd like to try. I'd regard it a challenge, given their native ingenuity. Arsenic in chewing tobacco suggests itself, or in their excellent Kentucky whiskey; but I find poisoning cowardly. I don't discriminate among people when it comes to killing. I'm an assassin, General, not a bigot."

The man was not lying; his gaze was level. And Cadoudal knew now the ring in his pocket was genuine. Its mere presence in a commoner's possession was cause for arrest.

He was shocked by the fellow's admissions. No, not admissions, or boasts: *Qualifications,* as he put it. Cadoudal had slain men in the field, but that had been in wartime, when all biblical restrictions were set aside. A man who avenged himself for personal reasons was a soldier just the same. François Carbon had killed without principle, but it had been just the one time. To repeat the offense on a regular basis—

He swallowed some wine. "You murder at random?"

"I murder for money. But I'm sure you knew that. What have we been talking about all this time?"

14

The man was the devil, there was no doubt of it.

Cadoudal had taken it for granted that the fellow must be compensated apart from his expenditures—there would be a great deal of money involved, considering the new security provisions that had been made since 4 Nivose, as the rabble insisted on calling it—but what he'd just heard, in that most civilized room in a civilized house, chilled his skin and turned the undigested meal in his stomach.

Roughnecks had been known to commit unsavory acts for profit, but this—*professional assassin*—was something infamous.

The man's quizzical expression remained in place.

"You're shaken. Why? You've been present at mass slayings: set them in motion, in fact. What's the difference between blowing a man to bits with cannon and stabbing him in a coach?"

"You've done that?"

"While it was in motion, and took my exit with the coachman unaware I was ever aboard. I asked a question."

"Mine was a field of honor. Yours—monstrous thing!"

"I was in danger myself; more so than if I'd stood on a hill directing fire. I'm not unique to history. The very word 'assassin' extends back to the eleventh century. The caliphs of Cairo paid their killers with hashish; *Hashishiyun,* they were called."

"But those men were fanatics."

"I am not, which is why what I say makes so much sense. It's a new century, General. We can't go on doing things the same way we did in the past."

"You make a good point, although I find it abhorrent."

"More so than blowing apart thirty-five men, women, and children just to kill one man?"

"I didn't authorize that."

"You'll pay for it just the same, unless you pay me."

"Am I to take that as a threat?"

"It would be empty, don't you think? They know where you are, and what you've been up to. It's only a matter of time before someone lures you into a trap. Your friend the earl, for example."

"Rexborough's a buffoon, not a Judas."

"He bores easily, or he'd have put up more of a fight when we sent him from the room. You're committed to your cause, monsieur. He joined it only because the shooting's so bad this time of year. It would amuse him just as much to turn you in, and testify during your trial about how he managed to infiltrate your ranks. He'll probably receive a decoration from that deaf and blind old fool in Buckingham.

"Your other friends may be more reliable," he went on. "On the other hand, they're Englishmen, with no real stake in the business, apart from vague fears for their own government. Do you find any flaws in my theory?"

Cadoudal felt drained. No argument had ever been devised to withstand a man without morals. "No. But nor can I be persuaded that the—our mutual friend—would undertake a transaction of the sort you suggest."

"And yet he did. He sought me out, through intermediaries, and is under no illusions as to its nature."

"You met with him? Where?"

"In Ettelheim, where the shooting is far superior."

That settled the matter. Apart from Cadoudal and select others—and of course Fouché's spy network—the place of their "mutual friend's" exile was not generally known. That this was a ruse designed to entrap the Royalist general was impossible, unless the ring had been forced from the man's own finger, and beyond doubt communication of the incident would have reached him through his own network.

"When the upstart is dead," said the other, "and the people of France demand Restoration and stability, the threat passes, and you go home a hero of the nation."

"Not that I'm considering your proposition, but what is the current market rate for murder?"

"Five million Swiss francs."

"Outrageous!"

"Two million, five hundred thousand upon agreement and the rest when I'm successful."

"Bonaparte conquered Italy on forty thousand."

The visitor's eyes had a smoky quality that defied connection. "You appear to admire the man despite all."

"As well admire a mad dog. Just for discussion, seven hundred fifty thousand—payable upon success. That's if my benefactors agree. Naturally we would advance you enough to make your preparations, provided the amount is within reason."

The man rose and bowed.

"*Adieu.* I did not come here to bargain."

Cadoudal had bartered with sharp practitioners for cavalry mounts and provisions for his troops. Feigned indifference had no effect upon him.

"Before you leave, perhaps you will be kind enough to tell me how you arrived at that preposterous sum."

"By being practical. Before this my targets have been petty public officials; one was a country constable, who made his rounds aboard a donkey. They were none who would be missed. This undertaking, as you call it, will make me notorious. I do not propose to be the next Charlotte Corday."

Cadoudal did not address that. The bitch had slit the jugular of the radical Jacobin Marat in his bath, and had been executed forthwith; vulgar whisperers had named the Cutthroat Club in her honor. But she had been no Royalist, merely an adherent of one of the many factions that had divided the Revolution into feral packs forever in conflict. Nothing could be further from what the Royalists were about.

"You seem timid for an assassin."

"Do I? Consider the situation. I will be forced underground. I'll never work again, and since I'm unqualified for any other labor, if my terms are not met I must resort to blackmail." He named all the members of the so-called Cutthroat Club.

The visitor's voice never rose above the level of parlor conversation. But each name struck his listener with the force of a blow. He'd thought them a secret even from Fouché.

He tried to keep his own tone steady. "I submit that there is a reliable remedy for extortion."

"My murder, you mean."

"That seems to be the fee simple of this discussion."

"It's been tried. But in that event, why engage me at all? Apply that same remedy to Bonaparte, and save five million francs."

He was down to his last argument. "What evidence can you provide that you are what you say you are, and have done what you say you have done?"

"Again, it was not I who sought this assignment. My accomplishments are better known east of the Rhine; celebrated, in fact. The Germans are fond of sensational literature, although I found the woodcuts less than flattering. Certain details made their way to Ettelheim, and some effort was spent in order to communicate with me. If it's trophies you require—ears, fingers, scalps—I cannot accommodate you. I make it a practice not to take them. They're difficult to explain at border crossings."

Georges Cadoudal suppressed an urge to shudder, sighing instead. A good captain acknowledged defeat when it was plain.

While he admitted to himself that he was no Bonaparte, he was at bottom a good captain.

"I must consult with my people."

"That could take months. Since Four Nivose they're scattered from here to America."

Where did this fellow get his intelligence? At all events, time was essential. Cadoudal's own liberty was a day-to-day thing; and what good was a counter-revolution without an able commander? Anarchy redux; the Terror restored.

"The first payment will take time to raise."

The visitor's smile was cold as the grave.

"I hardly thought you had it in your purse. I need time to prepare in any case."

"What shape will it take, this—business?"

"I don't know yet. Neither will you until it's done. There was nothing wrong with the Christmas Eve affair except the number of men who were in on it. One man can keep a secret, even two. Admit three, and you might as well issue a broadside."

"How can we be certain you won't disappear once you have the two million and a half?"

"How can I be certain you won't refuse to pay me the rest once the job is done? Don't respond, General: I'll supply the answer. A man who can kill the Strong Man of Europe can kill the commander of an army that no longer exists, without much more effort. On your end, a coterie of wealthy English nobles can kill a man such as I, friendless and alone, as easily as they can score at cricket. It's death in any case, you see. Better one than many. Even the Republicans learned that in the end, or the guillotine would still be in place."

A great cramp seized Cadoudal's inwards like a fist in a mail glove. He leaned forward again, affecting to study the matter with his chins folded onto his chest, until the spasm passed. At that moment he could quite willingly have killed Rexborough's cook; how bloodthirsty he'd become in half an hour.

The spasm passed. He straightened. "You're indeed a student of history. Are you seriously not familiar with heroic literature?"

"The men who write fiction know nothing and make up the rest. It's useless to my work."

When, he wondered, would he ever become accustomed to connecting assassination with honest labor? They would never be comrades, these two; in that he took some solace. The architect was not the grimy layer of brick.

"You'd be surprised at how often they stumble upon something practical." Cadoudal rummaged among the books on the table until he found the one he wanted: A copy of Alexander Pope's translation of *The Iliad*, bound in supple leather, peeled from travel and thumb-worn from study. He sat back with it in his lap, not bothering to open it to the passage he had in mind; it was enough just to hold the volume. It was his own, a work of war revered by all who practiced the art. The stoop-shouldered scholar who had assembled Rexborough's library was long on Shakespeare and Cervantes but short on Plutarch and Homer.

"According to the epics," he said, "when Troy was under siege, the Greeks saw something they interpreted to be a sign from the gods: A viper, snatched up by an eagle, bit the bird, poisoning it and forcing them both to crash to the ground and die. The Trojan horse was the result: The appearance of defeat turned into victory.

"You see the analogy," he said, when the fellow didn't answer. "The intended victim becomes the victor."

Still his visitor said nothing.

"You're aware, perhaps, that Bonaparte has chosen the eagle for his personal device? Already he takes upon himself the conceit of royalty. He'll crown himself king one day."

"I've heard this. A warrior would hardly embrace a sparrow as his signature." The visitor's nostrils expanded and contracted; he was stifling a yawn.

"If Bonaparte is the eagle, the one who destroys him must be the viper. With your permission, I'll call you *Le Vipère*, in person and in dispatches."

"No dispatches. Nothing is to appear about me in writing. If it does, I'll know where to look for the man responsible."

"Shall I take *that* as a threat?"

"I expressed it poorly if you don't." The muscles at the corners of his mouth drew his lips into a straight line. That part of his face was the most mobile, although scarcely more than inert. "Let's not take the omen too literally: Both parties died."

"Are you superstitious?"

"No. But nor do I tempt fate."

A most careful fellow, this. Georges Cadoudal began to approve of him, purely on a clinical basis and despite his lack of values—his loss, poor empty vessel that he was; but a worthy match for the unprincipled man who ruled France. Of course he would have to be eliminated once his services were no longer required. Such was expediency, and not the same thing as assassination for monetary gain. Leaders were sometimes led to unpleasant measures for the good of the nation.

"How shall we deliver the money?"

"You will send a courier—with an armed escort, of course—to deposit two million, five hundred thousand in gold in the Bank of Vienna under the name Colonel Franz Meuchel." He spelled it. "He's registered with the treasury department of the Austrian Army, so the amount will raise no suspicions. Once I'm informed that I may draw a note upon the account, I'll put my plans in operation. Under no circumstances will you attempt to make contact with me unless I initiate that contact."

"What's your connection with this man Meuchel?"

"That isn't your concern."

"You must trust him."

This brought no response. Cadoudal wondered if the treasury colonel was present in this room. It would explain a great deal, including the mystery of his true nationality. On the other hand, he suspected the man could not be explained away as easily as that.

"And the courier? Two and a half million can turn the head of the most honest of men."

"Surely not the *most* honest. In any event he's your responsibility, not mine. But if I may make a suggestion, I'd appoint someone who already has millions of his own."

Did the fellow tilt his head toward the door through which Rexborough had exited?

The houseguest frowned. "If the fool doesn't gamble it away."

"Commission him a general in the Royalist Army and put him in command of the escort. That should satisfy his pride and inhibit his self-indulgence."

"Just that?"

"Give him a sword if you like."

"And instruct him to have his tailor make him a splendid uniform!" Cadoudal beamed for the first time since greeting the visitor. "That's sound strategy. You *are* a military man."

"I said I was. I haven't lied."

Cadoudal committed the details he'd been given to memory. He hadn't written so much as a personal letter since coming to England. A man could commit suicide with paper and ink. "Will you make contact when the thing is done?"

"No. With any luck you'll never hear from me again. You will know when the time has come to remit the remainder. All the world will know."

15

Lady Carolyn awoke to a rapid knocking, sharp and insistent, not at all the decorous tap of a servant, or Geoffrey's thump when he'd drunk enough wine to tilt once more at her windmill. This was the knock of a stranger.

She threw on a dressing gown, slid her feet into slippers, and opened the door a crack.

It was the impertinent man from the entrance hall. She started to push the door shut, but he leaned his shoulder against it.

"I came to apologize for my behavior earlier."

"The only way to do that is to leave." She pushed harder, but his body was like an iron stop. She was a strong woman, athletic in the saddle and at bowls. She sensed in this man reserves of strength far deeper than he was showing.

"I came on business," he said. "I've finished it."

His face reflected light from the dying fire in her room in patches: forehead, cheekbones, the bridge of his nose. She thought of a Grecian bust. He smelled of wine, faintly and not displeasingly; Geoffrey's scent when he'd been drinking came mixed with vomit.

"What I mean to say is I make it a point to put work before the gentler pursuits."

Gentler was the word that occurred to her that same moment. His voice, which had cut across hers with a knife edge before, now seemed soft, almost vulnerable.

Still she resisted. "Now you've made your apology, and dispensed with business. It's late. I'm sure you're expected somewhere."

"His lordship was kind enough to invite me to spend the night."

She knew this for a lie. She'd seen Geoffrey go into his room an hour ago. He seldom emerged until he'd slept his full ten hours. The invitation had to have come from Cadoudal. His strange hold on her husband was as strong as ever: He was the auxiliary master of the house.

"My quarters are just down the hall," said the man.

"Does his lordship know you're at my door?"

"I think not. He sleeps in the Georgian wing, as you know."

"I know, because it was my idea to sleep in the Elizabethan. It hasn't the modern comforts, but it's private. No one tramps past on his way anywhere."

"Convenient."

Not just soft, that tone. Something feline crept through it. Yes, definitely purring: a cat on the prowl. The thought made the down rise on the back of her neck.

"Still insolent, I see. What became of that apology?"

"You haven't told me whether you accept."

"I'll think about it. When are you leaving?"

"Before dawn. You may not be awake. I'd hate to go without knowing your decision."

"I can't imagine it's that important, but if you must, ring before you do. I don't mind rising early."

"I will, if the bell connects with this room." The pressure increased from his side of the door.

She was mistress of the situation now. She'd wanted him, been rebuffed, and now the glove was on the other hand. Her lips twisted in well-bred scorn.

And then the door burst wide open. She was forced to yield as if she weighed nothing at all. A slippered foot caught on the edge of the rug; she fell backward into the arms encircling her, strong as girders. His lips pressed against hers, bruising them.

His tongue pried and thrust and flicked between her teeth. She tasted wine.

Straining with all her strength, she pulled her face free a half-inch. She was panting, as if she'd run up a long flight of stairs. "I must know your name."

"No, you don't." He pulled her even closer.

Later, when he'd gone, the air tasted sweeter; but only because she'd thought she'd tasted it for the last time.

His body naked was powerful; not knotted, like some trades-men she'd seduced, clumsy walking chunks of hickory and oak; the muscles were as smooth and as hard as oilstone, but supple in their action. He moved with savage urgency: How long had it been since he'd lain with a woman? Months? Years? Perhaps only days; the thought frightened, a man living with such constant fury, an animal in a cage.

Frightened? No! She was terrified.

Whenever she'd opened her eyes, she found he was watching her. She'd never had a partner who didn't close his lids at some point during the act. The intensity of that gray-green stare terri-fied her almost as much as the other thing.

He'd intimidated her with his brute strength, alarmed her with his animal drive—and at the moment of crisis closed his fingers around her throat.

"N—"

His grip was like steel cable. It choked the flow of air to her lungs, stopped the rush of blood to her brain. She clawed at his hands, drew blood with her nails. She might have been scratching at masonry for all the effect it had on that grasp. Her eyes strained from their sockets; the vessels must burst. The face above hers receded into gathering darkness.

Just as she'd begun to pass out, arching her back and scream-ing in her brain, she'd exploded in an orgasm that shook the an-cient house to its foundation. The fingers left her throat, although she would feel their pressure for days. Now came the scream, and with it her tongue, spilling out as large as a leg of raw mutton; but the scream was a squeak, lost in the whoosh of breath set free. She gulped in a great gout of fresh air, with a sob that was louder than any wail and ended in a racking cough.

When at last it ended he was gone, utterly and without a whis-per, like a snake through tall grass.

She took breakfast in her room the next morning. The maid who brought it informed her that last night's visitor had left even be-fore the servants arose.

The tea burned in Lady Carolyn's throat and she could not swallow a morsel of toast. She came out wearing a scarf to cover the bruises on her neck. That and her scratchy voice convinced Geoffrey it was time they returned to their comfortable house in London, leaving Georges Cadoudal in full charge of the estate and its staff. "You're looking positively wan," he said.

16

Martin Gaudin, recently minted French Minister of Finance under the Consulate, looked the part of an unsuccessful banker.

His watch chain and pince-nez were the only things about him that reflected light. Everything else was black or gray or brown, and in need of attention. He was chronically untidy. His trousers could no more contain his shirttail than a bedroom with an outside trellis could restrain a rebellious child. He cut his own hair and it showed.

He was a young man for his profession, but in Bonaparte's cabinet, youth was the prevailing feature and no longer a subject for conversation. The First Consul, for whom the phrase *enfant terrible* had been coined, loathed to surround himself with crepuscular remnants of the *Ancien Regime*. He violated this policy only in cases such as Joseph Fouché's; the Police Minister's capacity for deception could come only from decades of practice.

Gaudin was a wise choice. Unruly as he was in his grooming, he was meticulous in his professional responsibilities. He had proposed the establishment of the Bank of France, and within months the franc stabilized for the first time since the fall of the monarchy: "Sound as a gold Louis" was the old phrase, reckless now to employ; but true enough at the core.

Fouché received the nervous little man in his office. He noted that upon this visit Gaudin was more than usually clumsy; he lost count of how many times the fellow dropped and retrieved scribbled sheets of foolscap from the shabby portfolio he hugged to his chest, his spectacles springing free of his nose and swaying at the end of their ribbon.

"To what do I owe this honor, monsieur? Our jurisdictions do not often cross."

"To the First Consul, Citizen. He referred me to you."

The Police Minister allowed himself one of his rare tight smiles. He knew it brought no comfort to the observer; his gaunt yellow face was scant repository for any display of amusement.

"Amateur acrobatics in the books? I've suggested to his excellency that the government rotate financial personnel regularly. So much contact with bank notes and gold and silver coins leads to carelessness and chicanery. I maintain faith in the faithlessness of my fellow man."

"My people are above reproach." Spots of color stained Gaudin's gray cheeks, then withdrew like crocus in a frost. "You know this, as your officers watch them day and night."

And not just them, thought the other. He knew a bit about the Finance Minister's habits, including how often he visited his mistress in the Rue Saint-Jeanne. A cow; but there was no accounting for taste. Bonaparte had the inestimable Josephine, yet had salted the Continent with his bastards. The Police Minister was a bit of a prude. Adultery was the one Commandment he'd never broken and he cupped his hands around it like the last ember.

"The object of my visit isn't domestic," said Gaudin. "It has to do with financial adventures across the Channel."

Fouché was suddenly alert. Anything that involved England involved him inevitably. He'd made Great Britain a personal area of interest since 4 Nivose, like a suspect under close watch. "Continue."

"Officials with the Bank of England routinely report large transfers involving holdings on the Continent. It's a courtesy that benefits all countries, to prevent an international panic."

The Police Minister waited with an elaborate show of patience while the banker retrieved his papers once again and shuffled them into order. *Quel désastre!*

"Lord Chesterfield has sold his estate in Spain for the sum of two hundred thousand pounds. A similar sale went through in Belgium at the same time for the Duke of York, who transferred ownership of his hunting lodge and two hundred acres to a Monsieur Corbeil in Brussels for the sum of a hundred thousand."

"Nothing so unnatural in that." But Fouché was interested. Both men were outspoken opponents of the French Republic.

"I'm not finished, Citizen. A Mr. Edward Southern, a textile manufacturer in America, has bought for the sum of half a million pounds a manufactory belonging to Sir Humphrey Welden in Scotland. All of these transactions took place the first two *decadi* of Ventose."

The second half of February. The Republican calendar irritated the Police Minister: Wind, Flowers, Heat, Snow, Rain: how appropriate to the minds of the imbeciles who set the Revolution in motion with no clear course. He especially disliked having only one day of leisure with his family in ten, leaving five days extra to flap loose, as if a 365-day year could be forced into a decimal system. They were an excuse for an extended bacchanal. If the English were ever to steel themselves for a direct attack, that would be the time.

Sir Humphrey Welden had refused to do business with France since—well, Year One, by the infernal calendar. He saw a pattern.

"What else?"

Gaudin managed to separate a ten-day-old copy of the *Times* of London without spilling the rest of his papers and spread it on Fouché's desk. A bitten-nailed finger directed his attention to an item on an inside page, headed A COLLECTOR OUTRAGED.

A titled accumulator of antiquities had objected to the Earl of Rexborough's decision to sell his late father's ancient Greek statuary in one lot to the British Museum, destroying the market and reducing the value of the collector's own artifacts by forty percent.

> Lord Rexborough [wrote the reporter] responded:
> "I cannot see why there should be so much row over a
> few pieces of broken pottery."

Fouché's English was spotty, but he could make out the particulars well enough. As an enthusiastic amasser of canvases, statuary, fine furniture, and china, he found himself in sympathy with the complainant; but the advantage of the intelligence to his office was unmistakable. To avoid alarming the Finance Minister, he dissembled his excitement.

For months, Rexborough had been harboring Georges Cadoudal, the mastermind behind the incident in the Rue Saint-Nicaise; that was old news to Fouché's army of spies. He found it ironic that this fresh morsel should come his way by means of the popular press—and the *British* press, at that. Negotiations between the earl and the museum were speculated to fall between fifty and seventy-five thousand pounds. In his head, the Police Minister totaled the sums that Gaudin had reported.

"Eight hundred seventy-five thousand pounds. Nearly two million francs."

"One million, seven hundred fifty on the current exchange, give or take fifty thousand," corrected Gaudin.

"The margin is as wide as that?"

"We stride ahead on the strength of Citizen Bonaparte's victories; but at present we are at peace." He sounded disapproving.

Fouché smiled within himself. There were, after all, men more evil than he. A thousand men dead on some distant field meant less to this walking abacus than a thousand francs extra in the treasury.

"Thank you for bringing this to my attention, Gaudin. You were right to do so."

"It was the First Consul's wish, Citizen. I shall, of course, continue to monitor the situation and report."

"Please do."

Keep the fellow busy. It hardly mattered how much more these nobles raised. Another big wind was getting ready to blow from the west.

"It's probably nothing," Fouché said. "A fluctuation in the price of Australian wool will throw wealthy men into a lather. For the time being, let's not bother the First Consul again. He has enough to occupy him with the Civil Code and whatnot without fretting over the cost of bric-a-brac. Come straight to me. Tell no one else."

"Of course." Gaudin stiffened at this assault on his discretion.

The company had become tiresome. "Forgive me if I offend. I'm taking every precaution against an international panic."

Fouché's choice of words carried the moment. *Two* mentions of "panic" in one conversation made the banker's face pallid to the point of transparency.

After the man left, Fouché arranged the financial documents on his blotter and studied them the way Bonaparte pored over his campaign maps. Enjoying himself quite as much.

The Royalists were planning something, and were raising cash from both hemispheres the way Bonaparte assembled his armies from throughout Europe. That the something required pockets even deeper than the usual meant a great undertaking; and the greater it was, the more likely its details would soon be the property of the Police Ministry.

Plotters were easy to predict, even if their plots weren't. They were cautious to the point of absurdity, but inevitably they became bored with inaction. Men who ordinarily kept to themselves out of self-preservation began suddenly to convene, first in pairs, then in groups. They never met in the same place twice, a prudent maneuver—to their thinking. But merely by moving around they increased the risk of being observed and reported upon.

In this, the third year in his post, Fouché himself could not be sure whether the man who sold roasted chestnuts on a windy corner of the Quai Desaix was one of his own or just a man with wares for sale. He routinely replaced his household staff, in the suspicion they were spying upon him for the spies he'd hired himself. The fellow who'd filched wine from his cabinet had overstayed his welcome, and paid with his life. It wouldn't happen twice.

Secrecy was not a team sport. Fear and greed turned men into informants; aggressive interrogation had reached perfection under the Terror, and a healthy part of the Ministry's annual budget was set aside for bribery. *Discretionary spending*, for the bookkeepers. If some of the money went astray, who was to track it?

But the plunder was purely collateral. Joseph Fouché loved his work. Give him a conspiracy in the making and he took it apart, put it back together, and disassembled it again like a watchmaker on holiday.

He locked Gaudin's documents in a drawer and dribbled a bit of sealing wax on the lock to make sure it wasn't tampered with, then drafted a letter to be sent in code to all the operatives in charge of his intelligence network, beginning with all the provinces on the Channel:

> *Georges Cadoudal (description follows) to be*
> *detained immediately upon his appearance in France.*
> *In addition, strangers of every description are to be*
> *kept watch upon and their movements reported. In*
> *cases of suspicious activity, do not apprehend these*
> *individuals.*
> *But do not lose sight of them.*

He gave it to his secretary, a dull fellow who at least had the manners to keep his hands off his master's property. He read it.

"Shall I send a copy to the Paris Prefecture?"

"No."

No reason to burden Dubois with Fouché's little hobby. A city policeman broke up drunken brawls and domestic disputes in public places. It would be asking too much for a supernumerary who put together parts of dead cart horses to make room under his ridiculous hat for international intrigue.

And the less Dubois knew of this latest cabal, the less dependent the First Consul would be on his company. Everyone benefited.

17

Five days before his meeting with Cadoudal, the man who would be known as the Viper had made certain arrangements in London. The meeting itself would be only a formality, given the identity of his absent sponsor. The signet ring he carried—a death certificate in France—opened doors in England.

His errands began at a luggage shop in the Strand.

"You're Watley?"

"Yes, sir. Watley and Son; me being the son, though the old gent's passed on. I hope *my* son—"

"Surely every father does. I want to place an order."

"Yes, sir. We are equipped for anything, as you see."

On the evidence, this was no exaggeration. Shelves and tables contained portmanteaux in all sizes, stiff and shiny for travel abroad, butter soft for weekends in the country, rugged as bark for adventure on the outer stations. Hat boxes and satchels hung from the ceiling and tall steamer trunks stood on the floor, propped open to display their various drawers and compartments, chifforobes with grips; when the gentry went to get away from it all, they took most of it with them, on the backs of servants. An intoxicating, voluptuous smell of quality leather and peaty tweed permeated the place.

The proprietor approved of his customer at first sight: a tall slender man, English upper-class in appearance, in a conservative gray coat and knee-breeches.

"I understand you make all your goods on the premises."

Not an accent one heard often in the neighborhood. Not British, but there was breeding in it.

"Yes, sir, my apprentices and myself. All English materials, all English artisans. We serve the royal family by special appointment." George III had commissioned a pigskin shooting jacket with special pockets for the cruet set he carried everywhere to avoid being poisoned, hence the Hanover coat of arms in the window. The partridge would hear him clinking for miles.

"Have you someplace private? I'd rather not discuss details in front of all London."

The shopkeeper came round the counter to lock the door and pull down the window shade, then led his customer into the back room.

Here, punches, scraps of leather, spools of coarse thread, and unfinished pieces of luggage cluttered benches set against all the walls. There was an acid stench of dyes and curing compounds and a brownish smell coming from a teakettle leaking steam from its spout atop a coal-burning stove. Watley liked his tea strong enough to float a nail.

"We're quite accustomed to building luggage to order, sir. That trunk in the corner was designed for the head of a theatrical troupe, to accommodate all his costumes without having to fold them more than once. Over there is a dispatch case, a very special item—"

"Do you discuss all your customers' orders in public?"

He felt a client slipping away, and fell back to regroup.

"If discretion is—"

"It is. The article I'm about to describe isn't to be mentioned to anyone. You'll show it to no one and store it in a secure place out of sight whenever you leave the shop. You'll leave the shop as seldom as possible until the project's finished, and you'll allow no one to remain in the building unattended for any length of time.

"I realize these conditions are unusual, but you'll be recompensed for the inconvenience. If you find this unsatisfactory in any way, tell me now."

"Not at all."

"My instructions are clear."

"Yes."

The man desired a large valise, giving dimensions, with standard latches and straps, but with a panel installed inside that left a shallow recess in the bottom. He described its depth to the quarter-inch. The panel, he stressed, must be stiff and strong, to resist bulging, and attached permanently, so that it could not be removed without destroying it. There must be no release mechanism for anyone examining the valise to stumble upon.

The luggage maker looked up from his pencil. "But how will the item you wish to conceal—"

"Store."

"Store, of course. I beg your pardon. How will you get it inside?"

"I'll place it there myself when the panel is ready to install. You will wait until then before proceeding. I shall be alone in the room at the time. The item will be wrapped in opaque cloth. Under no circumstances will you disturb the wrapping. I shall watch as the panel is installed. How many apprentices do you employ?"

"Two. My son and another young man."

"Dismiss them."

"Dis—?"

"Not permanently. Place them on holiday. You'll do the work yourself. No one is to see it until it's finished."

He did not write this down. Surely he would not forget such requests.

"What is the lightest wood you have available for the frame?"

"I always use maple. It's stout and dependable."

"Too heavy. The bag must appear to be empty when it's presumed to be."

"Fir, perhaps; but it will not last decades, like maple."

"I won't have it even months. I want it to look well-used, not fresh from the shop."

"Certainly. Obvious newness can be gauche."

"In any event it attracts attention. The leather is to be stained with chemicals and distressed with sandpaper."

The shopkeeper made note of this, frowning. To mistreat fine leather was to him more sinful than beating a splendid horse.

"The valise must contain no label or other insignia that will identify its place of purchase. I know you take pride in your workmanship, but I must insist upon anonymity."

To this he had no objection. He would dread to attach his name to an item that was to look shabby and be framed with inferior wood.

"Now read what you've written and commit it to memory. It goes with me when I leave."

The luggage maker began to wonder if the man was a criminal despite his apparent breeding. The loss of overseas colonies and the ghastly last ten years in France had shaken one's faith in outward appearances.

He read his notes slowly and carefully, repeating the dimensions in a murmur, tore the sheet off the block, and handed it to his customer. To his surprise, the customer snatched the entire block from his hands and slid it into a pocket of his coat along with the sheet.

From another pocket he drew a leathern sack and placed it on a nearby bench, at an angle that enabled the other to see that it was filled with gold sovereigns. "I'll be back in a week and give you this same amount. See that it's ready; everything but the hidden panel."

It was more than Watley earned in a busy month.

"Is there nothing else?"

"What else could there be?"

"The color."

The customer smiled for the first time. "Brown, of course. No English gentleman carries black leather."

From there, the man whom we may call the Viper went to the Bank of England for a prearranged meeting with the head clerk. This was a young fellow who affected a lorgnette, which he used to read the fine print on the client's letter of credit and study the seal. The name of this "Colonel Meuchel" meant nothing to him, but his affiliation would please the directors. Austria was a British ally when sabers rattled, and the wealthiest empire in Western Europe.

At length he sat back and laid his lorgnette atop it. He didn't blink at the credit amount; so young a fellow was obviously acting on behalf of interests beyond his ken.

"How much would you like to draw at this time?"

"Ten thousand pounds, to start. In five-pound notes." The customer patted a dispatch case he'd bought in the shop on the Strand, a cheap one with frayed corners, unlikely to attract the attention of a cutpurse.

"These are uncertain times to carry around that much currency."

"Thank you. I shan't carry it long. I'm negotiating a purchase of property and the seller demands cash, in notes backed by the Crown. I'm sure he'd agree with you about the uncertainty of the times."

The clerk nodded. He had experience dealing with Tories who were convinced Great Britain was headed the way of Gibbon's Rome. He went to the vault himself to bring back the notes.

"I say, are there rats aboard your vessel?"

The grizzled mariner in the striped shirt and burlap coat scratched his back against the piling that supported him and spoke around the pipe between his teeth.

"There are for a fact, mate, but they don't take up much room, so I charge 'em only half fare."

The Viper nodded, as if this witticism were familiar. It served him on this occasion to Anglify his accent and season it with middle-class pomposity.

He proceeded with his arrangements for passage aboard the trawler tied up at the wharf. The master, whose name was Hubbard, had paid for it smuggling goods across the Channel the last time England and France were at war and a blockade was in place, so his passenger didn't trouble to confirm his ability to keep silent.

Refreshingly, he wasn't required to explain why he'd chosen such expensive accommodations when he could sail first-class for far less on more conventional craft; the countries were at peace, uneasy though it was, and excursionists traveled back and forth on a regular basis, with Joseph Fouché's police present when they docked in France, collecting names and stopping-places and following up on the answers.

Hubbard was no stranger to curiosity, but neither did he indulge it. He knew and was known by a charter member of the Cutthroat Club, which although he himself was a dedicated Royalist, he could not join because of low birth. He knew nothing about the passenger other than to expect him, and when asked about vermin on board, to respond as he had.

"Is it seaworthy?"

"She just came out of dry dock, fresh tar and I don't figure Lord Nelson would find fault with her brass."

"I don't care if it's green as grass. I want assurance we won't be semaphoring for help. I'd as soon capsize."

"Tight as a drum, sor." He gave forth the respectful address without thought. Something about the man suggested command experience. He may have come by that stick up his posterior by clear title.

Another thick stack of five-pound notes changed hands.

"Can you be ready to sail for France on the twenty-second?"

"Provided the tide don't change its mind."

That was eight days hence, and he would be busy every minute.

He'd taken a room in an old house off Knightsbridge, on the top floor with a window that opened onto a roof with an easy slope. He had no reason to think he'd have to take advantage of such a handy escape route, but caution came to him without thought.

The landlady was deaf in one ear and suffered from gout, so there'd be no climbing the stairs with trays of refreshment to surprise her boarder. In Brussels, he'd had to strangle an infatuated serving girl who'd come to his room in the middle of the night as he was cleaning his pistols; an activity impossible to explain away, considering he was posing as a seminarian. He'd locked her body in the wardrobe and abandoned both his lodgings and his mission. There was no abandoning this one, his last.

He sat at the tiny writing table, turned up the lamp, and removed a number of steelpoint engravings from a portfolio.

They were reproductions for popular sale in France made from recent portraits of the First Consul, his fellow consuls Emmanuel-Joseph Sieyes and Roger Ducos, and the archfiend Joseph Fouché.

The Minister of Police, that reptile, bore close study: The dossier the Cutthroats had compiled on him was twice as thick as any of the others. Fouché was fond of fine things, paintings and sculpture, fonder still of his authority, and jealously guarded the home he shared with his family from invasions friendly and otherwise.

The Viper thought that last fact useful. Fanged beasts tended to relax their guards in their own dens.

He laid Bonaparte's likenesses side by side and examined them closely. He could hardly fail to recognize the man in person, but time and circumstances wrought physical changes worth committing to memory.

The First Consul was putting on weight. The little man in the great position was no longer the gaunt hero of Arcole: The hollows had vanished from his cheeks and his middle had expanded where the facings of the famous green tunic parted to expose his waistcoat. "I grow fat in the saddle," he had declared for public consumption; but months had passed since his last campaign, and his notorious quick meals had filled the void as well as his belly. A roly-poly Bonaparte was difficult to envision, but the sallow cadaver who'd opened fire with cannon on his starving fellow Parisians on 13 Vendémiaire was history.

This was valuable, as the man employed doubles on some ceremonial occasions, and the fellows could not all have inflatable stomachs. The Viper concentrated on the ears, the chin, the nose; features difficult to change with wax and putty and fool the discerning eye. Fortunately, that swollen forehead and cake-knife nose were unmistakable. They belonged on a Roman coin; to one of the many Caesars whose blood had been shed when their vogue passed.

He slid everything back into the portfolio and tied the cord. The material was as good as could be expected, but inadequate. He'd have to get a closer look in person. That increased the danger manifold. But one didn't earn five million francs sitting at home on his bum.

The amount of written material on his subject was staggering. Everyone who had stood near enough to hear the Great Man fart kept a journal: Generals, mistresses, valets—the man who laundered his underdrawers, it seemed—had all found publishers eager to vomit out their observations. The Viper read them all: his fondness on campaign for fried potatoes and onions, how he brushed his perfect teeth, his sensitivity to odors, the whiteness of his hands; all these things were within access.

Of greater value were Bonaparte's own writings. Since the emigration of the nobility early in the Revolution, French newspapers were easily obtainable in local kiosks, and French books and periodicals in stalls and the library of the British Museum. The Viper read transcripts of the general's dispatches and bulletins in Italy and Egypt—comparing his monstrously inflated reports of enemy casualties to the monstrously downgraded figures in the British press—and made notes in the margins of the young artillery lieutenant's *History of Corsica*. Such material, dated as it was by the race of events, provided a revealing glimpse into the way the man thought and felt. It was like studying the migratory patterns of a game bird in order to anticipate its movements: in this case, an eagle.

On his second morning in London, the Viper visited the iron-fronted shop of Millbocker & Co., Gunsmiths, in Piccadilly, an old concern whose shelves were gray with dust but whose inventory gleamed. The atmosphere was a mix of vanilla-scented oil—pleasant, as in a Parisian *patisserie*—sulfur, and solvent, which stung the eyes.

"Mr. Molière!" The red-eyed proprietor glanced at the clock. "Right on time."

"By that I take it they're ready."

Eighty-year-old Augustus Millbocker produced a brace of flintlock pistols in a cherrywood box lined in velvet.

They were intricately engraved, with polished hickory grips, and nestled in form-fitted cutouts beside the ramrod and extractors and a brass powder flask, embossed with Bonaparte's profile. They were the work of Nicholas Boutet, the best gunmaker in France, and were duplicates of a set presented to the Corsican himself by their manufacturer to commemorate his victories in

Italy. The Viper had left them in the shop for necessary adjust-
ments.

"An excellent pair, and beautifully maintained," said the old
smith. "One would think they'd never been fired."

"They have." He removed each in turn and sighted down it.
The realignments were perfect.

"You haven't changed your mind?"

"I haven't. It's bad luck to sell one's guns."

"A pity. Boutet is hard to come by in this country. I wouldn't
have taken you for a superstitious man."

"I don't intend to be taken at all." He handed Millbocker a
sovereign.

18

"Monsieur Dubois, you are a breath of fresh air. Bonaparte has been locked up with lawyers all day; dull as brown soap, the lot. You can cast sunshine merely by not bringing up the Civil Code."

Prefect Dubois kissed the air above the slender, impossibly white hand that was extended to him. "Madame, you need have no fear of that. I enforce the law and eat soufflé, without the faintest idea how either is made."

Josephine rewarded this pallid attempt at wit with her chamber-bell laugh. It was extremely rare for Citizeness Bonaparte to greet a visitor to the Tuileries except upon ceremonial occasions, or to unbend herself from state protocol so far as to refer to her husband as "Bonaparte" outside her social circle. The tribute was not lost on the caller; he was regarded as a friend of the family.

Through charm alone, this woman had survived three radical changes of government when others with seemingly greater prospects had not. She had been the wife of an aristocrat, a prisoner of the state condemned to death, the mistress of a powerful politician, and now the First Lady of the Republic. Even a brief but infamous experiment in adultery had failed to shake her from her position. She had conquered the conqueror, and consequently all of France.

Tonight she wore a gown of filmy white muslin, with only an embroidered scarf standing between her polished shoulders and the drafts that stalked the two-hundred-year-old palace.

"Your hand is like ice, Madame," Dubois said, releasing it.

"It's the lesser sacrifice. Wool is warm, but it scratches."

Like Malmaison, the Tuileries bore the unmistakable stamp of its mistress. The flabby Bourbon furnishings had been destroyed or carried away by the mob that had taken the King; she had filled the void with paintings and tapestry looted from the Vatican and the royal houses of Europe and distributed them with taste. Josephine commanded decorators as ruthlessly as her husband led armies.

A comely general, she; although one couldn't help noticing fine fissures under the enamel the women were plastering on their faces this season. She was nearer Dubois' age than her husband's, and the Prefect considered himself *hors de combat* in matters of romance by reason of his years.

She opened the door to the First Consul's study without knocking. "Monsieur Dubois." She left them alone.

The room, vast as it was, felt close. A fire roared in the hearth, despite the relative mildness outside. The occupant was a Mediterranean, and not long back from the furnace of Egypt.

"The wine is there. Help yourself."

Dubois blinked. The leader of the Republic was sprawled on his stomach on the floor before his desk, like an infant rolling on a rug. He was in his shirtsleeves.

"Are you quite well, Citizen?" He wondered if the First Consul's famously nervous stomach had taken a turn for the worse.

"I am, but my navy isn't. It needs a dose of Nelson."

The Prefect saw then the large-scale map spread on the floor, as big as a bedsheet. Bonaparte lay stretched across the North Atlantic, his half-empty goblet standing on Scotland.

How he must envy that goblet! It occupied a prime position to strike south and annex the British Empire to his. England's army was pathetic, its generals inbred and incompetent, its ears and tail well and truly docked by the ragged American rabble, but its navy—well, there had been the Battle of the Nile, and Bonaparte's first bitter taste of defeat, courtesy of Lord Admiral

Horatio Nelson. In order to march on London, one must first cross the Channel, history's most formidable moat, teeming with full-rigged sharks armed with cannon commanded by officers as brilliant as they were ruthless.

"Shall I come back later?"

"No. The situation won't have changed." Bonaparte scrambled to his feet, scooping up his goblet, and took the decanter from his visitor. "A rare vintage, I'm told," he said, pouring. "The Italians I got it from worship everything ancient. Who can blame them? They've had a bitter harvest for a thousand years."

"I'm sure you're right, Citizen. History is a closed book to me."

"As is the science of winemaking, in my case. Burgundy and Madeira are all the same to me. What's happening in Paris?"

He'd come prepared. "We had an interesting suicide last week in—"

"A Royalist?"

"No, a butcher's wife. It seems she—"

"No, no gossip. What of Royalists?"

"Perhaps that's a question for the Police Minister."

"I've asked him. Now I'm asking you."

The Ministry had been closed to Dubois for weeks; Fouché had pled paperwork. The Prefect could report only what his own officers had told him.

"They've been quiet. I don't think two of them have sat at the same table in a tavern since Four Nivose."

Ventose, the month of wind—formerly the third week of February to the third week of March—was drawing toward a close, with Germinal, the month of budding, waiting in the flies; not that one would know it for the snow flurrying outside the casement windows.

"You don't *think*?"

"I would state confidently that they have not. Between my

officers and Citizen Fouché's informants, the Royalist taverns are not flourishing."

"That would explain why you're making your own amusement. I heard a rumor that one of your men attempted to detain one of his for questioning recently."

"Actually it was the other way around. They nearly crossed swords." Where did the man get his information? Certainly the Police Minister had been as chagrined as he over the incident.

Bonaparte chuckled. "You suffer from the necessary absence of uniforms. Chess?"

"Certainly."

Dubois had him checked in eight moves; a rare victory against this new kind of general, who cheated openly. He moved his knights and his pawns according to his own lights without regard to the rules of the game, the same way he made war.

Bonaparte was unfazed by his defeat. "Fouché's become quite the genealogist. At this point he knows more about the Bourbon family tree than they know themselves. There are Austrians, of course, and Hanovers, making the late Louis the Sixteenth a cousin of George the Third's; but I shouldn't be surprised to find a Jew lurking about the roots. Court morals," he said with a shrug.

Dubois suppressed a yawn. The wine was strong, and the atmosphere in the room was stifling. "It's an old line."

"It's still unclear just who is to occupy the throne in the event the monarchy is restored. Fouché says the man who stands to profit most is the man who'll be found closest to the center of the action. Do you share this opinion?" He began setting up the board again. The pieces were onyx on his side. Bonaparte always chose black, allowing his opponent to make the first move, which was frequently a blunder.

"It would stand to reason. Most thieves are in it for the gain."

"Spoken like a true policeman. But is it sound politically?"

"I can't speak for politicians, only criminals." Dubois led with a knight.

Bonaparte advanced his king two squares, leaping a pawn: a blatantly illegal move that put his most important piece in jeopardy. A trap, beyond doubt. "The difference between the two is immaterial."

Conversation ceased for several minutes. The First Consul suffered heavy casualties among his pawns. But while Dubois was slaughtering his infantry, an opposing knight advanced to within striking position.

He studied the shambles of a board. It would be a signal mistake to attempt to play the game according to his opponent's rules, or lack of them; that had been proven time and time again in the field. "The Minister's theory is not without flaws."

"Explain."

"That the other side may be aware of it, and has deliberately placed a lesser man in harm's way in order to deflect attention from the greater threat. A cat's paw, decorated in the raiments of royalty, with a tiger crouching behind." He moved his rook, ignoring the opportunity to capture the black bishop while blocking the black knight's path to victory. In three more moves he declared checkmate.

Color stained the First Consul's polished-pearl cheeks. Then he smiled genuinely, placing his excellent teeth on display. "Fouché underestimates you, to his peril. You look like a shoe clerk, but you think like Machiavelli."

He pondered whether Bonaparte was talking about chess.

The subject shifted to the domestic investigation.

"I fear whoever else was involved in the affair of Four Nivose has trickled through our fingers," Dubois reported. "The trail is cold."

"Doubtless"—Bonaparte's favorite word—"England is harboring them. It has, however, moved beyond the position of mere landlord. Last month a French patrol in Belgium stopped a courier traveling with an armed British escort on the way from the Channel to Vienna; transporting a shipment of broadcloth, the courier explained. The papers were in order, and after a brief search the party was allowed to resume its journey. In the light of Gaudin's recent revelations, I suspect the patrol didn't dig deep enough."

"Gaudin?" Dubois was vague on the name.

"My Finance Minister. Surely Fouché reported his findings to you." Bonaparte glanced up, brows lifted, as he rearranged his men on the board.

Paperwork indeed. The bastard. But the Prefect kept his face flat.

"When it comes to financial affairs, I'm out of my depth. Ask my wife."

"The fellow in charge of the escort was officious and annoying. The commander of the patrol was tempted to detain the party on the basis of his attitude alone, but emotion and instinct are two different things."

"Sometimes they're hard to separate."

"True. Incidentally, Fouché's informants in England report that Lord and Lady Rexborough have struck camp for their house in London, leaving Cadoudal in residence at their country estate. They did not follow the couple: Their orders are not to let the general out of their sight.

"The people the Police Minister had watching the house in London reported that while Lady Rexborough arrived safely, the Earl was not with her." Bonaparte paused, squaring away his men. "Difficult fellow, he, by all accounts," he said then. "Officious and annoying."

"Scarcely atypical of the British upper class."

"Just so. But Rexborough was prominent among the men who suddenly decided to convert their holdings—businesses, real property, even personal art collections—into portable assets, to the tune of two million francs. It would be just like those toffs to assign one of their own to safeguard their blood money."

They began a third game, but Dubois' mind was not on it. He was swiftly cornered and surrendered his queen.

"Another?"

The Prefect shook his head. "I have some things to attend to at the Quai Desaix before retiring. Thank you for the evening, Citizen." He rose and bowed.

Bonaparte kept his seat. "Austria is a British ally. I find it worthy of note that that fellow we were discussing, the one thickest among the thieves, is currently a guest of Emperor Franz the Second in Ettelheim. The Duc d'Enghien is the son of the Comte d'Artois, a cousin of the late Louis the Sixteenth's, and is one of several in line for the French throne."

Dubois' mind had been on what Fouché was about; clearly he had the scent, and that was why the Prefect had been pushed aside. Belatedly he realized Bonaparte was still speaking.

"Artois himself is too old and gouty to travel more than a mile at a stretch, and the others lack ambition."

"You consider Enghien the man behind these plots?"

"I don't consider a Bourbon prince capable of being behind anything, except a toady with a staff; they haven't the brains to dress themselves, much less conspire. This one is content to shoot partridges in Prussia and wait for Cadoudal to roll out the red carpet. The tiger behind the cat's paw, as you put it; and like most tigers, too fat and lazy to do his own stalking. For this the English pay him forty-two hundred guineas per year."

"This has been established?"

"When a coin falls to the pavement anywhere in the world, Gaudin hears it."

Then, apropos of nothing: "Succession, that's the secret to survival. The English haven't had to deal with regicide since Charles the First in sixteen forty-nine; and they settled that matter by disinterring Cromwell's corpse and stringing it up at Tyburn. The royals breed, they multiply. What's the point of slaying one, if another will just drop into his slot like a sou in a moneychanger's belt?

"Succession, Dubois. With few exceptions, it has been a guarantor against assassination ever since the fall of Rome."

Dubois was uncomfortably aware of being scrutinized; the great man appeared almost desperate for him to grasp what he was saying, without precisely saying it.

Of course he'd grasped it. How could he not? Bonaparte's ambitions were as bright as the sun, and as dangerous to stare into for more than a few seconds. To trade one monarch for another by seizing the crown himself raised cheating to a new plane.

Dubois made a strategic retreat. "Well, we can't risk war with either country over the trade in bric-a-brac."

"No. Not over that. Good night, Dubois. I hope next time you can keep your mind on the game."

"As do I, Citizen."

19

The Viper, whose visits to Great Britain usually restricted themselves to crowded, sulfurous London, marveled that there should be two hundred square miles of England as desolate as Dartmoor.

A man traveled leagues through green wooded lowland, ideal for fox hunting, topped a rise, and found himself suddenly on the surface of the moon: great gray stretches of bleak moors pierced with jagged projectiles of stone and rock huts. He wouldn't have been surprised to see a man emerge from one wearing animal skins and carrying a spear. At unpredictable intervals, swamp gas erupted in the mire, deploying eerie blue domes like umbrellas and stinking worse than an open sewer. The place existed perpetually on the verge, or in the aftermath, of a gray drizzling rain.

If a man believed in hell, this was it.

The local constabulary had posted signs to warn visitors away from the treacherous bogs, a well-meaning but perfunctory effort that seemed to have lost its novelty after the first few turnings. The danger didn't end where the signs did, only the campaign.

It was no wonder Georges Cadoudal should have chosen this place to train his people in the art of killing Republicans.

The property belonged to one of the general's Cutthroat benefactors, who if he had ever inspected it in person had probably blotted the directions from his memory. The absentmindedness of the English was often their best defense against a personal-injury suit: *Milord Chief Magistrate, I can scarcely be held accountable for accidents that take place on a tract of land I haven't visited in a generation.*

With a Swiss compass and a map drawn on vellum during the reign of Charles I, the Viper guided his horse along a path worn by wild ponies and feral hogs and at midday came upon the property, identified by a rocky tor in the east shaped like a reclining beast (locals called this the Sleeping Lion, and had named a public house for it) and a copse of ancient-growth oaks to the northwest, as broad in girth as castle keeps. He knew he was in the right place when he directed his field glass on a goatskin bag suspended from the gallows arm of a post in a large level patch some three hundred paces off the path. The careless fools had overlooked this makeshift target when they abandoned the camp.

Folding the glass, he dismounted and led his horse that direction, testing the ground carefully with each step as the sodden loam squished round his boots.

For a long time the bag seemed to maintain the same distance; it was deceptive country, designed for sinister purposes. The horse didn't care for it, and made no secret of the fact, snorting and blowing as it picked its way among rocks carried there by glaciers and left behind like jagged droppings.

At last the Viper drew near enough to see that the goatskin was torn open just below the middle. Clumps of sodden sawdust clung to the ragged edges and a heap of wet sand formed a cone on the earth beneath the bag, from where it had spilled. Here the earth was sound. He remounted, kneed the horse close to the object, leaned down, and gave it a push. The bag, roughly the size and shape of a human torso, moved reluctantly, swinging heavy and sodden from the frayed rope. Enough sand remained to replicate the heft of an adult male of average size.

Cadoudal had boasted of his lung power on the battlefield. His voice echoed in the Viper's head as if he'd been present during maneuvers: *Swing low,* mes enfants, *and put your backs into it.*

Brace yourself with your foot and twist the bayonet as you pull it out.
Men have been known to survive stabbing, but never evisceration.

The rider pressed his lips together in his phantom smile. Alien creature, this bellowing soldier, who would paint the earth with blood and entrails but scrupled against slaying one man to spare all the rest.

This dummy warrior spared him from having to fashion a target of his own.

He urged the horse another forty paces at a walk, swung down, and tethered it to a low twisted root to charge his fine pistols. He'd left the cumbersome cherrywood case behind. Now he reached inside the leather drawstring bag strapped around his waist, removed two paper cartridges filled with powder from the flask, and slid them down inside the muzzles, followed by balls and wadding. He tamped it all down using the slim wooden ramrod.

He handled the cartridges with extreme caution. The powder inside contained a substance called fulminate of mercury, last year's invention by Edward Howard of the Royal Society of London. It was several times more powerful than conventional gunpowder and expelled projectiles with greater velocity, using smaller amounts; but it was also several times more volatile. One errant spark, a tremor of the hand, and the world would hear no more from the Viper.

In his room off Knightsbridge, he'd tempted fate further. With a jeweler's saw he'd split the leaden balls in half and hollowed them out with an ordinary nutpick. He'd then poured fulminate powder into the hollows, varying the amount of grains and marking each ball distinctively with the pick after fusing the halves back together in the handpress. He carried the loads in separate pouches in his courier's belt, lest they collide with one another. It wouldn't serve to travel with them in his luggage for any employee of an inn to stumble upon while unpacking.

No one to his knowledge had ever attempted what he was about.

There was a high likelihood that when he pulled the trigger the charge inside the ball would ignite and turn the weapon into a bomb, and the shooter into the victim.

He experimented. He wedged one of the pistols between two rocks, tied a cotton cord to the trigger, and withdrew ten paces, unrolling the cord from the spool. Pulling the cord taut, he drew a deep breath, held it, and jerked.

The hammer fell, the flint sparked, the cartridge flared, and with a thunderous *crack!* Nicholas Boutet's beautiful workmanship split apart at the breech, flinging the firing mechanism and barrel in two directions.

The horse whistled and fought its tether. It held.

The Viper composed himself in thought.

At length, he retrieved the other pistol and charged the barrel, selecting a ball he'd marked differently from the first, containing a smaller load. He repeated himself, fitting the pistol between the blackened rocks, tying a fresh cord, and retracing his steps the same distance.

He hesitated, holding the cord. Another failure and he'd have to replace his weapon with an unfamiliar one, and likely inferior. But he must know.

He pulled the cord. The pistol bucked, but the ball flew from the muzzle and out across the moor until it spent itself, landing noiselessly on the wet ground.

But he was unsatisfied. If rocks could not hold the pistol steady, would his hand? Would his aim be true? He must know.

He cleaned and oiled the pistol with items retrieved from his saddle pouch, reloaded it with a ball containing the fulminate, raised the pistol to shoulder level, and extended it at arm's length, lining up the iron sight with the goatskin bag hanging from the gallows post. He'd be much closer to his target on the day—much,

much closer—but accuracy at a distance ensured success at close range. He filled his lungs once again and counted to three. . . .

Steel struck flint. The powder caught. A spurt of orange-and-yellow flame separated ball from barrel. The weapon pulsed in his hand like a living creature, but his grip held firm. His hand moved no more than a centimeter off level.

Time seemed to sag in the interval; in reality it was the smallest fraction of a second. Then the goatskin exploded with a report as loud as the first, but with results more satisfying. When the smoke slid aside, a scrap of skin no larger than a man's scalp swung free at the end of the rope.

He went down to investigate, walking through a rotten-egg stench of brimstone. Fresh sawdust and sand—the bag's entrails—lay in a pile at the base of the post.

The Viper knelt and ran a hand through the mess. Grains of sand slid between his fingers. Bits of sawdust clung to his palm.

He stood and wiped them off on his breeches. He was satisfied to the point of elation. No one could survive such destruction; not even the Strong Man of France.

20

Andrew Watley hated the luggage business.

His father had insisted he begin his apprenticeship in the tannery in Limehouse, where the raw hides were scraped and cured and the offal slung into the Thames. Those who exulted in the aroma of fine leather knew nothing of the stink of rotting flesh and the eye-stinging fumes of formaldehyde and tannic acids that went into its construction: All this on top of five centuries' accumulation of fish scales and green slime on the docks.

"How you exaggerate, Andrew! You should try a season in a stable."

What did the old man know? It had been twenty years since his own trial by stench. Things had reached the point where his son could no longer stand even the genteel smell of the merchandise in the shop. Odors of any kind seared his nostrils and soured his stomach.

When his father told him to stay away from the shop for a week, he was elated at first, then suspicious. He hadn't had more than Sunday morning off in two years. The old man had never before shown he possessed a bump of generosity on that thick skull.

"Why? Sneaking in a tart?"

He got his ear boxed for this suggestion.

"Find Virgil and go do whatever it is you two do when I'm not around to keep you from trouble."

Andrew, his head still ringing from the blow, stood watch from the doorway of the tallow shop across the street. He recruited Virgil, his father's other apprentice, to spell him.

"Sounds dull as paint. What's he about anyway?"

"If I knew that, mallethead, we wouldn't be doing this. Smuggling, maybe. If it's bad enough, he'll either have to cut us in or pay to keep our mouths shut."

"You would extort money from your own father?"

"I'd deem it the rise I've been two years asking for."

"Ballocks. He's too old and fat for a pirate."

Virgil had the brains of a born tanner.

They watched for most of the week. Customers came and went bearing nothing more interesting than satchel-shaped packages or claim checks for items they'd left for cleaning or repairing. It began to look as if Andrew had squandered his holiday on a bum steer. On the seventh day, Virgil didn't show up. Thinking he wasn't as stupid as he'd thought, Andrew decided to pack it in himself. He had a week's worth of carousing to make up for in one afternoon.

He was stepping into the street when a man carrying a large bundle stopped at the door. When he glanced up and down the street, Andrew retreated into his doorway out of sight. A shop that sold bags and briefcases was not a brothel; no one need be concerned about who saw him enter. And the bundle was intriguing. It didn't look as if it contained luggage.

He strode to the corner, crossed the street, and used his latchkey on the service entrance. This let him into the back room of the shop. He stationed himself in a corner beyond the lamplight, behind a dilapidated trunk stood on end with a stack of baggage balanced on top; torn and worn-out things, good only for harvesting hinges and latches.

His breathing quickened. His heart started thumping to get

out. He hadn't played hide-and-go-seek since he was small, and had forgotten the thrill when the seeker came near.

Time slowed to a stop. He heard only murmurs from the other side of the wall. No one seemed inclined to enter the room. Pulse and respiration slowed. Was it a wild-goose chase after all? The stranger had looked too ordinary for a brigand.

The door opened from the shop; the rush of stirred air made him jump. His father came in, followed closely by the man with the bundle.

Arthur Watley, the proprietor, had greeted his visitor without offering to shake hands. The man's right arm was engaged with the bundle he was holding, but in any event the luggage-maker sensed they were not equals.

This parcel, wrapped in brown muslin and tied with cord, was the approximate size and shape of a side of mutton, but much lighter, from the ease with which he handled it.

Watley dismissed it from his thoughts. He was not an incurious man, but he was being paid for his silence, which included asking questions that wouldn't be answered anyway. He turned the CLOSED sign round on the door and locked it.

"It's ready?"

"You said a week, and that's what it's been."

"A worthless thing to say. I'm not a calendar."

Watley raised the counter flap and they went into the back room.

The valise on the bench was large enough to contain two suits of clothes and a variety of necessaries, fitted with brass and secured with straps. The quality was obvious. The stitching was uncommonly fine and the leather was full grain, the best available. But from its appearance the item had seen much use and careless handling. The corners were scuffed, the brass nicked and tarnished by fumes from a bucket of common launderers' bleach; Watley knew all the tricks. The sides were cross-hatched with scratches applied with a copper scouring pad. The rolled leather handle was dark, as if soaked deep with the sweat of dirty hands (soot from a coal stove), but stout overall, although it was a shame the lightweight frame of brittle birch would not hold up as long as dependable rock maple.

The customer opened the case. It was deeper than it appeared from outside. The panel that would be inserted to create a false bottom lay beside it, a rectangle of birch veneer an eighth of an inch thick, nearly as light as New World balsam. The furniture maker who had supplied it had not been informed as to its purpose. Watley had concealed it between layers of paper-thin leather sewn together, from the same dye lot as the material he'd used for the valise.

The customer held it to the light, observing the holes round the edges where the panel would be stitched into place.

Watley considered the thing a masterpiece, both of construction and deception. It was a shame he could not advertise it.

"Satisfactory. I'll tell you when the panel can be installed."

"Yes." Watley returned to his shop.

The Viper made sure the door was on the latch, then placed his bundle in the bottom of the valise, smoothing its surface like a bedsheet, and lowered the panel on top of it. He pressed down on it with both hands, compacting the contents, but the holes did not line up with those in the case. An air pocket had formed, creating resistance.

He lifted out the panel, removed the bundle, and untied it, spreading the muslin and exposing the contents. He rearranged them and circled his palms out from the center in a kneading motion, distributing the pressure evenly. Air escaped with a faint sigh. He rewrapped and retied the bundle and replaced the panel. This time the holes were in line. Experimentally he closed the lid and tested the valise for weight. It lifted easily. Under casual inspection it would seem empty to anyone unaware of the flimsy framing material.

Something rustled in a darkened corner of the back room. He put down the valise, listened without moving. The noise wasn't repeated.

A mouse, probably. The shops on that street were old and teeming with vermin.

He strode to the door and rapped. Watley stepped in, wearing a sailmakers' palm strapped to one hand.

The customer stood out of his way but in full sight of the procedure. A large curved needle passed deftly through the holes in panel and case, sealing the one to the other with a thong, thin but supple, fashioned from bull's sinew. No motion was wasted and the stitches were even. This was the work of half an hour.

The luggage maker knotted the thong on the underside of the panel and cut it with a blade like a razor.

"You see, sir," he said, straightening, "how the stitching doesn't show. I stained the sinew with tea to match the case."

The customer handed him a second sack laden with gold sovereigns and left through the front, carrying his valise as easily as if it contained nothing.

After his father left the room, Andrew remained motionless, breathing as shallowly as possible.

His heart was pounding as before. What he'd seen when the man unwrapped his intriguing bundle had increased his curiosity rather than lain it to rest.

He'd expected contraband—arms, money, South American cane sugar, rubber from British colonies in Asia—something the

Crown either banned outright or imposed a hefty duty upon when it passed through its inspection posts. From there it set sail for the Continent or America, which levied costly tariffs: smugglers' bait. But of this—if it was what he thought it was—he could form no conclusions.

Except that if the stranger thought it worth hiding, its secret was worth paying to keep.

Andrew Watley, son of Arthur Watley, luggage-maker by appointment to the royal family, came out of hiding in a murk of thought. Whom to approach, his father or the customer?

The customer. He stood the most risk and would not bargain long. If Andrew moved fast enough, he would catch sight of the man carrying the valise and follow him to some quiet spot where he could make his proposition.

Virgil needn't be told. He'd lost interest; most likely he'd forgotten the affair already. That meant more for Andrew. That was only fair. It was his idea from the start.

He hurried out the back door, straight into a blow in the stomach.

It emptied his lungs of air. Gasping, he felt warm wetness soaking his shirt and coat and down the front of his breeches.

The man carrying the valise planted his boot on the boy's instep, holding him in place as he pulled the dagger from between his ribs with a rotating motion.

Brace yourself with your foot and twist; Cadoudal's orders to his rebels in training. The fool was an assassin at heart, whether or not he owned to it.

Their eyes met, Viper's and victim's. He saw the light go out, an ember among ashes. The pressure of his foot was the only thing keeping the boy upright. When he withdrew it, the boy collapsed.

The Viper bent to wipe both sides of the blade on the boy's

coat, and almost as an afterthought went through his pockets, retrieving a cloth pouch with a few shillings inside, a rather fine clasp knife with an ivory-inlaid handle, and a pair of plain keys on a ring. One would belong to the luggage shop's back door, making the youth either Watley's son or his other apprentice. He returned the ring but kept the money and knife. Since the arrival of fleeing French nobility and their servants, no one in London was safe from thieves who would kill a man for a handful of pence. The police would look into the atrocity, make routine queries, file the record with the other unsolved investigations, and move on. Pocketing the booty, the Viper surveyed both ends of the street, saw no one, and took himself away, scabbarding the dagger under his greatcoat and swinging the valise as he walked. At the first sewer opening he came to he committed the pouch and clasp knife to the sea.

That night he rode to Lord Rexborough's house, met with Cadoudal, spent his pleasant hour with Lady Carolyn, and left the next morning for France. The weather had turned foul. He anticipated a rough crossing.

21

"That's neither here nor there, Citizen. We're pledged to share all information in this matter. Not only by our oaths of office, but by personal agreement as well."

Prefect Dubois spoke quietly; an effort of will. There was something about Fouché's habitual calm that stood his nerves on end: the heavy reptilian lids, the length of lip beneath the long ecclesiastical nose, his air of knowing everything the Prefect had to say before he said it. All qualities Dubois lacked.

"*Monsieur le Prefect,* surely you don't mean we must burden each other with every trifling detail that crosses our desks. Shall I run my daily rubbish past you before it's removed?"

Dubois stood in the morning room of the Police Minister's pleasant house in the Rue de Bac—formerly the property of a marquis, since deceased—where its master drank chocolate from a translucent cup. The lace on the small breakfast table was spotless; Fouché's face was not. Patches of crimson stained the yellow skin. He was notoriously jealous of his time at home with his wife and children, and considered any breach an invasion.

The visitor was unmoved. "Forgive me, Citizen, but I'm a poor man. To me, two million francs is not rubbish."

"It's outside your jurisdiction."

"I'm confused. Which is it, too trivial for my regal eye, or not my business? Let me be the judge in either case."

Fouché retreated, folding his skeletal hands. With the sigh of a put-upon spouse, he reported what Gaudin had discovered, in detail and to the centime. When it came to monetary amounts, his memory rivaled the First Consul's.

Dubois stood in awe while the Minister reeled off names and titles of British nobles he himself had never heard of and how much each had raised, ostensibly to contribute to the latest Royalist plot.

"Citizen Bonaparte thinks the men questioned in Belgium were transporting cash from those transactions to the bank in Austria," Dubois said. "Do you agree?"

"Yes, but only on a contingency basis. The First Consul is not infallible. Had he his way, we'd still be rounding up Jacobins."

"I don't suppose we can count on the Austrian authorities to provide us with the details of a substantial recent deposit."

"I'll have to consult Foreign Minister Talleyrand on that. I am only a poor police official"—he gestured with a gold-chased spoon—"but last I heard, Austria was still allied with England. In any case they'd only confirm what we already know. The British are bankrolling a fresh assault on our chief of state. It's consistent with their standing policy of paying others to risk their skins."

"But what form will this assault take?"

"One can only surmise. Cadoudal isn't so foolish as to try the same thing twice." Fouché sipped from his cup. He was so deep in thought he left the brown stain on his upper lip. "*One* man may succeed where a band has failed," he said then.

"However did you arrive at that, Citizen?"

For once the Police Minister appeared at a loss for an urbane (and disingenuous) explanation. "I—cannot say. For some reason the thought just occurred. A pipe dream. Ludicrous, when you think about it."

Dubois was inclined to agree—until his superior changed the subject in the next breath. The notion had come so quickly he'd neglected to keep it to himself, for what advantage it might bring.

A lone assassin, thought Dubois. It bore looking into.

Fouché wiped his lips then and rose, in his silk dressing gown towering over the slight police official, and vanished through a door without remark.

He was gone several minutes by the ormolu clock on the sideboard. Waiting, Dubois pulled at his moustaches, wondering if he'd been forgotten or if the delay was intended to illustrate his own lack of importance; the Minister was not above such petty demonstrations. Crockery clattered somewhere, the blade of a shovel scraped the stone of a hearth. His host collected servants the way he did books and gimcrack. Finally he returned, carrying a sheaf of foolscap.

"I had my secretary copy this so I could study it at home. I confess this approach has been bootless so far. Perhaps that filing-case you use for a brain will spot something of minor import that will lead to something worthwhile."

"What is it?" The Prefect was so eager for anything new he overlooked the casual insult.

"I suppose you could call it an oral history. I sent men to all the ports of call on the Channel, to interview our informants on the off chance they saw something they left out of their reports. They're human, after all."

"Most regrettable." But his superior was immune to irony. "The Channel seems obvious. The English are nothing if not circumspect."

"So much so they may choose the obvious, thinking we'll expect they won't. But I think they're too clever to consider such a course as clever. Personally I expect the threat to come from the Continent, but who can say for certain? It's a shell game either way." He handed over the papers. "It's a summary, of course. I'll send round my secretary in the morning with details."

Dubois looked at the top sheet and was dejected at first glance. The reports hinted at droning accounts of comings and goings at various inns and taverns, dictated by illiterates to semiliterates; as if half-ignorance were an improvement. It was an unpromising beginning.

III

***

FLOREAL
(Month of Flowers)

22

Chief Inspector Limodin looked put out. His face rarely wore any other expression, but today it seemed significant.

"What?" Dubois asked his subordinate. "More anonymous letters implicating odious neighbors?"

"Worse. A parcel came for you in the forenoon. I made the messenger leave it outside. It might be another infernal machine."

The Prefect stepped outside the office and spotted the offending item at the end of the hall. It was a leather carton the size and shape of a bucket, with a strap handle.

"A hat box," Dubois observed. "Well, it's cheaper than hiring a horse and cart. In this case, however, I've been expecting it."

Limodin watched his superior stand the box on the heaps of paper on his desk and remove the lid. He looked eager.

Dubois lifted out an object that resembled an outsize pillbox with a square patent-leather visor, a brass eagle insignia on the front, and a strap with a buckle. He placed it on his head and fastened the buckle at his chin.

"First impressions? Be brutally honest."

"You look like a postman."

"Better a postman than a peacock." Dubois scowled at his plumed official fore-and-aft headpiece on its peg. "The uniform must not wear the man. Have you a looking glass?"

"If I did I wouldn't admit it. I'll see what I can find."

At length the chief inspector returned, dangling a hand-mirror by its mother-of-pearl handle between thumb and forefinger. He might have been carrying a dead rat by its tail. "Inspector Morage is fond of his imperials. He suspends them in a hammock when he sleeps."

Dubois seized the item, looked at his reflection, and made a small adjustment in the angle of the hat, squaring it across his brows. "I arranged with the quartermaster to have it made from my own design, based on an infantry shako, with a shorter crown. I like it, I think."

"Is it permitted?"

"I can't imagine the Police Minister would object. He already behaves as if I'm invisible. The First Consul separates himself from his generals on campaign by wearing the simple green uniform of a colonel. At all events, these two men run France. Do you think they care two snaps about my hat?"

Limodin registered disapproval in his customary way, by saying nothing.

His superior returned his attention to his reflection. "Yes, I like it. I intend to order one for every officer in the Prefecture."

"Excluding me, I hope."

"Then you'll be the only popinjay in the service. It's high time we all start looking like proper policemen." He admired the effect a moment longer, then returned the hat to its box; redirecting his attention to the mountain of paper with a sigh. The documents he'd brought from the Police Ministry lay atop the tallest heap.

Dubois was uncertain just when the business of government had fallen to petty clerks. The sheer volume of paper that passed through his office doubled by the day. One morning it arrived on pallets, left in slender sheaves, and returned the next day in trundle carts. It all required a volcanic personality to attend to it with dispatch; but there was only one Bonaparte, and he was busy drawing up a new system of law, and incidentally dreaming up another war.

Which would likely lead to more paper.

Dubois' method was to attack the piles of foolscap the way mounted lancers assaulted a redoubt. When there were no more enemy soldiers to kill, and his desk was empty (invariably after nightfall), he was free to turn his attention to police work.

He was a simple boulevard policeman, despite the grandeur of his title; a man who enjoyed patrolling the neighborhood of an evening, trying locks and questioning suspicious pedestrians. Limodin thought this beneath the dignity of Paris' chief keeper of the peace, but Dubois never felt himself more useful than when he was performing the duties of a common flic. He would rather rattle doorknobs and chivvy strangers than attend ceremonies of state wearing three rods of gold braid and a sword he never drew.

On the morning after his interview with Fouché in his home, the Police Minister's new secretary arrived at the Quai Desaix carrying a bulging dispatch case and laid it on a section of desk Dubois had just cleared. "The Minister sends his regards, Citizen. This is the material he discussed with you last night."

The Prefect could barely see over the case. "I was told to expect only those accounts that were collected from the ports on the Channel."

"Indeed. I shall be back with the rest. Is there a reply?"

"Thank Citizen Fouché for his promptness."

Alone again, Dubois fingered the hat box longingly, then pushed it aside and unstrapped the dispatch case. He would rattle no doorknobs this week.

He kept moving, like a viper after sundown.

He preferred not to stay in a place more than two nights in succession. Strangers attracted curiosity, and although he could speak the local dialect with or without a foreign accent (his choice, depending on the circumstances), blending in became more challenging the deeper he moved into the French countryside.

Regiments were on the march. War was in the wind, small surprise: 4 Nivose had reawakened Bonaparte's addiction to the smell of gunpowder; he inhaled it like snuff. Soldiers commanded rooms in all the inns, forcing a lone traveler to stay put until the troops moved on and lodging became available down the road. He didn't want another incident like Rouen.

There, he'd been evicted by an apologetic innkeeper on behalf of a lieutenant-colonel of Hussars, who'd requisitioned the entire establishment for himself and his staff.

"I understand. I shall leave at once." He could do nothing else, or risk being remembered.

The officer was a stout, red-faced man whose scarlet tunic barely contained his girth. With the country having been at war for nearly a decade, a man of his age who'd failed to advance beyond the rank of lieutenant-colonel was either incompetent or a martinet who'd managed to provoke those above and below his rank. This one suggested both. He yapped like a terrier at the corporal lugging a case of wine from a pack horse into the building. The Viper had tried to take advantage of the distraction to pass unnoticed.

"You, there! What's your name?"

He stopped and faced the officer. "Chaucer, sir."

"English?" His accent had been noted, as intended.

"American."

The lieutenant-colonel appeared not to disapprove. The fledgling United States had supported the Revolution.

"What's your business?"

He produced a letter on Bank of England stationery, identifying him as a courier in the employ of Major Meuchel, an officer in the finance division of the Army of Austria, which at present was at peace with France. He couldn't tell if the man could read English, but it looked official.

The "man on banking business" had bought a mare and two-wheeled cart—what the English called a dog cart, for the box under the rear seat where a good hunting dog could rest—from a stable in Doudeville. It was an unprepossessing outfit, and had excited little interest when he pulled it over to give the road to the columns of uniformed men on horseback and on foot flying the pennants of the Republic.

His valise was opened and searched, but the false bottom went unnoticed. His pistol and dagger were examined and replaced. *Not* to carry protection in a climate of unrest would have been suspicious.

"Where is the item you're charged to deliver?"

He'd transferred the money he'd drawn to a courier's belt strapped around his waist. He opened his coat to display it.

"How much is in it?"

Hesitation was fatal; if the man was a thief, so be it. "Ten thousand pounds, minus expenses incurred traveling."

A spark came to the fat officer's mud-colored eyes. The Viper let drop his coattails, freeing his hands.

The other bunched his chin.

"Money to fund the British Royal Navy, perhaps."

"A small sum for that, wouldn't you think?"

That was a tactical error; clearly the man preferred to ask the questions. If "Chaucer" was detained long enough to test his story, and his valise examined thoroughly . . . His hand crept to the dagger in its sheath in the small of his back. He might get three of them, and in the confusion make his escape. It seemed doubtful.

Just then another officer approached to ask about stabling arrangements.

The lieutenant-colonel returned the bank letter. "Be on your way, and curb that tongue. You'll find not everyone's as easygoing as I am."

Eavesdropping on gossip was the best way to keep abreast of great events. In a tavern in St. Germaine, the Viper learned that the country was indeed at war.

Bonaparte had signed the Treaty of Aranjuez, establishing peace with Spain and clearing the way for the French Army to cross through its borders and attack Portugal. Victory would open a port to transport troops to Africa and challenge British holdings there: This strategy had become vital in view of declining French influence in Egypt. Admiral Nelson had slammed that door with the British fleet.

When the Turks took Cairo less than a fortnight later, France swarmed with military activity, men and cannon trundling in to defend the frontiers in the event the British launched an offensive in retaliation for their threatened interests in Africa.

When the Viper learned of all this in St. Germaine, he altered his itinerary, wandering farther from the main roads, detouring miles out of his way in order to avoid any more confrontations. A false bottom was poor defense against a country at war.

Now he avoided hostelries of any kind. Even those that still had accommodations to offer were likely to quarter French troops; and there were always Fouché's spies to consider. He camped well off the traveled roads, building no fire and eating cold salted pork. When it rained he crawled under the cart for shelter.

The precautions were wise, but they didn't go far enough. At the next village he came to he entered an apothecary shop and bought poison.

23

"If they'd told me reading was involved, I'd have turned down this job and applied for a foreign posting."

Dubois smiled at Jules Limodin. His chief inspector spoke his mind whatever the consequences, and had been demoted twice under the Directorate for his candor.

"My friend, you'd have been singularly inept outside this country. You can barely speak French."

"You realize the Minister of Police dumped all this shit on us just to keep us busy."

They were seated facing each other across the Prefect's desk, with a canal cleared through the piles of paper so they could communicate.

"Not entirely. A fellow in his august position can't be bothered. He lives on summaries. Delegating the details frees him to meddle in the affairs of his peers. That's the secret to his survival."

"Why do we put up with it?"

"Because every now and then he puts aside his personal interests and does his job. We can do no less."

"He scans the world for foxes while we chase mice."

"Mice are more destructive."

"I agree. Here, for instance, is an incident of vandalism against the state. A goatherd's son was arrested last month in Blangy for scratching an inflammatory statement on a fence surrounding the house of a magistrate."

"Was it political?"

"You tell me. Is writing 'Eat my shit' constructive criticism or treason?"

"How was he punished?"

"He paid a fine of twenty francs and was made to repaint the fence. They should have added a mandatory session with the local schoolmaster. He spelled '*merde*' with three *e*'s."

"I think there's a place for him on the State Council." Dubois smiled beneath his moustache. "You see? We're having fun, you and I."

"What makes you so cheerful?"

"Who's to say? Maybe it's my new hat."

"I'd be happy too, if I knew what it is we're looking for."

"I would be as well, if only to see what you look like when you're happy." He rubbed his eyes. Hours of uninterrupted reading and the stench of Limodin's pipe tobacco had filled them with ground glass. "You should try my method. I begin by sorting the reports into piles on the floor: one containing details that invite further study, and a second to be returned to the Police Ministry as useless."

"There are three piles on the floor. What's the third?"

"Those are the ones I can't make up my mind what to do with."

"There's always the incinerator."

"That *is* treason. What would France be without its mountains of paper?"

"America."

The Prefect picked up a file. "A fisherman was jailed in Calais for failing to rise when someone proposed a toast to the Revolution."

"Where does he do his fishing?"

"The Channel islands."

"Maybe his French was faulty."

"It happened in a tavern. More likely he was too far gone in drink." He tossed the sheaf aside and picked up another. "This fellow paid full duty at a checkpoint rather than submit to have his barrow searched. The inspector searched it anyway, and found only sacks of grain. There's no tariff on that."

"No mystery there. In all probability he had a jug of rum hidden under the grain. The inspector confiscated it, and forgot to report it."

"Rum will do that to a fellow. And this." Dubois lifted another off the stack. "An innkeeper's daughter in Doudeville thought it odd that an English gentleman should arrive with pistol equipment, but no pistol."

"He had it on him, not in his luggage."

"Also no ammunition. Carrying around balls and powder is cumbersome. But I see no reason why the Minister's informants thought any of this worth bringing to his notice."

"It gets lonely on the coast. They were starved for attention."

Dubois was about to lay the last file on the discard heap when he glanced again at the first page. The report had, no doubt, been phrased more colorfully before a bored recorder had rendered it into bureaucratic prose:

> *Subject Englishman told innkeeper he was in France*
> *to visit friends. Innkeeper replied that it was a*
> *poor time to make such a crossing for that purpose.*

The Prefect agreed. But such an excuse for traveling put a handy end to the conversation. "Traveling on business" invited polite inquiries as to the nature of that business, while a stranger's social affairs interested no one but himself and his friends.

Perhaps that was the intention.

"Limodin, do you happen to recall what the weather was like on the Channel on the third Germinal?"

"I don't know what the weather was like this morning; but then I've been cooped up in here since yesterday. If you must know, go round to the papers and ask for that number."

"I think I shall."

He laid the file on the pile reserved for further study.

Right on top of the fellow with the petty rum-smuggler and the goatherd's boy who'd gotten a snootful of nerve and scratched a childish obscenity on the fence of a magistrate; who, for all Dubois knew, deserved to eat shit.

Camping out the night after he visited the apothecary, the Viper cut a slit in the heel of one hand, inserted two and a half grams of arsenic sealed in a capsule he'd fashioned from a sausage casing, then closed the slit with a stitch of thread.

It healed within days and he pulled out the stitch. He could tear it free with his teeth and swallow it. Painful as such a death was, it would spare him the protracted agony of aggressive inter-rogation by Joseph Fouché's officers.

Near Beaumont, some twenty miles off his course, he decided to put in with a contact whom Cadoudal had suggested, if shelter was needed that he couldn't provide for himself.

The man was a former viscount who'd renounced his title in 1788; an act which had spared him execution at the beginning of the Terror, although his motives had been entirely personal, not political. He'd fallen out with his father, the count, over the old man's second marriage, to a widow ten years younger than his son, and had renounced his claim to the family estate. It was a bootless gesture, as he was no longer next of kin, but it served to register his pique.

The ignorant Jacobins had looked only at the timing and granted him clemency as an early supporter among the nobility. After the father and young wife were executed, the Directorate awarded the son what remained of the family estate on the basis of a bribe. He lived there on the credit of his name and a monthly stipend from Royalists in return for putting up their colleagues in anxious times.

The Viper found him a bore, who kept asking meddling questions about his guest's purpose. He seemed unaware of the precariousness of his own position.

The guest stayed a week. During the day he strolled the grounds, unfolding his field glass to check the countryside for troops on the move. Twice he spotted columns of cavalry, and once an artillery crew freeing a cannon from mire with their backs and shoulders (and colorful blasphemies, without question), but they kept to the main road, no doubt scorning the ex-nobleman's modest stone house as unsuitable for quartering officers.

When the soldiers had made their way to billets on the frontiers, the Viper resumed his journey, carrying in the dog cart a case of wine his former host had pressed upon him from his own vineyard. This he parceled out at checkpoints along the road in return for being allowed to pass without inspection. The government functionaries were poorly paid, and now that the army had gone, they could relax their vigilance. The Viper went back to his original route along the Seine. In a few days he would be in Paris, capital of the civilized world.

24

Charles Eslée tipped over his queen, acknowledging defeat.

The Widow Deauville, in addition to being the most beautiful woman in Pontoise, was a chess savant, a fact she took pains to keep from the rest of her neighbors.

"It's difficult enough, Doctor, for a woman my age, not possessing a dowry, to find a husband; impossible, if the men of this village think I'm more intelligent than they are."

"Not precisely a distinction, Madame. The mayor himself would be hard put to use *cat* in a sentence."

"Oh, Rateau the miller's shrewd enough, and well off; but he's niggardly. I won't beg my husband for pin money. Poor León always turned his earnings over to me the day they were received. If you asked him the product of five times five, he'd shrug and say, 'You must consult Marianne upon this matter.' Also he trusted me."

"That's because he wasn't a cheat, unlike Rateau. I could dismiss a handful of pebbles in the occasional sack of flour as an oversight, but with him it's a given. The man should be in the gravel business." Eslée sipped wine and watched her produce another of her innumerable cigarettes. "You know, in my life I've known a half-dozen men who smoked those things, and no women."

"In both cases it's because they burn monstrously fast. You can raise blisters striking flint and steel all day long." She lit it off the lamp on the table, replaced the chimney, drew in smoke, and blew it at her kitchen ceiling, staining it further and exposing the magnificent long line of her neck.

The doctor suspected she knew it was magnificent and long.

It was no wonder women made good bookkeepers: They learned early in life to take regular inventory of their assets.

He sighed. He regretted the cynical turn his philosophies had taken since his own happiness was shattered.

"You speak of your age often," he said. "I'm fifty, and I daresay I was a grown man when you were born. I admire the way you wear your hair." It was blue-black, cut boyishly short, and suited the elongated shape of her skull.

"The style passed out of fashion when the last head fell into the bucket. Noblewomen took pains to see the blade cut clean. In my case it draws attention away from these." She gestured toward her breasts. It was true she was busty.

"I don't blame you. My own taste runs to women of an athletic build. But I'm not a fanatic."

She smiled, showing strong white teeth. "You always say what you think. It's a wonder you have any patients at all. Poor León loved my teats."

Marianne's husband, a first-class painter of houses, had traded his brush for a musket and departed this life at the end of a Royalist bayonet in the defense of the Republic. She'd gotten the news in the same post that carried his effects: Rousseau's *Rights of Man* and a popular romance, *Paul et Virginie*; the draft of a letter interrupted after "Dearest Pumpkin," a watch, no money. Some handler along the way had taken out his fee.

Eslée, who had befriended her in her time of loss, was a good listener, but beyond her brief marriage she was close with personal information. He knew nothing about her politics. It was dangerous to ask, and more dangerous yet to answer. Giroud, who kept the village records, seemed always at hand with his pencil and block, never in the courthouse. The doctor thought it safe enough to agree with her that while the Republic would likely have endured without León's sacrifice, the local houses had certainly suffered for lack of an experienced house painter.

He most definitely never mentioned *Pumpkin*. León's pet name for his wife was "Mouse."

She broke a quarter-inch of ash into a saucer next to the chessboard. "This bad habit of outspokenness aside, Doctor, you're both a generous spirit and an intellectual challenge. Why have you never proposed?"

"I'm too old for you, to begin with."

"You're the youngest bachelor in the village."

"Untrue. Grolier's not yet fifty, and he lives well."

"Creating floral arrangements. Need I say more?"

"Still, he'd be a good provider."

"What is age? I'm talking about marriage, not moving furniture. We can hire a man for that."

"I'm past such things, *Madame*. When Louisa left me I realized I had no talent for wedded life."

"You forget I knew her a little. She did you a favor. You could no more stand life with that brainless creature than an owl tied to a donkey. Marry me, and take me away from all these rags and thimbles." The kitchen—in fact, her entire charming cottage—was heaped with bolts of material and flimsy dress patterns.

"I don't believe you're looking for escape. You're a skilled seamstress, and just as successful as you choose to be. They know you in Paris, but you effect not to know them. What do the locals have that they don't?"

"A sense of responsibility. They pay promptly. Those harlots in society consider it a badge of rank not to have creditors howling outside their houses. A tradesman can do a hundred thousand francs' business in summer and freeze to death in winter because he can't afford coal."

"Still, you can do better."

"I settled for a house painter last time. Would you insult his memory by refusing me?"

He watched her ignite a fresh cigarette off the stub of the

last. Amazing. "I can barely support myself, let alone two," he said. "Here, people leave their medical bills unpaid not because it's fashionable, but because they can barely dress and feed themselves. On Tuesday I accepted a brood hen in return for setting a broken leg. On Thursday, I was asked to return it. A fox ate the flock."

"And did you return it?"

"I could hardly refuse. My practice is small enough without starving my patients to death."

"A doctor must eat too. You should have told him you'd eaten it already."

"You see? I'm not clever enough to keep a wife."

"You're a hopeless case."

"Thank you for agreeing with my diagnosis."

"How soon are you expected back?"

"I have no appointments. My girl knows where to find me in an emergency."

She put out the cigarette half-smoked. He understood she took them in barter from the tobacconist's wife, who liked embroidered handkerchiefs but couldn't afford them.

"Well, if you won't make me an honest woman, perhaps you'll mount me in the style to which I've become accustomed."

He finished his wine and joined her in the bedroom. She was naked already. Oddly enough, her bust was less prominent without the confinement of clothing; but wonderfully warm when he buried his face there.

The Viper fancied he could smell the French capital.

The odor was a pungent blend of horseshit, coal smoke, and perfume. Likely it was imagination, a lingering sense-memory from his last visit. A sign at a crossroads pointed the way to the village of Pontoise, three miles distant.

A pistol barked.

His mare pitched between the traces. The shot was so close a stench of sulfur swept Paris away from her nostrils. Her master hauled back on the lines with both hands. That kept him busy while the man who'd fired stepped into the road facing him with a fresh pistol in his right hand. The one he'd fired smoked in the left.

"Stand to! Just twitch, and it's a ball between your eyes."

The man wore a jerkin over a filthy shirt and trousers and a greasy tricorne hat cocked over one eye. The one visible was red as a cherry. A twisted nose ended in a hook. His bared teeth alternated gold with black, like the Indian corn the Americans were always trying to fob off as a New World delicacy.

The Viper sat motionless, still holding the lines. His pistol remained in his belt. "Stay calm. You're welcome to my purse, such as it is. I'm not carrying anything worth my life."

The red eye flicked toward the back of the cart. His victim crept a hand toward his belt.

Cold touched the bone behind his left ear: The steel of a musket. "A twitch, my friend said."

He left the hand where it was. He had not heard the man's companion creeping up from behind.

"Throw it out, friend. Let's hear it hit the ground."

He tugged out the pistol and flung it to the side. It struck the earth with a thud.

"I knowed he had it!" Tricorne's tone was shrill. "I wanted to draw him out was all."

"'Course you did, Crusher. I'm just here to shut the back door, like we agreed." The muzzle pressed tighter against the Viper's mastoid. "Now stand down and show us what's in the cart."

Crusher's friend had a seaside drawl; the other's was gutter Paris.

The Viper stepped to the ground, and with two firearms following his progress circled to the back of the cart and flung back the canvas covering the valise. The man with the musket looked disappointed. He was fair, younger and taller than his companion, and wore a blue uniform coat shorn of insignia, filthy breeches, and broken stovepipe boots. A military deserter, beyond doubt. "Empty your pockets."

The Viper hesitated, for effect. Crusher's pistol burrowed into his lower back. The Viper drew out his wallet. His hand shook, the thumb exposing the corner of a five-pound note.

Crusher snatched the wallet, lowering the pistol to dig inside.

His partner spread the Viper's coat with the muzzle of his musket. "What's in the belt?"

"Communiques. Nothing of value."

"Take it off."

He fumbled with the buckle. His fingers were like sash weights, clumsy and inert. He cautioned himself not to overplay his hand.

"Crusher."

The man in the tricorne hat obeyed, stepping in to tug at the belt, turning his pistol aside.

The Viper jerked the dagger from its scabbard under his left arm, jammed it into Crusher's body just above the pelvis, and jerked it upward, opening flesh to the spleen.

The bandit gasped. His partner stepped back, leveling his musket. The Viper tucked Crusher's arm under his, gripped the hand holding the pistol, and jerked Crusher's own finger against the trigger. Steel struck flint, flint sparked, powder ignited, and the ball struck the deserter's chest with a thump. The impact flung him onto his back, still holding the long-barreled weapon across his abdomen, which stained quickly with blood.

Crusher, held upright only by the arm pinning his to his body, worked his mouth. The Viper leaned his ear close to the lips, taking care not to step in the pile of intestines at his feet. It was one of his ambitions to partake of the wisdom of the dying at the moment of Understanding.

He was disappointed, as always. The man gulped at the air like a landed fish, then his knees folded and his weight became too much to support. His killer released him. He fell in a twisting motion, drawing the letter *S* with his body in the stained gravel of the road.

The Viper wiped his blade on the dead man's jerkin, retrieved his bank notes from cramped fingers, and stepped over to rescue his wallet and pistol from the dust. He changed hands on the pistol to put away his notes and the wallet.

A flint cracked.

He heard the pop of powder catching just in time to turn. The musket roared. Heat struck his right side, burning flesh and fabric.

The man with the musket had found strength to sit up, point his weapon, and snatch at the trigger. The flare leapt three feet, setting the Viper's clothes afire.

He staggered back a step, aimed, and fired. It was his off hand; he shot high. The ball entered Musket's right eye. The fulminate of mercury in the ball expanded against the resistance of gray-matter, spraying lead shrapnel and turning his head into a pink cloud studded with chips of skull.

The Viper swung open his smoldering coat and tore his shirt from his breeches. He'd bled down his hip.

He probed at the wound, clenching his teeth. His fingers found a hard knot an inch below the skin. He'd hoped it was a crease only, but the ball had entered.

Extract it himself? What if it had shattered a bone? That led to infection.

He folded his handkerchief and jammed it under his courier's belt, binding the patch to the wound. He mounted the dog cart, holding the bandage in place and making soothing noises to calm the agitated mare. When the animal responded, settling down, he turned it toward Pontoise.

He'd planned to avoid attention by staying out of provincial villages on the way to Paris. But he was unlikely to find medical attention in rural country.

The pain had started, a dull ache that would become a lancing throb, this much he knew. He felt himself growing light-headed, the blood pouring away from his brain.

"Fool," he said to himself. He'd been thinking miles ahead instead of a yard at a time, in a troubled nation crawling with predators. He'd made the cardinal error of considering himself unique.

Shabby fate for an international assassin, to die on a goat-path at the hands of a common highwayman, and a corpse at that.

Was there a doctor in the village? Small enough chance, but a chance just the same.

In her boudoir in Pontoise, Marianne Deauville was as skilled with her body as with a needle, but she was a difficult act to follow. Dr. Eslée came quickly. They lay side by side catching their breath when someone knocked on her front door. It was the rapid tapping of Eslée's serving girl. He had a patient.

25

When it came to a summing-up, Jacques Malroux allowed, the life of the country constable was not a bad one.

His hours were his own, barring rare urgencies, and a man with simple appetites could do worse when it came to money. He'd been the local postmaster for twelve years. That too had been a decent life until governments started changing with the wind from Paris, and when the mail went missing because some fool postman deserted his route to join the rabble or—as more often happened—the bureaucrat in charge of the province that week became frustrated with his backlog and chucked the lot into the stove, it had been Malroux who bore the wrath of the citizenry.

He'd been quick to put in for the constable's position when Old Zazou, his predecessor, became too rheumatic and fat to straddle a horse, and the bureaucrat in charge *that* week had stamped his application simply because it was on top of the pile.

Most times the horse, a gelding, grew as fat as Old Zazou while its master processed paperwork and heard the odd complaint, one neighbor against another, and nine times out of ten settled the matter by summoning both parties to his office above the bakery in Pontoise and encouraging them to shake hands and put their petty differences behind them. For this Malroux drew his month's pay and pocketed such fines as he saw fit to impose for petty vandalism and blaspheming within the hearing of women and children; drank strong coffee by the gallon and took snuff confiscated from smugglers caught attempting to swindle the government of the tax. These were the perquisites of office, and nothing like what highers-up claimed for themselves.

By sundown he was at home with his homely but affectionate wife and eleven-year-old daughter, who had inherited the uglier characteristics of both parents (her father's lumpy nose, her mother's close-set eyes and high forehead), sparing him concerns of unwanted pregnancy and the expense of a dowry.

The sole fly in his soup was Monsieur Blaq (Blaq insisted upon the *Monsieur*). The sallow, pockmarked city rat had been forced upon him by the Ministry of Police "to assist the local authorities by providing the latest investigative methods developed in Paris in matters beyond the purview of provincial officers."

Malroux had not been taken in by his promotion to plural, nor insulted by the suggestion that he was a bumpkin in need of sophisticated guidance: His objection was entirely impersonal. The man was a spy.

Whether he was expected to report upon the constable's own behavior or those of the citizens he served was mysterious— and of little account, because apart from diverting a few sous that officially belonged to the Ministry, Malroux had nothing to hide, and he knew his neighbors to be capable of anything but treason. But he resented the fellow's presence, and not just because he stank of toilet water: The sweet lilac reek permeated everything in the office, including the constable's chicken pot pie, lovingly prepared by his wife and sent with him each morning in his pewter lunch pail, along with a jar of beer. "Parisian soap" was the popular phrase for this layering of scents. The constable himself made it a point to bathe on the first and fifteenth of each month, regardless of drafts, but this fellow Blaq had never known immersion except in cologne.

Blaq was always *there*, circling like a vulture round every letter Malroux read and wrote, peering over his shoulder when he made a minor entry in the ledger—listening outside the water closet when the constable took a shit, no exaggeration; as if he might be hiding a traitorous message in a turd for the slops boy to extract and deliver to an accomplice. Malroux had exulted last month when Blaq took sick and was absent for a time, but the ailment proved to be minor, not at all bubonic, and at the end of ten days he was back, aromatic as ever, gaunter and sallower still, but evidently not terminal. It shook a man's faith in God, or Providence, or whatever universal truth was sanctioned at present by the state.

When the little peddler entered the office, holding his ratty hat in front of his overalls like a shield, Malroux could sense Blaq's feelers rampant, like a cockroach's at the scent of a piece of moldy cheese. The wretch hadn't the look of a put-upon local; he was a stranger to the constable, who knew everyone in the village and the rustics who visited it to secure supplies and provisions. And he was decidedly green about the gills. Any break in the office routine alerted Blaq to the possibility of some conspiracy against the Republic.

Malroux himself viewed it as a pleasant distraction from the oppressive existence of his resident spy.

The stranger, it developed, traded in kitchen implements, hauling a cacophonous load of pots, pans, graters, and skillets from one stone hut to another along his route, hoping to persuade some of the gimlet-eyed farmwives who reigned there into trading their patched and broken tools for shiny copper-bottomed vessels "forged in the shops of the finest artisans in Marseilles."

"Spare me your sales pitch, monsieur." Malroux patted back a belch flavored with chicken and peas. "There is nothing disgraceful in rescuing goods from junkpiles and patching them with tin. What's the purpose of your visit?"

"Murder, Citizen Constable. What I saw was no accident."

Whereupon he illustrated his point by vomiting upon the official floor.

Blaq, to the constable's satisfaction, turned green at the sight.

"Well, well. Congratulations, Crusher. I had you down for a tryst with the Gaunt Lady in Paris, but you stood her up. Well, what's one head more or less?"

Malroux was in a cheerful humor. The chill damp of Germinal was lifting, bearing an early promise of the bright blossoms of Floreal and evenings of warm late sunshine, and one less road-agent in the rotation.

He considered the dead bandit in the road worth the journey from town.

Malroux had spent much of his tenure a half-day behind one of the luckiest and dullest-witted brigands in western France, interviewing irate travelers minus their purses and luggage and studying the same holey boot-prints in the coach roads, which always seemed to lead to a dead end caused by a providential rainfall ordered by the patron saint of thieves. By the time Crusher was run to ground, the booty was gone, spent or hidden, and when it came to his word against his accusers', the fellow's skull-faced grin at close range had invariably cowed them into uncertainty. Today was the first time anything had stuck.

He wasn't smiling now, and it had taken the constable a moment to identify him definitively. His eyes and mouth were open in surprise, and no wonder. Anyone who had gotten close enough to tear open his belly and spill his inwards on the ground had either his trust or been considered by him to be harmless.

Malroux suspected a falling-out between thieves, and felt confirmed in the diagnosis by the presence a few steps away of a dead man wearing the remnants of a military uniform, still clutching a musket across his splayed body. Recognition was impossible with the fellow's face blown away, but the Crusher was known to work with a partner. Were it not for army deserters, the bandit population would not run so high.

But where was the plunder they'd slain each other to obtain?

The constable sighed. In the sensational pamphlets popular in Paris, clues were tangible items: broken penpoints, footprints in the rose garden, a compromising letter found in the hollow of a bedpost. In life, they were more often the absence of such things.

In any case he found it difficult to concentrate with Blaq retching noisily into the bushes alongside the road.

He found some satisfaction in that. He himself had seen worse as a young conscript in the service of the late king. But in addition to being useless the man was a nuisance, and the fact that he'd had oysters at luncheon remained obvious as long as he insisted on vomiting upwind.

Malroux sniffed all three weapons. Then he blew his nose into his handkerchief, expelling the rotten-egg stench. Fired. Crusher's fearsome injury was consistent with close range, but the constable was troubled by the absence of scorching on clothing and flesh.

Also—looking at the other corpse—was any pistol load capable of obliterating a man's head? Better a cannon.

Here in the dust were the signs of a horse and small vehicle, and of another pair of boots. A third accomplice possibly. More likely he'd been a victim waylaid by the Crusher. Hard to tell whether he was present when the partners quarreled.

If they quarreled. The evidence struck him as too consistent with so easy an explanation. Criminal investigation was rarely as orderly as sorting letters.

Unpleasant duty. Wrapping the handkerchief round his hand, he went through the dead men's pockets, came up with a pipe, a pouch of cheap shag, and eleven sous. Nothing worth fighting about there, and nothing fallen upon the ground.

He unwound the handkerchief and cast it away. For a moment he stood rooted to the spot, hands on hips, committing details to memory. Malroux had been an efficient postmaster, attentive to minutiae; there was not a deal of difference between keeping track of mail sacks and marking the positions of corpses.

He straddled his gray gelding. The Parisian's sorrel mare was picketed beside it.

"Take your time, Monsieur Blaq," he told the retching man. "I'll return in an hour."

"You're not leaving me with *them*?" The Ministry spy, sallower than usual, stood bent beside the road with his hands on his knees. Bits of his breakfast were ensnared in his beard. He gestured toward the dead brigands without looking their way.

"They can't harm you, but a stray dog or a resurrectionist may come along and drag them away before Dr. Eslée can have a look at them."

"What good is a doctor? They're beyond treatment."

"As usual, you grasp the matter very well. Beyond treatment, yes, but they may yet bear witness to a man who knows which questions to ask."

"What if someone comes along?"

"Show them your impressive credentials. But I suggest you wipe the vomit from your face first. Minister Fouché is fastidious to a fault, and will thank you for it."

26

Eslée was constantly amazed by the miracle of human endurance. Nothing in his training had prepared him for it; no theorem or formula provided for its infinite capacity, or lack of it. An ordinary hangnail turned gangrenous and slew a brawny stable hand in the prime of life. A stone cornice fell bang upon the skull of a consumptive clerk and left him with a buzzing in his ears only.

When the idiot serving girl, who could neither read nor write nor even sweep a floor with any show of competence (but who worked cheaply), led the way back to the doctor's quarters, shaking all over and raising clouds of dust with the hem of her skirts, he'd suspected more was afoot than a simple fracture, but since she was as incapable of a coherent explanation as she was of cooking a simple egg, he was left to speculate: Perhaps Linoc, the woodsman, had managed at last to lop off one of his feet with the double-bitted axe he handled so carelessly, or that drunken druggist Planchet had filled a prescription for a physic with arsenite of lead.

He had not considered a gunshot wound.

Such things were common enough among hunters; but there was no game to be had. Bonaparte's soldiers had scoured the country round on their way to defend the borders, and no one Eslée knew had the time to waste scraping for leavings. What little livestock remained, once the game vanished, had been hidden in barns.

Nor had he expected the severity of the injury, or the bare thought that a man who had taken a musket ball in the hip should have made his way to the house of the nearest physician without fainting.

Human endurance? No; the man was a bull on two legs.

A strange cart and horse stood at the end of the sunken-stone path to the front door of the hovel Eslée called home, without affection. He was always eager to flee its bleak walls to play a losing game of chess with Marianne Deauville.

And to do more, perhaps. But he'd reached that measure in life where a spirited competition of wit and will was recreation enough. To mesh the flesh with the widow was a contest of another sort. The physical pressure upon his member between her loins; well, suffice it to say the woman might have inspired the guillotine. Had her poor León joined the Revolutionary Army for a holiday?

His patient awaited him in the horsehair armchair in his consulting room, which doubled as a parlor. Novels were shelved next to medical journals in the glazed bookpresses, and bottles of Cognac stood among the tubes and retorts on a bench.

The doctor heard then the drip-drip as of a leaking pipe, and saw the scarlet puddle at the foot of the chair.

The man in the chair followed the track of his vision with glazed eyes. Muscles tugged at the corners of his well-shaped mouth.

"My apologies, Doctor," said he, in court French. "I've defiled your rug."

He fainted then.

Eslée took him gently by the shoulder and eased his body away from the arms of the chair. That was when he discovered the source of the bleeding.

He sent the girl home. She was no nurse, and was barely a servant.

The man came around.

"I haven't any opiates," the doctor said. "They're a smugglers' staple and too dear." It occurred to him the fellow may be a smuggler himself. "I'll dull your senses with Cognac."

"No. I'll stay awake."

"I don't think you know what you're saying. The pain—"

"Awake, I said."

A belt of some kind, made of buttoned canvas pouches rein-forced with leather, held a bloody fold of cloth to the wound. When Eslée leaned in to unfasten it and examine the injury, something prodded his belly. He looked down and saw a pistol clamped in a bloody hand.

A criminal, definitely; or some kind of official messenger, which came to much the same thing. Paris fought pirates with pirates.

"I'm not a thief, monsieur."

The pistol didn't move.

"You'll faint again, and who will defend your property then? Trust me with your life, trust me with your purse."

"Where will you put it?"

"I'll lock it in my desk, how's that? I have the only key."

"Let me see you put it there."

Eslée removed the belt, produced the key attached to his watch fob, and made a broad business of opening the drawer, placing the belt inside, and locking it after. The belt was both heavier than it looked and lighter than expected. He started to return the key to his waistcoat.

"Give it to me."

"But where will you put it? I must undress you."

He repeated the command, lowering his weapon only when the key was in his fist.

"My valise is outside. Bring it in."

"I am not a footman."

The muzzle came back up.

Eslée folded his arms across his chest.

"And what will you do once I'm shot?"

The wounded man was silent for a moment. Then he lowered the hammer gently and rotated the pistol, offering the handle.

The doctor took it and laid it on his desk.

"Put it out of sight. You don't know what a danger it is in igno-rant hands."

"I know about firearms."

"Not this one, I assure you."

The doctor opened a bookpress and placed the pistol behind *Diseases of the Stomach,* a weighty volume. He closed the door gently.

"The valise, now."

"No. The bleeding needs to be stopped."

"Please. It contains everything I own."

Which was not the case, or there would have been no nonsense about the belt. But it was the first sign of supplication; plainly he was at the end of his strength.

A distraught patient was hard to treat. The doctor went out-side, brought in the large piece of luggage, and slid it inside the kneehole of his desk.

He found the man docile after that. Eslée helped him to his feet and through the door into the next room, depositing him on the worn leather couch he used for an examining table.

The patient drifted in and out of consciousness as Eslée stripped him, but the key remained in his clutches; the will was stronger than the man.

The bleeding gash was a hideous flaw in an impressive exam-ple of male anatomy.

Eslée probed the wound. The man flinched, but made no sound.

"The ball isn't deep, but removing it will cause more damage, and more pain. It can't be helped. Will you take Cognac now?"

"I suppose I may as well."

He went back for it, but found the stranger insensate when he returned. The doctor put aside the bottle, picked up his forceps, and burrowed until the jaws closed on a leaden ball the size of a walnut. The flesh recoiled, but the man didn't wake up.

Eslée shook his head at the bloody lump he'd extracted: the things Man came up with to destroy his fellows, as if nature weren't ruthless enough. He flung it ringing into an enamel basin, cleansed the wound with alcohol, and applied a patch. He was holding it in place when he saw the patient's eyes were open, looking at him.

"You're lucky, monsieur. There's no bone damage and the ball didn't separate."

"When can I leave?"

"You'll be here a week at least."

"Too long."

"You won't think that when you try to stand. You've lost a great deal of blood. There's nothing to be done about that except rest and broth—and prayer, if you're a religious man. I can treat infection: alcohol, fresh dressings. I don't subscribe to the popular theory that filth is a barrier against disease. Quite the opposite."

"I'm inclined to agree. Otherwise, certain men would live forever."

"Your sense of humor is a good sign, like a healthy appetite."

"Spare me your bromides. A man can die laughing and with a bellyful of beef."

"That would depend upon the quality of the beef."

He unrolled three yards of muslin round the abdomen. The man obliged him by sitting up with a grunt. The effort cost him. He paled, and sweat pricked out on his forehead and upper lip. His skin was clammy to the touch.

"No one must know I'm here. Tell your girl I left after treatment, and give her a week's holiday."

"It won't work. She's far from bright, but she knows you're too badly injured to have gone away on your own."

"Would she go to the authorities?"

"She'd be afraid not to, I think. The times—"

"Yes, one can't travel more than a mile without being reminded.

Tell her I was hurt when my cart overturned, and give her the holiday."

"That may work. After a week she'll forget the whole business."

"For her sake I hope so. You'll need to conceal the horse and cart. I'll pay you well for the inconvenience."

"Are you sought by the police?"

"They don't know I exist, and I intend to keep it that way, with your help."

"I can't be an accomplice."

"Very well. I'm a courier, charged with a mission of international importance."

"A very old story."

"You'll find a letter in my coat that will identify me. My mission must remain secret. I can't tell you anything beyond that."

"Whoever wounded you must share the secret."

"There was no one. I was careless. I caught the hammer of my pistol on a nail while climbing a fence and it discharged."

"So far I've seen no evidence of carelessness on your part. Quite the opposite."

"Give me a reason to believe you won't betray me."

"I saved your life. I shouldn't want to think it was a waste of time."

"Try again."

"If I told you the real reason, a man like you wouldn't understand."

"You consider yourself bound by your oath?"

"It isn't a matter of consideration, but of fact."

The stranger's lids were heavy. He was keeping them open with visible effort.

"I'm a desperate man, Doctor. If you betray me, I'd have nothing to lose by tearing off my bandages and opening my wound with my bare hands. My death won't sit well with your creed."

"You're quite mad."

"Madmen are invariably truthful, isn't it so?"

"I wouldn't know. I wasn't trained in diseases of the mind."

The man smiled then. The expression brought no warmth.

"You shouldn't have admitted you cared about your work. I owned you from that moment."

Then he slept. The fist holding the key to Eslée's drawer remained clenched tight.

No, the man was not human; but neither was he a bull. Something more nocturnal and closer to the ground.

27

Cold.

Raw cold, the kind that crept through three layers of wool and lay like steel against the spine.

In the dream it was Vendémiaire, the month of vintage, and the pre-dawn chill made his breath smoke and made a brittle skin on puddles that broke beneath his feet and filled his boots with ice water.

He'd flung off his covers in the heat of fever, but the movement taxed him of all his strength. He hadn't enough to draw them back over him, or even to fight sleep. He shivered in his own clammy sweat.

Forty guns.

Forty, forty, forty.

A biblical number: days and nights of rain, lashes from Pharaoh's oxhide whip, years wandering in the desert.

Bronze giants, these pieces, scarred and tarnished blue-black; veterans of Lyons and Toulon, a few pieces rescued by blockade runners from Gibraltar, muzzles charred inside like the bowl of a pipe. Garrison guns: Gribeauval twenty-four-pounders, their carriages grinding cobble stones into dust beneath their ironbound wheels.

No, not mechanical grinding; nothing so remorseless. Voices. Two men were speaking in the next room.

"Monsieur le Docteur," that much he made out, in its officious tone. The rest of the conversation was too low.

The door opened. Automatically he groped for his pistol, then remembered it wasn't there.

The General spoke.

"Tell me, Captain, the best way of bringing a drunken man to his senses?"

"I don't know, sir. I rarely drink."

"An aggressive dog, then. Use your head for something other than a place for your hat." As high as this singular man would rise—and in this autumn of 1795 even perverse history could not predict just how *high*—he would ever retain the coarse battlefield manners of a master sergeant.

"I've heard a dash of cold water in the face helps."

"The cold hasn't stopped this rabble. What else?"

He thought; a difficult thing to do with those gray eyes boring holes in his face. Inspiration then, sudden as a spurt of flame when a log split in the hearth.

"A whiff of pepper. Even a dog must stop to sneeze."

"Excellent. You may yet deserve those bars. But the pack is large, and we haven't the pepper. We'll give them a whiff of grapeshot instead. Yes, a whiff of grapeshot. Good man."

Sensing movement in the room, he exerted every ounce of pressure and opened his eyes.

Dr. Eslée, wearing a hat and overcoat, had a satchel open on the zinc shelf of the cupboard where he stored his instruments. They clinked when he put them in the bag. He glanced at his patient, started when he saw he was awake.

"I'm called out," he said. "I won't be long."

Church bells chimed the hour: four strokes in the watery afternoon. The insurrectionists had blundered, postponing their attack on this latest government, this Directory, for hours while the guns were deployed.

"Ready!" The General's voice was a bellow.

Flint struck steel, ignited rope-ends saturated with slow-burning powder. They hovered over the touch-holes of the hair-trigger cannon.

No command to aim was given. There was no need: All forty guns had been elevated properly on their wooden rails under the General's personal supervision. In his heart he would always be a lieutenant of artillery, as he'd begun.

He raised his saber, paused to observe the crowd surging into the courtyard, into the center of the circle of heavy guns. Into the valley of the shadow of death.

"Tenais"; gentle now, like a stable hand soothing an excited horse; yet it carried. "Tenais . . . tenais . . ."

Holding, holding. Sweat trickled into the captain's eye, red-hot and stinging.

Silence then; acres of it, building, pulsing, pressing tight enough to make a man mad. Then—

The saber slashed down. "Fire!"

And once again hell came to Paris.

The doctor's satchel snapped shut. His patient felt his covers being drawn back up under his chin, but he was still half submerged in 13 Vendémiaire—the Royalist revolt that made Bonaparte a butcher—couldn't stir. A hinge squeaked. The patient opened his eyes and saw the doctor hasten through the gap and pull the door shut behind him.

Not fast enough for the Viper to miss the dusty-blue tunic of a country official loitering in the next room.

He struggled into a sitting position, ignoring the lancing pain in his hip. But he was no longer light-headed; his skull was

packed with mud. His body would not support its weight. He fell
back into blackness.

"I said you would have no need of equipment." Constable Malroux sounded peevish. "I asked you to accompany me in order to
determine if the men died the way I suspected. It doesn't require a
degree in medicine to prove they're dead."

"I'm sure your diagnosis is sound." Eslée shifted the sling attached to his satchel to a more comfortable position on his shoulder.
The contents tinkled merrily. "But I always travel prepared."

"Will you measure their wounds with calipers, to determine
whether they were broad enough for their souls to escape? They
look ample even to the naked eye."

The doctor guided his mount carefully along the furrow that
passed for a road.

He and the brown mule had never been comfortable with their
arrangement; he suspected the animal of honoring it only until a
rock or a rut gave it an excuse to stumble and dump him off its
back. The previous owner had inspired loyalty in patients and
animals with his good cheer; Eslée was solemn. He knew he'd
lost business because of this, and most assuredly the esteem of his
mount.

"You say they were highwaymen?"

"One was, for certain. The country won't mourn long. Jean-
Luc Écraser was the name he answered to: Crush, in ugly English. He seemed to prefer it, for some reason. And so we called
him Crusher, not being disposed to offend a felon of his talents.
The other no longer has a face for me to identify."

"No face?"

"As if a charge of powder went off inside his head. I never saw
its like, apart from a direct hit from a mortar."

"You were a military man?"

"I served. It isn't quite the same thing. If it were, I might know how Crusher managed to cause so much damage with just his pistol. I'd think the other man's musket was the greater weapon."

"Is it possible the man who lost his face was the robbery victim?"

"I considered it. But there was a third party at least. A horse and cart left fresh tracks. No horse and wagon was to be found."

"Perhaps the animal bolted during the shooting."

"The possibility suggested itself. However, I suffer from a narrow throat."

Eslée was distracted. The road had entered a decline littered with treacherous rubble. He wound the reins tighter around his wrist.

"A narrow throat, you say? I treated you for diphtheria a year or two ago. I noted no deformity then."

"And yet I find it impossible to swallow certain theories. They catch in my craw like fishbones."

"A goose has instincts. They wouldn't stand the test of law."

"Yet he always finds his way north in the spring."

"I wasn't ridiculing you," Eslée said. "I've seen men survive when medical science said they were dead. It can't be explained, but there it is."

"You and I are refugees, Doctor, from the Age of Reason."

"Take care, Constable. Even the hills have ears."

"So does Monsieur Blaq. But he also has a weak stomach." Malroux let his gelding pick its way down the grade. "Mind you, there are features about my theory I also find difficult to choke down. That's why I'm imposing upon you. I trust you have no matters more pressing."

"None whatsoever."

"Then we're both fortunate in the timing."

The doctor wondered if the constable was being ironic.

He went over all his precautions.

He'd put his patient's horse and cart in the carriage house behind his home, which was big enough as the cart was small and he kept no carriage, only the mule; rubbed down the mare and given it straw. No one had seen him, he felt sure. He'd made sure Malroux had not been looking when he went into the examining room for his supplies and when he came back out, leaving his patient asleep.

Still, there was something about the little man in the shabby uniform that put him on his guard.

A horse and cart, the constable had said.

Well, they were anything but rare. A stranger with a gunshot wound and a brace of brigands shot dead could be coincidence. The past dozen years were an anarchist's dream. No village, however quiet and remote, could claim that it had not witnessed a villainous act.

The courier story held up. The letter in the patient's coat, which had escaped damage when he was shot, bore the name of the Bank of England embossed and a gold seal. Eslée hadn't much English, but the charge was brief and the vocabulary simple enough to grasp its meaning.

Men would be careless with their own weapons. Two years ago, he'd removed a ramrod from Emile the tailor's cheek after he forgot to discharge his fowling piece before cleaning. He'd nearly lost an eye.

So what if his patient lied? If Malroux was right and the man who'd escaped was the intended victim of a robbery, it wasn't the physician's duty to surrender him.

28

Now they were climbing a steep bank. The infernal mule quivered with eager anticipation. Eslée stepped down and gathered its halter. It balked, infuriated by disappointment, but he exerted all his strength and it resumed climbing with a snort.

"Now, what is that fellow about?" said Malroux.

Eslée looked up. A gaunt creature in a tricorne hat and long black coat stood atop the rise, holding a handkerchief over the lower part of his face. The doctor thought him a highwayman: the constable's third party, not a victim at all.

Then he recognized stooped shoulders, the rodent cast of his features when he lowered the cloth. Blaq, that was the name. He haunted the bakery in Pontoise, where a flight of steps led to Malroux's office; some kind of government functionary.

A spy, no doubt. Malroux had said as much.

How important their little village had become, to warrant the attention of this fellow and Giroud, the clerk who never clerked.

The constable spurred his horse to the crest. "Why are you here? I left you to guard the bodies."

"They started to stink. The flies—"

"Which did you not expect, the stink or the flies?"

"You were gone two hours!"

"All the more reason to anticipate nature. Did I say, 'Stay here two hours, then do as you please'?"

"No, but—"

"Did I say, 'Stay here, until these fellows begin to smell and the flies arrive'?"

"See here! I—"

"That's when the vermin come to dine, which as I made clear was the reason I told you to remain. I didn't invite the doctor to see the place where the bodies *were*, before they were dragged away and devoured by wolves, but where they *are*."

A dirty flush stained the other's dead cheeks. "Take care, Malroux. I answer to Paris."

"And Paris will hear you deserted your post in a death investigation. What will you say when you're asked to defend yourself? 'Citizen Fouché, they began to smell. The flies!' *He* doesn't shrink from such unpleasantness."

"You dare to insult the Minister of Police?"

"Forgive me. I meant only to insult you."

"I *warn* you, sir!"

"Gentlemen." Eslée joined them, his hand on the mule's bridle. "I wish to experience the smell and see these flies for myself."

The constable had given the village gravedigger directions to the site. This round, ruddy fellow arrived, singing to himself, as Eslée was finishing his examination. The man pulled his wagon off the road and sat watching from the driver's seat, munching peanuts from a sack.

The corpses had bloated under the sun, and there were certainly flies and stench enough to go round. Malroux and Blaq stood several yards upwind.

The doctor smelled only garlic. A clove was a handy thing to bring along on such errands: crushed and applied round the nostrils, it was better than carbolic.

He poured alcohol into his palms, rubbed them together briskly, then returned everything to his bag and joined the men from the constable's office. Malroux had lit a pipe against the stench; the exhaust seemed to cause his companion as much distress as the other. It was a powerful blend.

But then, yellow-gray was Blaq's natural coloring. Eslée suspected long exposure to potash, a lye-based caustic commonly used in fumigation. An indoor rat, this, who would live to be no one's grandfather.

"The man you call Crusher was not shot," Eslée announced.

Malroux smoked. "You're certain?"

"He was stabbed; gutted, actually. The wound was made with an edged weapon and there was no ball to extract."

"Bayonet? Saber? The other fellow wears the rags of a uniform."

"Did you find either weapon?"

"No. But the man belonging to the horse and wagon might have taken it with him. What about the gentleman without a face? His musket was fired. Perhaps he missed, and Crusher emptied his pistols at him at close range. We have the pistols, and both were discharged."

"You are the policeman, and know about such things. I found shards of lead; but even if both balls shattered on contact, I don't see so much destruction of tissue by ordinary loads. As you said, it's as if a mortar struck. Then again, there is this." Eslée opened his hand. A ball of lead lay in the palm. "I found that in the chest of the man in the uniform. I think it accounts for one of the Crusher's shots. That leaves only one ball in Uniform's face. But what a ball!"

"You're part policeman yourself, Doctor."

"Or criminal," Blaq suggested. "For a country practitioner he knows a great deal about violent death."

Eslée ignored him. "Crusher wasn't slain by a saber or bayonet. The gash is vertical, directed upward from the point of penetration. Such wounds are usually delivered at extremely close range with a short blade."

"The man incriminates himself with every word."

"I studied in Paris, Citizen Blaq, from before the Terror through Thirteen Vendémiaire. The university didn't lack for cadavers."

Malroux took his pipe from his mouth. "You were present at Thirteen Vendémiaire?"

"The aftermath. It's no small thing to separate the maimed from the dead after forty cannon are fired into a crowd."

"What happened here, Doctor?"

"Again, I'm not a professional investigator. As you suggested, these two waylaid a man traveling with a horse and cart. Whether they fell out between them, or had the tables turned against them, perhaps you can supply the answer."

"I should have stayed a postmaster."

"You may need this." Eslée thrust his palm closer.

The constable's pipe had gone out. He bent and knocked loose the plug against his boot. "You may keep it as a souvenir, *Monsieur le Docteur*. It's an ordinary ball, as you said. I must look for an infernal machine in a package no larger than a pebble."

Eslée tightened his lips, as if to prevent anything incriminating from escaping. *"Put it out of sight,"* the man had said, relinquishing his pistol. *"You don't know what a danger it is in ignorant hands."*

29

"Thirteen Vendémiaire?" said the patient. "You were there?"

Always the same question, thought Eslée, when the subject came up. It was as if he had no past apart from it.

"Were *you*?" he replied.

The other shook his head. He was sitting up partially, pillows bunched behind his back. Eslée had lent him one of his nightshirts. It fit him well enough, although short in the sleeves. His color was good. The fever had broken and the wound was healing with no pink flush of infection. The doctor prided himself on his treatment.

"I knew someone else who was. A captain of artillery serving with Bonaparte. Is it true they opened fire on starving Parisians with cannon?"

"They were a rabble, put up by Royalist agitators to storm the palace." Eslée shrugged. "That's what the newspapers said. I was there in the capacity of a physician, not a coroner. My responsibility was to the survivors. I hadn't time to examine blasted corpses to see if their bellies were indeed empty or full of brandy from aristocrats' cellars." He shipped a spoon with chowder from the bowl he was holding, blew away the steam. "The blood was red enough, that much I remember; not royal purple."

"What sort of man can give such an order?"

"The Directory—our third government in six years—appointed him to manage the crisis. Bonaparte was an artillery officer, like your friend. I doubt his superiors expected him to settle things with a stern word and a swat on the arse. Open."

The patient obeyed, swallowed when the spoon was withdrawn from his lips. "It's very good."

"I can't claim credit. A local widow was kind enough to oblige. She's an excellent seamstress as well."

The man on the couch stiffened; winced when the action pulled at his dressing. "She knows about me?"

"I told her you're a clerk on an errand. A very mundane one, of no popular interest. But if the people who sent you found out you fell ill, you might be sacked."

"Did she believe you?"

"Does any woman, when it's a man talking? But I vouch for her discretion. We've been acquainted for years, and I couldn't tell you where she lived before she came to this village. I like to think she sailed across Europe from some fairy kingdom in a hot-air balloon. Again." He held out the spoon.

"She'd do that?" The patient accepted the broth.

"I wouldn't put it past her. Or anything else, for that matter. I sometimes wonder what keeps her in this sleepy place."

"The way you speak of her, I think I can guess."

"Less talk. More soup."

Conversation fell off for a few minutes while the meal continued. When the man in the bed shook his head at another spoonful, the doctor set aside the bowl.

"What is your name?" he asked.

"We agreed that you'll call me Meuchel."

"*You* agreed. I abstained. Meuchel is the name of the major you represent. I saw the letter."

His patient ceded the point with a nod. "English domestic staffs traditionally address visiting servants by their masters' surnames. It avoids confusion belowstairs. A practical people, the British. Let's leave it at that. I'll be gone in a few days; there's nothing to be gained by cluttering up your memory with superfluous detail."

"Are you English?"

THE EAGLE AND THE VIPER

"An undiplomatic question. France and England are at war."

"Not an answer."

"The answer is no."

"I thought as much. You have no accent."

"I speak with a Parisian accent, like you. I have no nationality at present."

"A lonely thing to confess."

"Try to contain your probing to your skill with forceps."

"You must throw me some little morsel, to surrender under torture. We're a two-spy village, monsieur."

"Not so sleepy a place, after all."

"We're a stone's-throw from Paris. Bees swarm about the hive."

The man who called himself Meuchel paled a shade. Eslée couldn't tell if the pain was real or feigned, to avoid further questioning. His powers of endurance were superhuman, and he seemed able to dissemble not only in speech and expression, but in the flow of blood to his face; he could flush or become ashen at will.

Eslée got up, opened the same cupboard where he kept his instruments, and poured an inch of liquid from a small brown bottle into a glass, then returned to his chair beside the bed. He pressed the glass to Meuchel's lips.

Meuchel smelled the contents. He clamped his mouth shut.

"A weak solution of morphine, diluted with alcohol," said the doctor. "Just enough to deaden the pain, not bring on sleep."

A smoky hazel gaze studied him. The man drank, then screwed up his face. "Faugh! I smoked opium once. It tastes just as bad either way."

"You've been to China?"

"One needn't go so far to chase the dragon. Are you asking these questions for yourself or the policeman you went out with this morning?"

Eslée hesitated, nodded. "I should have known you saw. I didn't want to upset you, but Constable Malroux was most insistent. I think you know I kept your secret. Otherwise he'd be here, asking these questions and more. Unlike the widow, I have but one skill, and interrogation isn't one. In any case, my lips are sealed by the oath of my profession. Do you still insist you shot yourself with your own pistol?"

"I thought we'd laid that to rest."

"I said I knew a bit about firearms. The ball I took from your hip is a musket ball. I confirmed it by comparing it to the muzzle of your pistol. It was too big."

"Of course it lost its shape when it struck bone."

"The apothecary here has scales, to measure his pills and powders. I can ask him to weigh the ball and compare it with one of these." He drew something from his waistcoat and opened his hand under Meuchel's nose.

The Viper stared at the ball of lead. He smelled fulminate of mercury. He snatched at his sheet, pulling back the corner near his head.

"Yes, I examined your belt with its curious pockets. Did you think I couldn't find where you hid the key? Not even a man of iron can hope to hold it in his hand indefinitely."

"Doctor, that's no ordinary ball."

"I know. I saw what one did to one of your victims."

"You must lay it down."

"And these too?" He reached into another pocket and showed him what he'd withdrawn. The balls whispered against one another as he rolled them back and forth on his palm.

"Doctor, believe me when I tell you there's enough explosive material in that handful of lead to blow this building to splinters."

"I'm prepared to believe you killed those two men in self-defense. You were carrying a lot of money, possibly as part of your mission, whatever it is. You lied to avoid being questioned by the authorities. I can overlook all that, but I must know if these devil balls are intended for French use."

"They're intended for mine. I was chosen in place of an armed escort, for purposes of traveling unnoticed. It's a dangerous assignment for one man. The protection is necessary."

"Evidently. Your grand mission was nearly brought to calamity by a pair of ordinary brigands."

"I was careless. I never make the same mistake twice."

"Are you a mercenary?"

"I'm paid, the same as any soldier."

"Ten thousand pounds?"

The man's expression was bland.

"It *could* be nine thousand, Doctor. I'm allowed some discretion as to expenses."

Eslée shook his head. "If I could be bought, I'd have kept it all. In any event, what would I do with so much money? I couldn't spend it without attracting notice. No, Meuchel, you can't tempt me."

"Then I appeal to your patriotism. At this stage of the transaction, the motives of my superiors may be misinterpreted and my mission declared an act of war. The fate of great nations rests with you."

"You exalt me."

"I entreat you."

"I've seen governments fall like tenpins. I'm no longer certain whether I'm a citizen of France or of whoever occupies Paris at the moment. You wave the flag, I say, 'Which one?' The white flag of the House of Bourbon or the tricolor of the Republic or one of Bonaparte's guidons? Is this treason?"

"Nothing so committed. Boredom, perhaps."

"I wonder what *that* flag would look like." Humor entered the doctor's tone. "How I'll miss these talks when you're mended and gone. You'll be on your way to glory, but for me it'll be back to my corns and carbuncles."

"You agree to my terms?"

"I haven't a choice. My first loyalty lies with a Greek physician dead more than a thousand years."

"Then put those damn things back in my belt, and be careful about it. The town needs a doctor, and your balloon woman her friend."

"Depend on that. I'd rather handle tarantulas."

"I'd be more confident if you'd accept money."

"You can repay me by walking out a whole man at the end of the week."

He said nothing. Eslée hadn't that long to live.

IV

PRAIRIAL

(Month of Meadows)

30

In a small room near the Quai Desaix, two men read late into the night.

A lamp smoked, worse than Chief Inspector Limodin's pipe. The vile domestic blends he chose, in a virtuous effort to deny profit to Channel smugglers, offended Prefect Dubois' senses. But without the extra light, the reports swam before his weary eyes.

"Here is something," Limodin said.

Dubois removed his spectacles. "How many does this make?"

"I haven't an inkling. If you wanted me to keep a tally, you should have said so at the start."

He took the papers with a sigh and laid them atop the stack on his desk. "I feel compelled to tell you there is such a thing as being *too* outspoken, even for a policeman."

"That, too, comes late."

"What makes *this* something something?"

"Well, read it. For me to summarize would be a waste of my talents."

Dubois decided they'd been shut up together too long. They were like the miserable married couple who were too poor to divorce and so had taken to hounding each other into the grave for sheer spite.

"This is dated day before yesterday."

"It didn't come far. The nearness to Paris alerted me. If there's anything to it, we haven't time to waste."

As Dubois read, boots crunched gravel directly below his window. The noise was like a maul breaking up ice, monotonously and in rhythm. The Prefecture's courtyard had been commandeered, as had all the other vacant ground in the city, for the drilling of troops. Was that a bull treading on its own testicles? No; just a master sergeant bawling commands in an indecipherable soldiers' dialect.

When he finished the report Limodin had handed him he went back over it more slowly, sliding his spectacles across the dilapidated lines like a convex glass.

"This was written by someone with a quill between his arse cheeks. Does this say Formerie or Rochefort?" He stabbed a purple-stained finger at the page.

"Neither. It's Pontoise. A charming village, if you like them mired in the Dark Ages; it's very near here, as I said. In addition to his wretched penmanship, his instincts must be unreliable, or the Police Minister wouldn't have thrown him in our laps. Blaq is the name; a spy assigned to the local constabulary."

"If I had a tenth of the Ministry's resources, I'd have every bag-snatcher in the city behind bars." There had been an epidemic of late, no doubt caused by the distraction of war; the papers were calling, quite literally, for Dubois' head. "Even if his story can be credited, two dead highwaymen outside Paris doesn't fall into either jurisdiction."

"Still, a highwayman without a face presents points of interest. The village constable said it was as if he'd been hit with a mortar, or something equally explosive."

The Prefect's mouth twisted under his smudge of moustache. "Another infernal machine?"

"A coincidence probably. But how many others have come to light?"

"What do you know of assassins?"

Limodin frowned. "They climb to balconies with daggers clamped between their teeth and slit the throats of doges. Don't ask me what a doge is. My mother read to me from novels. Is that what this is about?"

"Perhaps. A pipe dream, the Police Minister said. Rather too quickly to ignore. For once he seemed to have let the mask slip. 'One man may succeed where a band has failed.' His words."

"Likely a misdirection."

"And yet it made good sense."

"It would explain two dead men, one with his face blown away. The doctor corroborated that at the scene."

"Don't speak of the wisdom of country doctors," Dubois said. "Some would treat an ingrown toenail by amputating the leg, and the wrong one at that. What would even an able one know of explosives? Pontoise is not Toulon."

"Still, it's one of the villages travelers pass through on the way here from the Channel. It may be significant."

"You place too much faith in geography." Dubois, who rarely ventured outside the city, distrusted maps, which seemed to exist with the specific intention of misdirecting him. "I suppose one of us should have a talk with this Dr. Milieu."

"Eslée." Limodin spelled it.

"Are you sure?"

"When I was a boy I earned a franc a week making deliveries for a druggist. His scribble was worse than this. Shall I go?"

"No. I will. There's no telling what the dregs of Paris will get up to when they learn the bulldog chief inspector is away."

"Meaning you get the holiday while I stay here and grub through Citizen Fouché's leavings."

"At least you'll be making more than a franc a week."

"I'm asking a favor," Eslée told Marianne Deauville. "I can't tell you why."

She frowned at her sewing. "I already did you the favor of making chowder for your patient. Now you want me to give him room and board."

"Please respect my wishes in this matter. I wouldn't impose if I didn't think it important."

"Then the answer is no."

He breathed in and out. He'd begun to see why the men of the village were intimidated by her intelligence.

"I'll say this much," he said. "That man Blaq who hangs around Malroux's office is a government spy. He suspects me of harboring a criminal. He'll be watching my place, and if he thinks he has the evidence he may come in with an arrest warrant. My patient's recuperating faster than I thought possible, but any rough handling at this point—"

"I'm to harbor him, then. It's all right if I'm the one being handled roughly."

"If we're careful, you won't fall under suspicion. Our situation, yours and mine, is hardly a secret in this village. My visiting your house won't be thought irregular. Meanwhile I can continue treating him.

"You'll be reimbursed for the expense of feeding him," he continued, "and I'll come by to check on him daily. Surely no one will question the frequency of my visits after all this time." He smiled wickedly, hoping to draw off her annoyance with ribaldry.

"And so you seek my cooperation by informing me I'm compromised."

He resisted the urge to roll his eyes. He never knew when her prudish streak would surface; another time, a bawdy joke would make her laugh like an uninhibited child. Women! What was one to make of the race?

"It's only a few days. He agreed to a week's rest, and he really is coming along remarkably; almost supernaturally. If I had an ounce of academic ambition I'd publish a paper on this case."

"Would this have anything to do with two dead bandits on the road outside town?"

"Where did you hear that?"

"I altered a dress for Citizeness Beloit, the wife of the baker. The ventilation duct goes straight to Malroux's office upstairs. There isn't a runner in the country who spreads news as fast as village gossip."

"She may be a spy herself. Blaq thinks I'm connected with what happened. Even if he's right, the death of a known highwayman and of his probable accomplice are scarce reason to endanger the life of a third man who may or may not be involved. At all events my only concern as his physician is to bring him back to health."

She manipulated the needle industriously, concentrating on her work in the light of her parlor, where a haze of discarded thread carpeted the floor.

"How will you get him here, with Blaq watching day and night?"

"Not at night; even a rat must sleep. Then he'll be spelled by Giroud, if I'm any judge of how the Police Ministry works. I've been treating Giroud's weak bowels for years. He's good for an hour at most before he scuttles round the corner to use the necessary room in the tavern. He's good then for twenty minutes; enough time to deliver Meuchel to your door in his own dog cart, return it and his mare to my carriage house, and re-establish myself in my consulting room as if I'd never left."

"Meuchel is your patient?"

"That's what he says. I know what you're thinking. Austria is an old ally of the English, and the name may as well be Austrian as German. But a man can't be condemned on the basis of just his name."

"If you think that, you slept through the Terror." She bit off a piece of thread. "You must think you know me very well, to enlist me in this game of cat and mouse and ask me to put up a stranger in my home."

"I know you're brave as well as merciful. Also that you've kept poor León's bayonet all these years, and sleep with it under your pillow; although you'll see for yourself this stranger is still too weak for you to need it."

She rethreaded the needle, and for a few moments stitched so furiously her hand was a blur, the thimble on the opposite thumb flashing in the strong sunlight coming through the window. Then she stopped.

"I suppose you'll want to move him tonight."

"I'd do it now, if Blaq weren't on duty and if I thought the neighbors wouldn't see. There's no telling when he'll pounce." He hauled out his old pewter watch. "In fact, I should be getting back, in case he decides to break in, warrant or no. It's all just a matter of his own certainty. Fouché will hardly stand on principle if he's satisfied with the results." He kept his tone from rising. He didn't dare hope her remark was a sign she'd help. Marianne was a deliberate chess player who considered every alternative before making the simplest move. And she usually won.

"Fly back, then, to your precious patient. I'll expect you any time after dark. You'll find the back door unlatched and one lamp burning. And me waiting—with poor León's bayonet."

He stood up abruptly, almost overturning his chair. "You're a heroine, Citizeness Deauville."

"And you're a little shit. But I still hope you'll make me an honest woman someday."

And for as long as it took Eslée to walk back to his house, he thought that might happen after all; he could do worse, and in fact had.

Then he spotted Blaq's drab gray presence in the doorway of the tanner's across the street and remembered how much he resented anyone bearing witness to his comings and goings.

———

The Widow Deauville was under no delusions that Charles Eslée would ever link his name to hers, short of desperate measures
on her part. A confirmed bachelor couldn't conceal his condition
beneath the litany of the divorced man. But he was her only prospect, and she had no doubts about her determination to wear him
down. (Just getting him into bed had been a rigorous campaign,
months in the execution, a severe test of her pride. Yet she'd pre-
vailed.) If that meant agreeing to an impossible appeal, so much
the better for its impossibility. It was one more arrow in her quiver.

She hadn't played hostess to an overnight guest of either
gender since before poor León had marched off to defend the
Republic. She'd offered countless times to make breakfast if
Charles would stay until morning (wretched cook that she considered herself, she could improve upon the greasy fare in the
tavern where he dined daily), but he had old-fashioned notions
about protecting her honor and always left by twilight at the
latest.

Now, as night fell, noticeably later than only a few days before,
she chose personal vanity over domestic appearances and reached
for a pot of rouge instead of a broom.

No one, after all, had ever commented upon the cleanliness of
DuBarry's chambers, and *that* lady had commanded the attention
of a king.

She sat naked before the mirror on her dressing table and filled
in the tiny fissures at the corners of her eyes with powder; wish-
ing she could afford the ingenious enamel she'd heard the ladies
of Paris employed to disguise the tracks of age. Mediterranean
rouge, applied sparingly and cunningly blended with a fingertip,
counterfeited the blush of youth, and so far there wasn't so much
gray in her roots it couldn't be dissembled with a grease pencil.

Men. Boys, really. They worried about their honor, their wives,
their mistresses, their business affairs, whether they were being
swindled by their bankers, their sexual abilities; their lives, if they

laid their wagers carelessly in the game of politics. What did they know of the importance of beauty, the only currency exempt from devaluation, if one could but maintain it year after year?

Her neck, at least, was unlined, becomingly long and slender. Her arms were slender as well, the underflesh firm, and she'd made her peace at last with the pale cicatrix of the smallpox vaccination Eslée had insisted upon giving her. She was no wraith, but men were loath to embrace a rack of bones.

Her breasts—she hefted them and let them fall, frowning at their irresiliancy, the way they flopped like sacks of meal—were a problem that would increase with time. But then, the ladies of Paris were getting on as well, and she had faith they'd provide some solution, either of engineering or dress. She herself, wizard with a needle that she knew herself to be, lacked the vision to create, had only the skill to follow patterns drafted by others.

But the goods were good; Charles seemed never to get over the novelty of her casual display of them in broad daylight.

Not that she cared if they were accepted by her impromptu guest; if she stooped to offer them at all.

Impossible. Men who resisted robbery were brawny oafs, placing their purses before good sense. This one had been lucky, that was all. She'd bring him down to earth by treating him as a baby mouse, motherless and bald, too inept to feed itself or stir from its own filth.

Meuchel, was it? She would call him *Moule*: her little mollycoddle.

31

Giroud, the spy, Eslée noted, appeared to have discovered a cure for his watery bowels.

As his physician, Eslée should have been happy; but even if it bent his oath a bit, he'd welcome one more night of hasty trips to the facility for the spy.

It was growing late. He was afraid that if Marianne was forced to wait much longer, she'd change her mind.

He stood at a window in darkness, watching the figure in the tanner's doorway opposite his consulting room. Nearly two hours had passed since the so-called records clerk had relieved Blaq at his post, and Giroud had shown no sign of physical distress. Was he wearing a diaper?

This explanation, indelicate as it was, had just occurred to him when Giroud emerged from the doorway and started round the corner to the tavern, his feet moving with grim urgency.

Eslée waited a moment, in case it was a ruse, then swung into action.

He had on a cloak and hat. He went out, unlatched the door of the carriage house, and brought the dog cart and mare, hitched already, to the back door. He found his patient sitting up on the couch, wearing his own hat and coat over a shirt and breeches from his valise. His courier's belt was buckled round his middle, loosely to avoid chafing his fresh bandages, and his dagger was in his belt-sheath.

He held his pistol in one hand, pointed at the doorway. Eslée froze in his tracks.

Meuchel—or whatever his name was in truth—tucked the weapon under his waistband. "I had to be sure it was you."

He started to rise. He looked pale in the light spilling from the consulting room, but he wasn't perspiring. When the doctor stepped forward to help, he waved him away. He pushed himself upright.

"How do you do it?" Eslée said. "It's been only four days."

"I have a good doctor."

Once outside, he accepted help climbing onto the seat of the cart. Eslée started to join him.

"My valise."

Eslée went back for it and put it behind the seat. The man's obsession with his bag was mysterious. It contained nothing but clothing and books and a kit for cleaning and oiling his pistol.

The horse was obedient; probably it had become bored with inaction. They hadn't far to go, but they moved slowly to avoid jolting the recovering passenger. *God, let Giroud's session on the toilet last long enough for our purposes!* When they passed through the light from a window, Meuchel's jaw was clenched, but still he made no sound of pain.

At last they took the turning that brought them behind Marianne's house, dimly illumined by a single lamp. The back door opened the moment he drew rein. He saw her silhouette briefly inside the frame, and knew by the way she held her left arm that she held poor León's bayonet.

When Eslée helped his patient inside, she set the blade down on the table where she and the doctor dined and played chess, and came forward to take his other arm.

"Thank you, Madame. I regret the imposition."

She hesitated, possibly surprised by his flawless dialect. No doubt she'd expected bad French with a coarse Teutonic accent.

"At least you're polite."

Eslée shared her curiosity. To his dying day, he would wonder about Major Meuchel's ethnic origins. Through all the turns in his life, the small victories and great tragedies, the man would seldom be far from his thoughts.

She hadn't expected a man so well set up. He wasn't exactly handsome, but his features were regular, and though she was sure he was suffering, his posture made him look taller than he was. Perhaps he was a military man after all. His eyes were a smoky color she associated with meadow frost, and their expression was frank.

If this was the impression he made when ailing, she regretted not having met him in the peak of health.

He slept in her bed. This was no hardship. When she worked late, she simply drew a blanket over herself in her rocking chair. She didn't sleep well under the best circumstances; had anyone, who'd seen what she had, done what she'd done to survive? Poor León had rescued her from all that, but she'd never expected that situation to last, and she'd been right.

For the stranger, at least, it would be an improvement over the stiff couch in the doctor's examining room. She had painful memories of spontaneous passion there, followed by a week of spinal purgatory.

That first night outside her room, Charles seized her hands. "I have to go. You're a saint." He kissed them.

"And to think a few hours ago I was only a heroine. It must be a battlefield promotion."

"If he wakes up hungry, let him eat what he wants. He's strong enough now for solid food."

"He'll eat what I give him. I'm not running an inn."

After he left, she looked in on her guest. His eyes were closed, his breathing even. He didn't snore or talk in his sleep. A gentleman even when insensible.

She would have to watch this one.

Eslée drove back as quickly as he dared, detouring onto a side street to approach his house from behind. He lost no time unhitching the mare and putting it and the cart away in the carriage house. He was eager to get back to his window and learn if Giroud was still indisposed.

"Dr. Eslée."

He was fumbling out his latchkey when the speaker stepped forward from darkness. His heart lurched.

"Citizen Giroud! You gave me a turn."

"Why, Doctor? Have you something to hide?"

The records clerk was androgynous, with a high voice, womanly hips, and a suggestion of breasts under his frilled shirt. He wore the same flat-brimmed hat and tailcoat in all seasons.

"I thought I was alone. Only a few days ago, two men were slain just outside the village in a falling-out between thieves or somesuch. It puts a man on edge."

"So Monsieur Blaq informed me. You were quite interested in the case."

"Constable Malroux asked me to examine the corpses."

"Where were you just now? I knocked at your door."

"Why? Are you ill?"

"My question first, Doctor."

"If you must know, I came out for air."

"Is the air in your house staler tonight than usual?"

"Is your stomach in distress, Giroud? I can give you apricot oil."

Giroud blushed. "The, ah, effect of that particular treatment has been rather the opposite of its purpose."

"I'm sorry to hear that. Perhaps you should change your diet.

I advise patients who complain of constipation to leave off eating boiled fruits. If you were to reverse that prescription—"

"That doesn't seem very different from apricot oil."

"I'm a physician, not a scientist. I don't always know why the treatments I suggest work, only that they do."

"Or don't, as in my case."

"What have you to lose? And stewed pears can be quite tasty."

"We're drifting off the subject, Doctor. There's a war on, and a curfew's in effect. I should report you."

"What makes that the duty of a records clerk?"

"Upholding the law is every citizen's responsibility."

"War or no war, there's no law against strolling in one's own backyard."

"I heard a hinge squeak a few moments ago. Were you in your carriage house?"

Dangerous to deny it. Any curiosity on the part of this spy might lead to a search of the building, and a connection to the wheel tracks at the scene of the double killing.

"I looked in on my gelding. Madame Jote is expecting any day. It's a long ride out. I can't afford to have the animal take sick in the damp."

"Did you find it well?"

"Very much so, thank you."

"Still, perhaps I should have a look. My uncle was a very fine veterinarian, you know. I served as his apprentice for a year. It turned out I didn't share his gift, but I learned some things."

"Thank you, but it's not necessary. The horse is fine."

"But as long as I'm here."

The tips of Eslée's ears burned. He riffled through his card-box of excuses.

A long, ominous, gurgling rumble issued from Giroud's stomach. He doubled over; and to his credit managed to turn it into a bow of leave-taking, marred ever so slightly by a Homeric fart.

"I just remembered I have work that can't wait. I must offer my services another time. Good night, Doctor."

"Good night, Citizen. Consider those stewed pears."

He was speaking to Giroud's coattails, flapping above clenched buttocks.

A temporary reprieve. Eslée fretted about that cart and horse throughout the night. It was evidence that could put him to arrest and torture.

But where else could they be hidden?

Marianne had no outbuildings. The carriage house would be searched, that was inevitable, and when its contents were exposed, both households examined. He'd placed Marianne in his own dangerous position, just as she'd suggested.

He sat up abruptly before dawn, determined to come clean and warn her. It would mean the end of their relationship; but what of that? A monk's life was light penance.

Dressing, he realized he was being selfish. He was only trying to clear his conscience. She was better off ignorant. Innocence was difficult to pretend, and Fouché's interrogators were practiced in detecting lies and excavating the truth, ruinously and at great length.

The burden was his alone. He dared not share it, even with the woman whose life meant—

More than my own; was that where he was headed?

"Charles René Eslée," he said aloud, "if you're not married to this woman by the end of Thermidor, you're a donkey, and I want no more to do with you." He went back to bed, to sleep the sleep of the guilty.

Marianne found herself humming over her sewing.

It annoyed her greatly. She was a woman who concentrated

on her work, neither enjoying nor disliking it unless something went wrong. Work was work, and complaining about it or taking pleasure in it didn't shave a second off getting it done. Whenever she heard some lout whistling as he dumped out a bucket of slops or shoveled horseshit into a pile, she knew him for an idiot. She would whistle when she was paid.

Why, then, was she humming? And an insipid little romantic jingle from her childhood at that?

There was a man in the house, to be sure. One comely enough, with a spice of danger that brought back memories of her romantic youth, which she'd thought buried with the victims of the guillotine. How could mere fancy survive the events since 1793?

The weeks succeeding the King's execution had been harrowing. Brigands swarmed the countryside, believing that the natural order of society had broken down and all laws were suspended indefinitely. She'd caught one of the scum leering at her through the window of her bedroom when she was undressing, and had chased him all the way out to the street, wearing nothing but her stockings and brandishing a pair of shears for a weapon.

She no longer needed a brawny champion, to barter his services for ten sweaty minutes abusing her snatch. The Revolution had made everyone equal, genders included, and put an end to the rite of the caveman; the stranger's strength, obvious despite his present condition, wasn't why she felt happy sharing her roof with him.

Or was it?

A woman wearied of being self-sufficient, and longed to lean against a firm breast and feel safe. Eslée was a good man, an attentive lover, but she could no more see him dispatching two bandits in the space of as many heartbeats than she could imagine a faithful terrier vanquishing a pack of wolves. He would *try*; but it would end in tragedy.

"*Ouf!*" She pricked her finger; rare event. She prided herself on her concentration. She sucked at the wound, tasting salt and iron.

"You've hurt yourself. May I help?"

She looked up sharply. She'd heard fewer than a half-dozen words from Eslée's patient, and his faultless French had so distracted her she'd failed to note the pleasing timbre of his voice.

He stood in the bedroom doorway, wearing the same shirt and breeches: A hasty cleansing of his wound and changing of bandages had been all Eslée could manage considering the restraints of time. With one foot placed before the other and a hand bracing his weight against the doorframe, he looked like one of those heroic Renaissance statues the First Consul had brought back from Italy and scattered throughout Paris.

He wasn't wearing the bulky belt she'd noticed when she'd helped him to bed. Perhaps he'd put it in the valise Charles had brought in. Such belts always contained something valuable.

Which explained the pistol and dagger still in his waistband.

She snatched off the spectacles she used for close work; they weren't flattering.

"Thank you, monsieur, but no. It's a hazard of my occupation. You shouldn't be up. Are you hungry?"

"That can wait. I'm bedsore and bored. If you'll let me sit here with you, I promise I won't disturb."

She inclined her head toward the chair Charles always sat in.

"They say boredom is as good a sign as hunger. If so, I am in the best of health. I welcome the disturbance."

He made his way to the seat, touching the back of her rocker briefly for its support. She had the queer feeling he was playacting, and not as weak as he appeared.

A lock of hair had fallen over his right eyebrow. He wore it long, against current fashion. She found it a relief from the shorn heads that filled the village. Ears that stuck out like jug-handles offended her taste.

As she sewed, she found herself looking up from under her lashes at his hands resting on the arms of the chair: large hands,

with thick veins like ship's rigging on the backs. One could sense
a great deal about a man from his hands (not that old charwom-
an's legend about proportions in one area echoing those in another; she was a woman of the world, and had seen the flaws in
that theory), but things like strength and endurance were to be
found in a man's hands. Charles's were narrow and delicate in
appearance, well-suited to healing, but in other areas he was a
sprinter rather than a long-distance runner. In bed she invariably
finished second, when she finished at all.

"You're a machine, *Madame*."

She looked up quickly, her cheeks warm. Without her glasses
she'd been working almost entirely by feel, her experienced fingers moving swiftly, making up for shortsightedness, like a blind
man's hearing and touch. It was this display of industry that had
caused his remark, not her impure thoughts: No man could read a
woman's mind. In self-disgust she hooked the spectacles back on,
and saw immediately her stitches were crooked.

"Not a bit of it. I'm vain of my aging eyes; and now I must
undo all I've done." She bit off the thread and tugged it free.

"Strong teeth, too. I admire a woman who takes care of such
things."

"You're very observant for a man." She threw away the tangle
of thread and reloaded her needle.

"Have you and Dr. Eslée been friends for long?"

"Not in terms of years. I did some dress work for his former wife,
and he set my late husband's leg when he fell off his ladder—he was
a house painter before he became a soldier. I consoled the doctor
when his wife left him, and he comforted me when poor León was
killed."

"You're lovers?"

She concentrated on her sewing for thirty seconds. "You're
presumptuous, Major."

"I didn't mean to offend."

"I don't offend that easily; but I'm jealous of my privacy."

"Then you *are* lovers."

"That language is old-fashioned. We fuck, monsieur."

He smiled; or so she thought. The muscles of both his face and body seemed to reserve their power for more important things.

A dangerous man. She felt the downy growth rise on the nape of her neck.

"I find you refreshing, *Madame* Deauville."

"You may as well call me Marianne, if there's to be no pretense between us."

He smiled in truth, exposing strong teeth of his own.

"And I am Franz."

32

Dubois quite liked Constable Malroux.

He hadn't been prepared to, given his convictions regarding things rural: hex signs and the like.

Here was a policeman after the Prefect's own heart, with sound instincts and a village postmaster's memory for detail, remarkably on a par with the First Consul's; and he was swift to confess when he did not know something—which the First Consul was increasingly unlikely to do, as Dubois himself had observed lately, to his alarm. A man learned nothing listening to himself.

The pleasure of the man's company, together with a glass of full-bodied local beer offered to comfort him after his journey, soon made him forget what a devil's own time he'd had finding Pontoise. The maps of Paris' suburbs and environs made no allowances for a questionable sense of direction; signposts in particular seemed to have been engineered to discourage visitors who hadn't memorized every road, lane, and goat-path that wandered outside the city. In many cases they didn't even exist—evidence of the hard winter recently passed, and the lust for firewood—and where they did, stiff winds or malicious vandalism had turned them in directions that brought him maddeningly back to a landmark he'd passed twice.

He owed his success to the occasional native who overcame suspicion regarding official uniforms long enough to point him in the right direction. Even so, night birds and not swallows welcomed him to a village only a few hours' journey from Paris.

Malroux didn't return his affection; but that was expected. Villagers distrusted city folk, and village authorities city police.

The air thawed when it became clear the two shared a strong dislike for Monsieur Blaq, the Ministry informant who'd insisted on joining them above the aromatic bakery where justice was sought in Pontoise. When the rat-faced menial demanded to know why the Minister had sent a city policeman instead of one of his own, the Prefect detected a glimmer of sympathy in the constable's weary eyes. Plainly the man had been saddled upon him without his consent.

Dubois sipped from his glass of beer.

"You must understand, Citizen," he told Blaq, "that the Ministry receives daily dozens of reports of doubtful activity, from all over the country. It can't pursue them all, so I'm assigned to take up the slack. Common criminal behavior doesn't normally interest the government."

"But surely the evidence of an infernal machine—"

"A journalistic phrase, Citizen. You won't find it in any government report. But your point's taken. I'm here because of the intriguing nature of the weapon involved. Otherwise I'd leave things in the capable hands of Constable Malroux."

That worthy individual rolled his shoulders.

"Quite the opposite, I regret to admit," he said. "That's why I consulted Dr. Eslée on the nature of the facial injury. He too thought it excessive. I assume that's why Monsieur Blaq, assiduous public servant that he is, considered it proper to inform the Ministry."

He sat behind a homely worktable stacked precariously with papers, some bound with cord, others poking out at all angles, like bookmarks in a zealot's Bible. Dubois found the arrangement similar to his own, and more likely proof of an industrious mind than Fouché's orderly regiments of foolscap. An untidy desk suggested a tidy mind. Indeed the office itself resembled the Prefect's, absent distracting gimcrack, and small enough for a true crafts-man to reach all his tools without stretching.

The intoxicating smells of warm pastry rising between the floorboards were a diversion; Dubois hadn't eaten since dawn. But he supposed the constable took notice of them no longer through familiarity.

"I'd like a few words with this doctor."

"Of course. Ten doors down, across from the tannery. Just fol-low your nose." Malroux pinched his nostrils significantly between thumb and forefinger. He disregarded pleasant odors, noted foul ones. A good policeman.

"I'd consider it a favor if you'd accompany me. Some of these provincials—forgive me, but you know the type—shrink into their shells in the presence of a strange uniform."

"I'll come along, but you'll find the doctor a man with nothing to hide."

Blaq snorted.

Dubois looked his way. "Something, monsieur?"

"I suggest Malroux is prejudiced in favor of the locals."

"Then it's good I'm here, a disinterested third party, at the constable's own request."

Blaq shot up from his hard chair. "I'll go along as well."

Dubois steeled his expression. "You're not invited. This is a Paris affair now. I've chosen my local liaison."

"I represent the Ministry!"

"The Minister himself has ceded jurisdiction." Which was technically true; although Fouché remained unaware of what use Dubois was making of the files that had been placed in his charge.

"Then I'll accompany you as a private citizen. This is a free Republic, after all."

"If you persist," put in Malroux, "I must place you under arrest for interfering in a criminal investigation."

"You can't do that!"

Dubois interceded.

"He can. Any officer can. You'll find it spelled out clearly in the Civil Code."

"That hasn't been signed into law!"

"Noted. Should you care to take it up with the First Consul, who is drawing it up—"

Blaq backed off from that line of argument. "I shall file a protest with the Ministry."

"That's your privilege," Dubois said. "It's a free Republic, as you said."

Blaq flushed an unhealthy orange under his sallow pigment. He hastened out, banging the door behind him. The current stirred the stacked papers, freeing one to drift like a leaf to the floor.

The constable was beaming. He unstopped another beer bottle and filled both glasses to the rim.

"That was better than a physic. I'd have thrown him out months ago if I didn't think I'd be shot for it."

"I may yet be," Dubois said. "But I didn't get myself lost all day on your diabolical roads to worry about it tonight."

"They make sense, once you get to know the place. I myself could no longer find my way across Paris without a native to guide me."

"Nor I, some parts. Fortunately, I have a chief inspector who grew up doing odd jobs throughout the city. Not that I'd praise him in his presence. He's insufferable as well as indispensable."

"I'd trade him for Blaq."

"If it weren't Blaq it would be someone else. Perhaps even someone competent. Count your blessings, Citizen."

Malroux groped for his watch. "We have plenty of time, *Monsieur le Prefect*. Eslée is a bachelor and stays up late."

"Please call me Dubois. Only my wife uses Nicolas, and my official title annoys me nearly as much as this ridiculous uniform."

"I like the hat."

Dubois smiled beneath his caterpillar moustache.

"We must meet again, Citizen, when this thing is through."

"Malroux, if you please. What thing is that?"

"Who can say? We policemen must take events as they come." Dubois finished his beer with a flip of his wrist and put on his flat-topped cap. "Let's talk to this remarkably honest man Eslée."

33

Marianne was gentle to start, thinking the patient could neither support her weight nor exert himself in the dominant position. She turned away from him on the bed and spread her thighs to reach between them and guide him inside her from behind.

She was shocked when he seized her shoulder and jerked her over onto her back. He was upon her in an instant, already stiff and panting, and entered her with such force she felt that he would impale her to the mattress.

The violence alarmed her. She twisted her face away from the heat of his breath and tried to struggle free, but his body was heavy as well as hot, constricting her chest, suffocating her. She knew blind panic; and (to her astonishment) the tingle of approaching orgasm. She stopped resisting then. It would be over soon and sweet.

In the next moment she was fighting again; for her life.

His hands clenched round her throat. Corded fingers dug into the arteries, stopping the flow of blood along with her breath. She clawed at his naked back. She drew blood, but the pressure increased along with the pumping of his pelvis. She got her hands between them and pushed. His body wouldn't yield.

Her vision shrank. She was looking up through a long narrow tunnel into the eyes of an animal. The vessels of her eyeballs were closing like wire nets. Her tongue swelled and slid out between her lips. She was strangling.

Charles! She could only think the name; her voice was gone.

Would *he* be her last thought? How curious life was, in the leaving.

Suddenly Meuchel's breath caught in his throat with a croak. His body shuddered, but not with release. His expression went from surprise to agony. That terrible grip slackened. Marianne sucked in air with a sob.

In her panic, her vagina had closed tight, strangling his member as he was strangling her, stopping the blood in the thick veins that upheld his erection, starving the rest of his body. Charles had often complained of the razor action of her loins. *Like the scarlet lady of Paris,* he'd said with a gasp; meaning Madame Guillotine.

And in that moment something had given in Meuchel; broken loose. Not sexual release. She felt a sudden warm wetness, but it wasn't semen. Instinctively, she plunged both hands down and tore at his bandages. The seep became a gusher.

He let go of her and sprang from the bed.

Sounds of rustling—clothing thrown on, scraping—the valise being slid from beneath the bed—the jingle of a belt buckle. Then measured breathing. She sensed he was looking down at her, weighing some decision. She lay still. Only her breasts moved, the lungs beneath gulping air. Then more rustling, as of something being put away under a coat.

Pistol? Dagger? It scarcely mattered which. Another close call.

Bang!—she flinched, but it was only the door, swung wide on its hinges and striking the wall, followed by a fall of plaster. Footsteps retreated. More rustling in the adjoining room; muttered curses. Then silence.

The Widow Deauville lay for what seemed an hour in a pool of sweat, hers and his, until it felt cold as ice; then found the energy to roll from bed and claw poor León's bayonet from the drawer of her nightstand.

She stood holding it flat to her bosom with both hands, shivering half-naked in the night air but drawing strength from tempered steel. When at last her hands were steady enough, she released one to turn up the lamp, and saw a scarlet smear on her chemise, the only clothing she wore. The blood wasn't hers. Major Meuchel's wound had reopened; that was the reason he'd quit.

She hoped the rupture was fatal. Such a thing would be more certain than to die from asphyxiation of *le coq*.

He paused long enough in the damnable slut's house to seize the dress she'd been sewing, and once he was outside tore off a piece and jammed it between the bleeding and his bandages, cinching it tight with the courier's belt. It needed fresh dressing, and possibly stitches.

He hurled away the rest of the garment. *Merde!* He'd let his beast get the better of him. It was always a danger when he was bored.

First carelessness on the road, now this.

The bitch! It had been like sticking his member into a steel snare. He should have killed her.

But no. He'd been wise to relent. The trail was bloody enough without an unnecessary death to draw more attention.

He'd kept his wits about him during the ride from Eslée's house and remembered the way. He paced himself to avoid jarring loose his rude dressing.

He needed the doctor just once more, and then it would be time to finish him. He was an inquisitive man with a lively mind, and his patient had sandwiched too much truth between his lies, in an effort to make them plausible.

A horse and a mule were tethered in front of Eslée's house. He heard three distinct voices coming from inside, one belonging to the homeowner.

He'd have to find his medical treatment somewhere else.

He went round the back, picking his way carefully through darkness toward the carriage house.

"Your pardon, sir."

Turning in the direction of the voice, he made out the vaguely womanish shape of a man standing near the corner of the house. The Viper stepped toward him, grasping the handle of his dagger.

34

"The time has come to face the facts, General," said the new-comer. "Your gladiator has lost his way to the arena."

"Not now, Villon. A few moments, if you will." Georges Cadoudal sipped Lord Rexborough's superb port and watched the sun setting on England from the rear veranda.

The Royalist general held most of the island in contempt; it was one great brothel filled with whores to be thrown on the ash heap once he got what he needed. But that scorn didn't extend to its spring when the sky turned copper. Rainy April was forgotten, May well along, its lush teal grasses shuffling in the breeze like a deck of new cards, streaked with colorful wildflowers. A flock of sheep made its way across the meadow, bleating greedily; one could set his watch by them at feeding time. They were as predictable and gluttonous as their British masters.

"If you're quite through admiring the view," Villon said, "let's discuss the likelihood that someone has trod on your precious Viper."

Cadoudal sipped and regarded his co-conspirator. François Villon was a caricature of the old French court in powdered wig and silk slippers, a corset under his waistcoat, and no doubt a jeweled lorgnette in his sleeve. With Rexborough back in London with his ailing wife (she'd seemed quite sturdy before the assassin's visit; could she have divined his purpose?), their houseguest had persuaded the cook to change her menu for the sake of his belly, but this impatient emissary from the aristocracy in exile threatened to bring back his gastric complaint. One didn't have to like one's accomplices, with the great cause they had in common; but even on brief acquaintance, everything about Villon rubbed him the wrong way.

"I'll entertain the possibility," Cadoudal said, "but likelihood and possibility aren't fact. When I fought in the field, I regarded casualties as facts: a man wounded, a man captured, a man dead; these things are indisputable. Do we know our friend is any of those?"

"Why hasn't he reported?"

"I understood we wouldn't hear from him unless he needed help. His silence is reassuring."

"But what was his plan? You should have insisted he confide in you."

"Those fools in the Christmas Eve affair were splendid at confiding. Fouché cracked the plot in days. The fewer people know what he's about, the better; myself included."

"The Comte d'Artois—"

"The Count is a dotard, as I'm sure you know. More pity to us all if he ascends to the throne. Come, Villon; speak for the man you truly represent."

Villon lowered his voice to a hoarse whisper. "The walls have ears even here."

"What walls? That ewe there, the one at the end of the feeding trough. Is she a spy in disguise?"

"You know very well what I mean. If you could smuggle an ally into the domestic staff, so could that pig in Paris."

Cadoudal took pity on this fellow, despite his antipathy. Probably he was a government clerk with no hope of title, sacked by the Republic for his associations, but not important enough for Paris to prevent his emigration.

"I confess I anticipated some news before this," said the general.

"The Corsican has been uncommonly vulnerable lately, inspecting his troops and even joining them at campfires, coarse creature that he is. Why *Le Vipère* hasn't struck already, I can't say. Can you?"

"Of course not. I'm not a murderer for hire. I don't know how they think."

"Thank God for that. He made me uneasy just being in the same room with him. But we use the weapons available. I wouldn't break bread with this British vermin if I didn't think that."

"I suggest we've been betrayed. Your man has absconded with the loot. You should've considered that before you agreed to his terms, without consulting the rest of us."

"It occurred to me, of course. But there's always that danger, and whatever deficiencies he has in his character I doubt they include larceny. At all events, to seek counsel outside this house would risk word getting out."

"Then he's been taken. In either case our situation is the same. We're a cause without a champion."

"What, then, are you asking?"

Villon brushed a bit of snuff from his waistcoat.

"Go to France. Take personal charge of the counter-revolution. I assure you a prince is on his way to reclaim the throne. We have Moreau and Pichegru in our camp. You need only show your face to raise our friends' spirits. *Mon général,* you *are* the Restoration."

"As Bonaparte is the Revolution, in his very own words. We're truly lost if we have to borrow rhetoric from our enemies. *Which* prince is our savior-to-be?"

"I'm not at liberty to say. As you said, some things must remain secret, even from you."

"I'm glad *some*one was listening. But I know who it is." Cadoudal fingered the ring in his pocket, bearing the signet exclusive to the Royal family, a bona fide from the Viper. "Our high-placed friend is young and in good health, with a sound head on his shoulders. None of these things applies to his—to d'Artois." He drained his glass to settle his nerves. He'd caught himself just short of identifying the man aloud, in a place crawling with servants he knew nothing about. "General Moreau is a hero of the Republic. Why should he fall in with us?"

"He doesn't like the direction it's taken. He thinks the Corsican has betrayed his glorious Revolution."

"I wish that were so, although Bonaparte has all the makings of a despot. A civil war would make things much easier. But I don't like throwing in with a man who's turned his coat once. He'll find it easier next time."

"All the more reason to keep him close." Villon moved a shoulder. "For now, the enemy of our enemy is our friend. Once the usurper is dead and we no longer need Moreau, we'll clear him away along with the rest of the trash."

Cadoudal's smile was thin. "Remind me, Villon, never to get on your bad side."

"Your pardon, monsieur," Eslée said. "Who did you say you were?" Despite his uniform and odd hat, held politely in the crook of his arm, the drab little man at his door resembled a pushcart peddler.

"Nicolas Dubois, Doctor. I'm the Prefect of the Paris Police. I believe you know Constable Malroux."

Eslée smiled at the village official, whose personal neatness and reputation as a good family man spoke well of his post. "I do. Pontoise lost a fine postmaster when he decided to become a policeman. Enter, gentlemen. Cognac?"

They declined, no surprise; they both smelled of beer.

Dubois confirmed his suspicions. "Malroux was most generous in his office, and I haven't dined since breakfast. At end of day, all I have are my wits."

When they were all seated in the consulting room, the Prefect drummed his fingers on the hat in his lap—drummed, literally; the tight fabric resonated. "Are you treating anyone at present, Doctor?"

"Not here." Which was true. His patient was under Marianne Deauville's roof, not his. "I have a local woman about to give birth and two cases of ague, but apart from that it's been quiet. We're indecently healthy here." He smiled.

"Splendid! Then we're not keeping you from anything. Malroux says you were most helpful in clearing up the details of an unfortunate incident outside the village this week."

"Some may think it *fortunate*. As a physician, of course, I deplore the loss of life, bandits or no."

"A noble sentiment. You agreed with Malroux that an explosive device was used on one of them."

"I was guessing, but the condition of the victim certainly seemed to indicate it."

"That's what brought me here. Malroux's description of the corpse convinced me I hadn't wasted a trip. It's the nature of the device I'm curious about. If heavy artillery were used, the carriage would have left deep tracks, but your constable says he was all over the area and found nothing fresh, apart from traces of a horse and cart. And of course *some*one would have reported hearing the thunder of cannon. That eliminates any theory that the military was involved, either intentionally or by accident. Also it's unlikely this man Cruncher—"

"Crusher," corrected the constable. "We may never know the identity of the other man, but from his uniform, stripped of insignia, I suspect he was a deserter or a rogue who was drummed out of the army. Perhaps the one led to the other."

"In this case the corpse is more important than the man. It's doubtful this Crusher shot his partner with the ordinary round you extracted, Doctor, then reloaded with the explosive one to finish the job. That would be a classic example of overkill, wouldn't you say?"

"I'm afraid I've given you all the help I can."

Eslée saw the Prefect's moustache twitch. Had he said something that betrayed him?

But Dubois moved on.

"Do you own a pistol, Doctor?"

"No."

"Dear me. I may retire to this gentle village, where bandits have the good grace to die in pairs and a country practitioner can go about his rounds unarmed."

"Look around you, monsieur. Do I give the impression of someone worth waylaying?"

"I *would* like to look around, if you don't mind. It's a matter of being thorough in my report to the Ministry."

He hesitated. He'd just had time to strip the couch in the examining room when the two men came to call. He hoped he hadn't overlooked anything. "Be my guest."

The two officials worked efficiently. Malroux read the labels on medicine bottles, unstopped one, sniffed, winced, and restopped it. Dubois passed behind the desk, opened and shut drawers, riffled through the papers on top.

"May I ask what you're looking for?"

The Prefect smiled shamefacedly. "I wish I could answer. I'm like the stable boy who inspects the horses' teeth every day because he's paid to, never knowing why. We're a bureaucratic nation now."

Malroux opened *Diseases of the Stomach,* paled when he came to a color-tinted illustration, closed it, and put it back on the shelf. "I declare this to be a doctor's office."

"So it appears. May we see the rest of the house?"

They entered the examining room. Dubois placed a palm on

the couch. Surely the man's body heat had dissipated by now. As Eslée turned to watch Malroux opening the cupboard that had contained Meuchel's clothing, he spotted a scrap of bloodstained bandage on the floor beside the trash bin. He felt himself blanch. It must have fallen out undetected when he'd emptied it earlier.

"You could do with a proper cot," said Dubois, straightening. "The horsehair is so lumpy I think they forgot to remove the horse."

"I hadn't realized it." Stepping forward, Eslée kicked the bandage under the cabinet where he kept his instruments. He pressed his hands on the couch, testing it. "You're right. I never lie on it myself. You've saved future patients discomfort."

"It wouldn't do to send them home suffering worse than when they arrived," Dubois said.

They looked through the kitchen and the narrow bedroom where the doctor slept. Eslée's unease began to lift. His patient had never been in those rooms.

Dubois started to put on his hat. "You're quite certain you haven't treated anyone in this house recently?"

"Yes. Why do you ask?"

"It's possible the man who blew off that wastrel's head was injured himself during the exchange. If it was severe enough, he'd seek the nearest medical help."

"Perhaps he came away unscathed."

"Evidently; although I caught a strong scent of liquid opium in your examining room. It's a pain medication. Has a bottle been opened there recently?"

"I inspect my stock from time to time, to make sure nothing's spoiled."

"Of course. I have a sensitive nose. My wife says I should have been a chemist in a perfumery."

"You police are anatomical oddities. With Malroux, it's his throat."

"Indeed?"

"A conceit," said the constable. "It's constricted now, as a matter of fact. It happens whenever—"

Eslée spoke quickly; kicking himself inward for his clumsy remark. "May I prescribe tea and honey?"

Dubois appeared oblivious to the exchange. He donned his hat. "Thank you for your time, Doctor. We'll—"

Outside, someone shouted, an unearthly howl.

Dubois made for the door, drawing a pistol from under his tunic. Malroux followed, armed also; the pistol in his belt scabbard wasn't a stage property after all. The doctor trailed them outside and round to the backyard.

Pale light came from an inside window, illuminating a series of images:

The doors of the carriage house splayed open, Meuchel's mare and cart boiling out at a gallop;

A figure standing in the front seat, shaking the lines and shouting at the animal for speed;

Dubois and Malroux scattering from its path.

Malroux was the first to collect himself. He unshipped the pistol from his belt and fired at the retreating cart. Orange flame leapt from the muzzle.

"For God's sake, don't step on me!"

It was Giroud, the village records clerk, Police Minister Fouché's junior man in Pontoise, seated on the ground, rocking back and forth and cradling his bleeding arm in his lap.

Dubois swung his own pistol, but didn't fire; cart and horse were out of sight, hooves clattering on cobblestones.

He straightened, panting. He turned toward Eslée, who knelt beside Giroud, knotting his handkerchief round the man's upper arm with shaking hands.

The Prefect scabbarded his weapon. His face was grim. "Doctor,

I think it's time we resumed our talk. Here is convenient, but if necessary in Paris, and the offices of the Ministry of Police. The choice is yours."

Eslée nodded, weary beyond words. "Can it at least wait until I prevent this man from bleeding to death?"

"But of course." *I am not Fouché*, he might have added.

35

This time, Fouché and Dubois were met by Méneval, the First Consul's personal secretary, at the Tuileries. Although Méneval was a civilian, his immaculate appearance in black tailcoat, snow-white breeches, and glistening boots gave the impression of a military aide-de-camp. He bowed to the visitors and led them to his master's study.

Outside the massive double doors, he hesitated with his fist raised to knock. Bonaparte's parade-drill voice could be heard bellowing through the heavy oak panels.

Méneval turned with lips pursed. "Another time, perhaps, Citizens. The First Consul is in conference with the Foreign Minister."

"I wonder what Talleyrand's done now?" mused Fouché. "Made peace with Britain, possibly, without consulting the palace. He dictates policy as if he were the head of state. But I suspect he'll survive. A spider is impervious to most poisons, being himself venomous."

Méneval made no response. Indiscretions, from both above and below, stopped with him.

Fouché popped open his watch. "We'll wait. What we have to report won't keep till tomorrow."

The secretary bowed again and conducted them to an anteroom.

"Fouché! What news? Are you here to arrest one of the other Consuls?" Lucien Bonaparte, Napoleon's younger brother, arose from a chair. A bird of paradise in plumage and velvet, he bore a close enough resemblance to the First Consul to make even Dubois glance back toward the study.

The Police Prefect, who knew Fouché's every mood, saw a twitch of irritation in the reptilian face. It was gone by the time he turned toward the speaker.

Lucien held the office of Minister of Internal Affairs, and as such meddled in all departments of government. Dubois considered him an even more accomplished theatrical performer than his brother. He'd saved Napoleon from being mobbed by the late Council of Five Hundred by placing the point of his sword at Napoleon's breast, promising to run him through if he betrayed the Republic. The result was a bloodless coup, and France's fourth government in ten years.

Dubois held the uneasy conviction that there wasn't so much theater in the performance; that the promise he'd made on that historic day was literal. Lucien bore all the marks of a dangerous fanatic, Jacobin to the core.

Fouché's expression changed. His response was blandly urbane; the guise in which he was most dangerous.

"Quite the reverse, Citizen Bonaparte. We're here to save the Consulate from a serious threat. Unfortunately, your brother is occupied."

"With Talleyrand, yes. Perhaps this time he'll dismiss that club-footed ogre. You may report to me, and I shall inform the First Consul of your concerns."

The Police Minister gestured with the worn leather portfolio under his arm. "With respect, Citizen, this is for the eyes and ears of the First Consul only. He'll bring you up to date, I'm sure."

"*Méneval!*"

Napoleon's shout shook the door panels. The secretary bowed a third time and turned toward the study.

Lucien affected not to have heard.

"Yes, I know all about your secret newspaper, and how its

columns are filled. I found one of your spies under my bed the
other night, masquerading as a roach. How are you, Dubois?"
His demeanor softened visibly when he addressed the Prefect.

For some reason, both Bonapartes held Dubois in the same
affectionate regard. This pained him. Lucien wasn't above persuading Napoleon to put him in Fouché's place—a perilous
presumption with the Police Minister still very much in power.

How he envied the common patrolman, with only his ring of
keys to fret about.

"I'm well, Citizen. Thank you for asking."

"That's happy news. So many gifted individuals have lost their
stations—indeed, their heads—to ambitious bureaucrats. Who'd
have thought such gray men would prove worse than a king?"
Lucien clicked his heels. "Dubois. Fouché."

Fouché observed his retreating back from beneath heavy lids.

"You know," he told Dubois, "the First Consul might have perished in Egypt, with Nelson in control of the Nile. His brother
was president of the Council of Five Hundred, and would in that
event have taken charge himself. There, but for the grace of a
good blockade runner, goes another Robespierre. We might have
had the Terror all over again."

Dubois made no remark. It had been the Terror that had cat-
apulted the Police Minister into power. With each new government he'd thrown off the last without a backward glance.

The Prefect drew a deep breath. His sole ambition was to do
his job. Greatness kept getting in the way.

They wandered back out into the corridor just as the study
doors flew open and Charles-Maurice de Talleyrand, France's
Foreign Minister, burst out and swept past them without stopping,
leaning on a gold-headed stick. Alone among the First Consul's
inner circle, he clung to the powdered wigs of the *Ancien Regime*:
a tall, aristocratic figure with an implausibly long neck bound
with a silk stock, threads of gold glittering in his state uniform.

He powdered his face with white lead to conceal the scars of smallpox, but even so his cheeks were aflame with rage.

"Best to leave the conversation to me," Fouché told Dubois, as Talleyrand clumped away down the passage on his crippled foot. "For the First Consul, it's the next best thing to doing all the talking himself."

Dubois thought it just as well. Intrigue was beyond his depth.

Méneval came out of the study. "Citizens, the First Consul will see you."

Bonaparte fidgeted behind his ornate desk until Fouché finished speaking, then said: "What do *you* think, Dubois?"

Dubois glanced at the Minister, seated beside him. His expression was impassive, a sure sign he was seething. It would go badly for the Prefect if he were not absolutely diplomatic.

"Citizen Fouché put the matter thoroughly and succinctly, Citizen. I can't add anything."

There was no trace on the First Consul's face of his earlier rage. The Strong Man of France shifted from one humor to another as easily as turning a lamp up or down.

If in fact he'd been honestly angry to begin with.

He took a pinch of snuff and wiped his nostrils with silk. "We're all equals here. What's your interpretation?"

Dubois marshaled his recollections.

"Dr. Eslée was lying when he said he knew nothing of the double killing and that he wasn't treating anyone at the time we spoke. I suspected as much, but I lacked evidence. After what took place behind his house, Constable Malroux and I made a thorough search of his examining room and found a scrap of bloody bandage. The rest of the story came out as the doctor worked on the man Giroud."

"One of mine," Fouché put in.

Dubois continued as if he hadn't been interrupted. "Thirty-two stitches were required to close his wound. Giroud was lucky; he managed to block the dagger with his arm. Unfortunately, the fugitive escaped despite Malroux's best efforts. A good man, the constable."

"Is the doctor in custody?"

"I thought it unnecessary to detain him. He certainly withheld evidence, but he was misguided by his oath to his profession and by the man Meuchel's plausible story that he was acting on behalf of peace."

"Hardly plausible." Fouché's tone was even. "I'd have brought this quack to Paris for further questioning."

Torturing; but Dubois resisted the urge to shudder. He'd liked Eslée, deluded fellow that he was. He cleared his throat.

"He's being watched, of course, by Malroux and by Citizen Blaq, the Minister's other man in Pontoise."

Bonaparte turned his eyes on Fouché. "Why two, for so small a village?"

"In light of what took place last night, your excellency, there should have been twice that number at least."

Dubois resumed.

"I think the doctor told the truth at last. The constable and I interviewed Citizeness Deauville in Eslée's presence. We were satisfied by his reaction to her story that he knew nothing of the man's real nature: He honestly thought he was protecting an innocent, and was appalled when he realized the depth of his error. The man he knew as Meuchel tried to take advantage of her in a most brutal fashion. She was naturally reluctant to enter into detail, but she's lucky to be alive."

Fouché's nostrils expanded in a suppressed yawn. "I'd like to interview her as well. I suspect the Prefect didn't go deep enough."

"Yes, they often scream rape when the *fait* is *accompli*." The First Consul scowled down at his desk. "And the man who calls himself Meuchel? Where is he now?"

"By now I suspect he's in Paris." The Minister retook the conversation, emphasizing some points with a bony index finger extended.

"The description both the doctor and his mistress gave us is similar to the one my people in England provided of one of Georges Cadoudal's visitors at the Earl of Rexborough's country estate early this spring. He's the only man we were unable to identify definitely; all the known members of the so-called Cutthroat Club are on file. Until she was interviewed by Ministry professionals, a fool girl we recruited in an inn outside Doudeville near the English Channel failed to report the anomaly of a stranger who carried equipment for the maintenance of a pistol, but no balls or powder to load it, at least in his luggage." He moved a shoulder. "We must make do, your excellency, with the materials we have."

Dubois said nothing as the Minister assumed the credit for this discovery.

Bonaparte said, "No excuses, Fouché. Talleyrand is a diplomatic genius; yet I just sent him scurrying out with his tail between his legs for committing a blunder which may cost France all its victories to date."

Fouché lowered and raised his head; no doubt collecting that information for his voluminous files.

"During the interview the girl provided a description which I believe belongs to our mystery man," he said.

"Why am I learning all this just now?"

"Until now, we had only two vague descriptions, which although similar didn't mesh until this latest report. But if one were to draw a line on a map from England to our west coast, and from there to Pontoise, it would form an arrow pointing directly to Paris. I don't believe in coincidence."

"And yet you thought little enough of the double killing to fob it off upon Prefect Dubois rather than follow it up yourself."

"Your excellency—"

The First Consul held up a palm. "No use to protest. The greatest victories and the most inglorious defeats turn upon such trifles. Which is why even the lowest infantryman in the field sometimes is worth five generals. Splendid work, *Monsieur le Prefect*."

Dubois could not decide if the First Consul intended to compliment him or stoke the fires of jealousy in his colleague. He was capable of setting those around him at one another's throat for his own amusement.

Bonaparte lifted the copy of the *Bulletin de la Police* from his blotting-pad, put it aside, and picked up a steel-edged ruler, the one he used to draw lines on a campaign map. He stood it on end, slid his fingers to the bottom, let it topple, repeated the action. The man simply could not sit still.

He smacked it flat on the desk. The report startled Dubois. Fouché, that amphibious creature, didn't react.

"I learned a bit of German while fighting the Austrians in Italy," the First Consul said. "Do either of you understand the language?"

Fouché shook his head. "I have a Breton's fair understanding of English, but none of that barbaric tongue."

Dubois shook his head. "I'm an uneducated man, Citizen."

The head of the Republic smiled, showing his unnaturally white and even teeth.

"It's the barbaric tongue of Frederick the Great, of Mozart, of the poet Goethe, and of the composer Beethoven. The barbarians who spoke it toppled Imperial Rome. With that tongue I persuaded the Emperor of Austria to cede Central Europe to France. It's a mistake to regard ignorance as a virtue."

Fouché folded his hands across his spare middle, stifling one of his infamous yawns. Dubois—more astute, for once, than the master intriguer—listened closely.

"Meuchel, I believe, is the name our subject of interest gave Eslée?"

"The only one," said Dubois. "He said he acted on behalf of a Major Meuchel, an important official in the Austrian Army. To Madame Deauville he confided his Christian name was Franz, which is also German or Austrian. It isn't unusual for an emissary traveling incognito on an errand of state to adopt the name of the man he represents."

"Meuchel is the German word for 'assassin'; which even our euphemistic friends the English haven't seen necessary to render into a gentler term. It's clear that Herr Meuchel, whatever his name may have been at birth, is in Paris at this moment to murder me."

Fouché and Dubois sat in silence.

Dubois had guessed the man's intentions, but he was stunned by so simple—no, simple-*minded*—a subterfuge.

What the Police Minister was thinking, he could not fathom.

The First Consul flipped over the ruler.

"Were I slain, the man who takes my place—if he'd keep it, and if he isn't a Bourbon—must declare war on England and all its allies; meaning all the other civilized nations on earth. I'm as interested in surviving as the next man, but if it must happen, I shouldn't mind dying if to avenge me the entire world went to war."

36

Georges Cadoudal, Bonaparte's mortal enemy, sailed for France aboard an English frigate under the command of Captain Wright, in whom the Cutthroat Club had placed its confidence. The waters were calm and the journey uneventful. The ship landed near Biville, in Normandy, where local sympathizers lowered a rope to help the passenger scale the cliff.

It was a hardship, and no mistake. His great belly, and the rich fare at the Rexboroughs', had him panting at the top, with alarming pains in his chest and a tingling in his left arm; yet another reason to cut his alliance with the perfidious British when the time came. If Bonaparte failed to defeat them, their diet surely would. It would represent the victory of *vichyssoise* over treacle and tripe.

"Are you all right, *mon Général*?" The speaker had learned his French in some British university.

"Right as rain." There wasn't a thing to be gained by admitting weakness; the mission, after all, was to restore morale.

Which did nothing to restore the health and strength of youth on the field of battle. He felt the first faltering steps of age, and the unpleasant possibility that he would not live to see a king once again on the throne of France.

Chief Inspector Jules Limodin was more peeved than usual.

Which was like saying a simmering cauldron was abnormally hot. If ever a man enjoyed living in a constant state of apoplexy, thought Dubois, his trusted subordinate must be the happiest in Paris.

"I don't see that any shame should fall to us. On top of being bloodhounds and seers, must we be multilingual as well?"

"It appears friend Meuchel is," Dubois said. "Dr. Eslée said he spoke French with a Parisian accent, yet the girl at the inn said his pronunciation was English."

"On the evidence, it's a wonder she could speak the language of her birthplace."

"The innkeeper corroborated her story. One could scarcely expect Fouché's interrogators to overlook him."

The two men charged with the safety of the capital were burning lamp oil well into another night on the Quai Desaix.

"He's thumbing his nose at us all," Limodin said, "boasting of his intentions through his choice of a *nom de guerre*. So reckless a gambler must soon ensnare himself."

"We can't count on Providence. It appears he has as many lives as a cat, and a name for each. He registered at the inn as Chaucer. Do you find that significant?"

"Should I?"

"Really, Limodin, when your mother read to you she should have included epic poetry."

Limodin pouted.

The Prefect sighed wearily. "Forgive me, *mon ami*. I am the pot and you the kettle. A simple village constable was quicker on the uptake than I, discharging his pistol while I watched our quarry escape with my *coq* in my hand. I've been too much in this cupboard and not enough on the pavement."

"Water under the bridge." Limodin looked uneasy; not the same expression as his customary sour mien. "The English are behind this; it is confirmed?"

"*Oui*, if Gaudin, the Finance Minister, is correct in his figures.

I haven't his skill with arithmetic to argue. The English aristocrats have raised a great deal of cash, in some cases taking large
personal losses in the interest of time. When men of that class sell
short, be assured it isn't caprice. They're financing an ambitious
project, and the Police Minister and I are in agreement on what
it is. Odds were we would see eye to eye on something someday."

"Just malcontents, then. Not England itself."

"I shouldn't go so far as to say that. A number of them belong
to its House of Lords."

"Why do they hate us so?"

"They don't. They fear our Republic and its principles, that it
might overtake them and cast out their king. Then they should
all be like you and me, mere citizens of a great nation. To avoid
that, they will gladly let go of their silver at tin prices."

"They should fight us face-to-face instead, as men do."

"I'm sure that's how the First Consul sees it. But he hasn't their
treasury, nor allies willing to spill their own blood on his behalf.
This, it pains me to say, is the privilege of empire."

Limodin glowered; an aspect he found more comfortable. "Just
when did you become political?"

"Have I? Well, be it so. The only people who know truly how
to run things are too busy peddling fruit and shoveling shit."

"What's our next step?"

"None, I fear. We wait until Meuchel resurfaces. We can but
hope that it will not be within pistol range of the First Consul."

"Isn't that counting on Providence?"

"Foolish optimism, rather—and faith in all the keepers of the
peace we have alerted to a stranger recovering from a serious injury, and who may seek medical help, or failing that a bolt-hole
where he can rest and gather his strength. Meanwhile the Police
Minister has the scent at long last, and is releasing his hounds
as we speak." Dubois shook himself; he had no reason now to

dissemble emotion. "I would not be Georges Cadoudal for all the beer in Germany."

Fouché's people among the Earl of Rexborough's staff lost no time in reporting that General Cadoudal had packed his bags and left the estate.

Every informant in western France received his description. A stable boy in the employ of a known Royalist who lived in the district took care to notice a remarkably ugly customer who matched the man described in the broadsides, including the fact that he spoke French with a Brittany accent, and borrowed a horse from his master to report to his Ministry handler in person. Three days later, the handler's written account was on Joseph Fouché's desk.

"A gold Louis to the young man," said the Police Minister to his secretary. "I leave it to his master whether to penalize him for the time spent when he should have been sweeping out the stalls."

He issued a general order:

> *Do not detain subject under any circumstances.*
> *Keep him under close surveillance and observe his*
> *movements and everyone with whom he comes into*
> *contact. Failure to do so will be considered*
> *treason, punishable by imprisonment or death.*
> *This directive comes from the highest authority.*

Surveillance: a term dear to Fouché, and which he'd coined. He'd been pleased to see how well it was catching on, even in England.

37

"I'm recovering from a serious illness, Madame. I'll pay extra to have my meals brought to me in my room. I ask you not to disturb me otherwise. My physician has ordered complete rest."

As he spoke, the Viper laid pound notes one by one on the lace-covered table where the proprietors of the rooming house served their guests and conducted business. The notes were crisp: He'd evidently obtained his currency at the bank very recently, but had wisely not changed them for French francs, whose value fluctuated daily with the situation in Europe.

The expression on Madame Frontenac's heavy features changed from avarice to sympathy as she regarded the stranger. He was pale, and obviously in discomfort. She thought his accent Belgian or Swiss. There was always some malady stewing in those land-locked countries, with no sea winds to blow away the miasma.

"It will be no imposition at all, Monsieur"—she glanced down at the register—"Marechal. My husband came down with dis-temper of the throat this past winter. He isn't whole yet. I hope your complaint is less severe."

"It's an inflammation of an old injury. I'm assured of a com-plete recovery in a fortnight."

She smiled congratulations, and swept the money into an old candy box bearing a chipped image on the lid of Bonaparte, the sallow shaggy-haired twenty-one-year-old hero of the Bridge at Arcole in Italy. "Is this your first visit to Paris?"

"No, I was here some years ago, before the Consulate."

"Ah. You'll find it a more orderly place now."

Just then a wagon struck a loose cobblestone outside. The bang startled the visitor, who winced and placed a hand to his side. "It seems a busy neighborhood for one so far from the center of the city."

"That's the brewer down the street, bringing back the empty barrels." She spoke quickly, lest he change his mind about staying. "We have a quiet room in the first floor back, overlooking an alley no one uses. You'll swear you're in the country. May I carry your bag?"

"Thank you. I shall manage."

"Our cook is simple, but her lamb stew is popular with all our guests. You'll be strong as a horse by Bastille Day."

Muscles twitched at the corners of his mouth.

"Thank you. That is my wish also."

Days passed peacefully. The husband whose health was taking so long to return was a confirmed egalitarian who insisted upon being addressed by everyone, even children and peddlers, as Jean-Baptiste, not monsieur (he found the Republican "Citizen" stilted). His wife, Claudine, was annoyed by this and thought it common. He was even more rotund than she, with a shining bald head and no outward evidence he was under the strain of illness.

"Just between us," he told their guest in a low voice, "I'm much recovered. But my late inconvenience spares me mundane chores."

"Your secret's safe with me, Jean-Baptiste."

The host set a tray of covered dishes on the side table in the lodger's room. "More mutton, I'm afraid. Our Juliette seems to know all the butchers in the city who sell it cheap."

"I won't hear a word against it. Thanks to her I grow more stout by the day."

The landlord thought this a true statement. The man, who had

seated himself on the edge of the bed after admitting his visitor, was less gaunt than when he'd arrived only days ago. His
dressing gown no longer hung in loose folds and he didn't per-
spire so easily after a minor exertion. Jean-Baptiste found him
never less than civil, and at times cordial. He wished all their
boarders would learn by his example.

"The whiskers are coming in nicely," he ventured. "I envy you
your ability to grow them."

The man on the bed stroked the sandy growth.

"I can't claim credit for something I can't control. But at least
they itch less with length."

For whatever reason, possibly to spare himself the effort of
shaving completely, the lodger had begun what promised to be
a fine set of fierce muttonchops. They were darker than his hair,
and gave him a military demeanor—enhanced, perhaps, by his
name: Marechal, the term for a groom in the cavalry. He wondered if the fellow had served. He seemed of an age to have de-
fended the Republic in its early days, a foreign convert. The man
was Breton; he'd swear to that on a stack of Bibles. Perhaps it was
in that service he'd sustained the injury that had come back to lay
him low.

"Your Christian name, sir, if I may be so bold? I promise not to
address you by it without your permission, and never in public."

Jean-Baptiste's lodger gave no evidence of offense, however
independent his smile seemed of the rest of his face. "León."

Fouché was livid; which meant that his complexion was a bit less
waxlike.

"That imbecile on the coast has lost our chief conspirator."

Prefect Dubois did not so much as twitch his moustache at this
news.

"Cadoudal, you mean. Is this confirmed?"

"The fat swine stepped into a tonsorial parlor in St. Germaine and never came out. After thirty minutes the man assigned to him decided to investigate. It's never taken me more than fifteen to have my hair cut."

"Perhaps your creature thought he had his nails trimmed as well. What did the barber say?"

The Minister passed the report across his desk.

Dubois put on his spectacles. "A man answering Cadoudal's description walked in, said, '*Bonjour*, Citizen,' and went on out the back door, he claims. Is he trustworthy?"

"He's on his way here for questioning, but I suspect he is. He has a son in the army—that's confirmed—and he was given a citation by the Committee of Public Safety commending him for harboring fugitive Revolutionaries from the King's soldiers in the old days. He framed and hung it on the wall of his shop."

"Such things can be faked."

"It was yellowed and flyblown. My creature, as you call him, turned out to be a dunce, but he has an eye for detail."

"Except how many doors a barbershop has. At least we know Cadoudal is on his way to Paris."

"Most likely he's here already, and meeting with our friend Meuchel."

"I fear we shall never hear again of anyone by that name. What now? Alert the press?"

"We'd be inundated with false reports. It would be the Terror and the Christmas Eve Plot rolled into one great *mélange*. Given the opportunity it's only human nature to denounce your neighbors."

"That's Limodin's view. We must take steps to protect the First Consul. When's his next public appearance?"

Fouché's smile was piteous. "What would be?"

"Bastille Day, of course." *What a prize booby he must think me,* thought the other.

"He and Madame Bonaparte will appear on the balcony of the Tuileries and wave to the crowd on the anniversary of France's liberation." The Minister's thin upper lip folded over its mate like the flap of an envelope. Fouché himself shunned the center of the light. Like a grub.

"We must persuade him not to take part in the celebration," Dubois said.

"Bonaparte, the son of Mars? Impossible. Even if he agreed, our conspirators would remain underground. The object is to flush them out, falcon and falconer together."

"Is it? I wasn't told."

"I'm telling you now. We've wasted enough time hunting this assassin when we should have let him come to us."

"Risky." Dubois did not mention that this was the plan he himself had confided to Limodin. The situation changed with the direction of the wind.

"I'm open to any suggestion less hazardous."

"You should place faith, *Monsieur le Ministre,* in our two agencies. Both men's descriptions are in the hands of every officer and informant in France. We must pull them all into Paris, place them behind brooms and pushcarts and in all the inns and taverns. Sooner or later, one or the other will show himself. If Cadoudal, your people will sweat Meuchel's whereabouts out of him. If Meuchel—and we shall call him that for now—we can proceed to the capture of the prime mover at our leisure. Perhaps *his* creature will flee from the pressure and give us room to breathe."

"Do you really think he would flee?"

No. Aloud: *"Je ne sais pas."*

"What you're suggesting may take weeks. We haven't that much time."

"Which is why we must buy some. Citizen Bonaparte must sit out Bastille Day."

Fouché contemplated a headless bust on a corner pedestal; some prosperous Roman merchant, no doubt, dead since Christ.

"You're right."

Dubois, surprised by this admission of defeat, sympathized; it had to have come with a wrench. "I shall speak to the First Consul myself," he said.

The Minister shook his head. "That's my responsibility. I shall approach him tonight, once he's rested. A glass of wine may help him see reason."

Dubois didn't say what was in his head: There wasn't wine enough in France to persuade Napoleon Bonaparte to stand down from a cowardly threat of murder.

Claudine Frontenac smiled at her lodger.

"Another constitutional, Monsieur Marechal? Are you quite certain you're not overtaxing yourself? To lose my favorite boarder to a chill would devastate me."

"Small chance of that, in such balmy weather. At all events I must put myself to the test. I'm feeling much fitter than yesterday."

He stood at the base of the stairs in the light topcoat he'd asked Jean-Baptiste, the master of the house, to purchase for him, giving him more than the necessary amount in notes. At that it was too heavy for the season. Messidor, the month of harvest, was nearly half gone, with blistering Thermidor waiting in the wings—July, according to the old calendar. Dogs lay stupefied in the gutters.

True, Madame Frontenac considered, there was color in the man's face, framed by his striking new sidewhiskers, and although he carried a stick he didn't lean on it. In less than a week he'd passed from invalid to *boulevardier*.

A handsome man, she decided: It was the facial growth. She had thought him quite ordinary-looking at first, apart from his illness, which she saw now as romantic. Perhaps an old duel was the source of his complaint: *Un affaire du coeur*, she hoped. When he'd left his room for the first time, she'd scarcely recognized him. Men transformed so easily, without daily recourse to paints and powders, alchemic extremes. She wished Jean-Baptiste could grow something more than gin-blossoms on his round face.

"Enjoy your walk, monsieur."

He did. It was a fine day, with the sun warm on his back. He swung the stick as he strolled, feeling the not-unpleasant tightness of new skin on his wound. Absent a musket ball, the Paris physician who'd stitched it up had accepted his story that he'd been gored by a bull on a shortcut through a farmer's field; there was no reason to report the visit to the authorities. He'd discarded the last of his dressings, and with them all regret.

He ran a hand over his sidewhiskers, a pleasant sensation. They'd foil any description that might have been broadcast from Pontoise.

The tailor's shop he found bore a tricolor in a wall frame, smaller than the dark patch where the Bourbon fleur-de-lis had once advertised it as of service to the King.

When the proprietor heard his request, his cheeks cracked in amusement. "An accident?"

"An atrocity." He assumed the indignant air of a loyal servant. "A street tough threw a ball of horseshit at my master, knocking it off his head."

"I don't know what's become of our youth. They should all be conscripted."

"Can you have it by Bastille Day?"

When the tailor hesitated, he dealt bank notes onto the counter. "Of course. Come back in three days."

Claudine was involved with her accounts when her boarder returned. "Your *Moniteur*, monsieur. The boy just left."

He thanked her, gave her a newly acquired centime for the newspaper, and unfolded it.

She returned to the receipts spread out on the table. They were beyond Jean-Baptiste, or so he claimed; she'd begun to wonder if his glacial recuperation wasn't merely a strategy to avoid work.

Intrigue surrounded her.

In keeping her books, she suspected Juliette exchanged more than small talk with the merchants who sold her provisions for the kitchen; but she wouldn't challenge her. Prices were so high, with so many foreigners visiting now that things had settled, domestically, anyway—more of them than at any time since the days of the Court—and after all it was Year IX, in which all the prudish old ways were buried with the past. Jean-Baptiste was Republican enough for them both, but if five pounds of potatoes could be got for twelve centimes when more exacting households were paying fifteen, she could wear the red cap and wave the Tricolor as zealously as any Jacobin.

A sudden violent crackling of newsprint returned her attention to Monsieur Marechal. He'd torn a page of his newspaper.

He looked from it to the landlady, seeming to come to himself. Color stained his cheeks.

"Your pardon, Madame. I overexerted myself, just as you predicted. I need rest." He refolded the paper and dropped it into the trash basket on his way to the stairs.

A most curious man.

She got up and retrieved the paper. She skimmed the gray columns from front page to back, but the news was less than alarming.

French diplomats were meeting with representatives of the King of Naples in Florence to discuss peace: That was good. A slave grandly calling himself Toussaint L'Ouverture was leading an uprising against colonial control on the island of St. Dominique: too far away to fuss about, and the man was black. The First Consul expressed his regrets that negotiations with Rome over a possible accord between France and the Vatican would keep him busy with the Foreign Minister at Malmaison over Bastille Day, preventing him from taking part in the ceremonies in Paris: A disappointment, surely, but these things happened.

No, there was nothing there to upset her guest. He'd exhausted himself, as he'd said. Away with the paper, and back to her potatoes.

V

THERMIDOR

(Month of Heat)

38

Bastille Day broke heavy and hot.

The press of unwashed bodies in the old *Place de la Revolution* made it more oppressive yet. As the Viper neared the Tuileries the air grew thick as paste.

In just a dozen years, the Day of Liberation had become a combination Easter, Christmas, and harvest festival, complete with women in elaborate bonnets, peddlers hawking roasted offal, masqueraders in costume, and effigies on every corner: It was difficult to determine whether a toothless scarecrow decked out in a powdered wig and shingles of lace was making fun of aristocrats or paying them tribute.

Indeed, there were those who'd never laid eyes on a count, a duchess, or even a footman in livery. Such figures would appear to them as fantastical as goat-bottomed satyrs prancing in an illustrated book on pagan mythology.

A generation too young to remember the fall of the prison so emblematic of Royal repression would soon come of age. It had no concept that things were not always as they were now, under the orderly rule of the Consulate. That boy there, the one licking grease off his fingers from his baked potato; was he aware he stood on a patch of earth soaked yards deep with the blood of the decapitated? Would he care if it was explained to him?

The Viper doubted it.

The crowds were not so dense in the courtyard of the palace as they would have been were the Bonapartes in residence. The balcony was dark where the First Consul and his lady usually stood on such occasions, a pair of primitive islanders basking in the adoration of the rabble. The grenadiers guarding the entrance sweltered in their dress tunics and bearskin shakos, stifling yawns. Heat, and a palace deserted by its luminaries, had made them soporific.

Monsieur Marechal—a hasty invention, that name, adopted on the run from Pontoise—made a circuit of the grounds, shouldering his way through throngs of revelers reeking of beer, jug wine, cheap scent, and sweat, and returned to his quarters. He had the house to himself. The landlord and landlady were out enjoying the pageantry. Their cook, Juliette of the incomparable stewed lamb, had deserted her own post within minutes of their departure.

He stretched out on the mattress with his hands behind his head, staring at the cracked ceiling, restructuring his itinerary, and wondering if the First Consul had in fact been warned away from public exposure.

The announcement in the *Moniteur* that affairs of state would keep Bonaparte away from the celebration had been a bitter disappointment. There was no telling when the First Consul would offer himself next as a target. Behind this came a surge of panic: The Viper was known: quarry now for that godless ex-clergyman Joseph Fouché and his pack of vicious rat-terriers. But now that one had time to think about it, he took careful inventory of the things he'd done that might have betrayed him to the men in charge of security.

What evidence had he left behind in Pontoise? Two dead highwaymen, a wounded local busybody, and possibly a hysterical seamstress with an incredible story she probably would try to pass off as rape. He was grateful more than ever for his restraint. Dead, she was proof of something more sinister than two brigands slain in the pursuit of their trade; alive, she would be dismissed as a whore, and an irrational one at that.

The tale the doctor would tell was more outlandish yet.

The Viper's courier story explained the money and explosive rounds on his person, but it would unravel under close questioning by the provincial police. It would play out as cock-and-bull, and Eslée a liar. In that light, the happenstance that had spared him the fate the Viper had planned for him was another stroke of good fortune. Just as it was with the Widow Deauville (that man-eating baggage!), a slain physician would have posed a far greater danger than a live one with an axe to grind.

Even if the local constabulary believed them both, there was nothing to connect Meuchel with the Cutthroat Club and its intentions. The provincials would canvass their jurisdiction, make a fine show of energy; yet when all was said and done, the bandit population was the only loser in the affair. But others would be only too eager to fill the void; there would be no repercussions from the *demimonde*. And there was no reason for Paris to involve itself. Cosmopolitan authority was already predisposed to disregard anything that came from the hinterland. The "Age of Reason" to the contrary, France remained the feudal nation it had been in the time of the Huguenots, divided into fiefs, each of which feared and distrusted its neighbors.

The more he thought about things, the more convinced he was that the newspaper had reported the truth. With new laws to pen and a war to fight, Bonaparte had no time for mummery. Josephine rarely appeared in public without him; her fear of the mob stretched back to her own imprisonment before the cyclone blew in from Corsica.

He got up and tilted a straightback chair against his door, wedging it under the knob. He distrusted the latch, and there was no predicting how long he'd be alone under that roof. The greedy wife and clownish husband who owned the place were meddlers. Claudine Frontenac could be silenced with a franc, but Jean-Baptiste was just the sort of buffoon who'd blurt out colorful discoveries to anyone within earshot.

The item his lodger had ordered from the tailor to the King—now the Republic and its officers—was certain fuel for idle gossip if it were found in that room.

He'd smuggled the tall cylindrical box into the house while the couple was out, and slid it under the bed behind his valise, which he'd left packed. A flock of dust balls told him the girl who came in to clean would be too indolent to discover it.

At all events, that was his hope. For it to be found in that room meant arrest, trial, and execution.

He lifted off the lid, unwrapped the blue cloth protecting the contents, and examined it again. He blew on the hairs, spreading them, rubbed at the glossy black leather with his thumb and inspected it for the stain of cheap dye. The thumb was clean.

Adequate. In fact, altogether a superior piece of craftsmanship. But impossible to conceal under the false bottom of his valise. It was the one piece of his plan he couldn't arrange beforehand.

He put it back and returned the box to its hiding place. Then he cleaned and oiled his pistol and inspected the ammunition. The Republicans who drew up the calendar had named that month Thermidor for a reason. Heat, fug, and mold could be nearly as destructive as the explosive balls themselves.

39

"It's all so—*Roman,* Cadoudal. You should take your nose out of Plutarch once in a while and read a newspaper."

"Please remember to address me as Couturier, General. The Republican vermin have raised eavesdropping to an art."

Charles Pichegru waved off the admonition. "Had you consulted me, I'd have advised against using a name belonging to a designer of dresses. No woman would ever commission a frock from anyone so ugly."

Cadoudal smiled over his Cognac; an indifferent label, but he no longer had Rexborough's cellars at his command. His host here in Paris—whose name he'd misplaced—lived meanly, drinking inferior vintages in cheap surroundings. Like the English earl before, the fellow had been barred from this meeting; but he'd taken no offense. He'd harbor a conspirator, but shun the details of the conspiracy. The simpleton thought ignorance would spare him the rack.

"You're trying to bait me," Cadoudal said. "I'm not so easily angered. You scarcely qualify as handsome yourself; we are neither of us a gay dog. I selected the name at random from the Paris directory. Like most occupation names, it filled a column. It's almost as anonymous as Pierre Robért, but not so obviously an alias."

The other steepled his hands, elbows planted on the arms of a homely chair. He managed to appear martial in civilian dress; but at forty-two he'd spent half his life in the army, and half of that plotting to restore the King.

"You've been too long in the company of the English," he said. "They never use one word when ten will do."

Pichegru's features, hacked from an oaken stump, were burned brown from three years' hiding in French Guiana. He owed his repatriation to Cadoudal, who had helped haul him up the cliffs of Normandy as he himself had been hoisted by his predecessors. But the man was ungrateful.

"You're no doubt right," said Cadoudal. "It's hard to remain idle and not acquire bad habits. For instance, you're more irritable than I remembered. I assume Guiana isn't as accommodating a place of exile as England."

"It's a shithole. Call yourself Marie Antoinette if you like. You speak of bribing Bonaparte's Hussars to fall upon him with daggers when he comes to inspect them. It's romantic shit. It was shit in Shakespeare's time, and before that it was shit in Livy's. Bonaparte is a student of classical literature. He'd spot a Brutus at a thousand meters. And what if they won't be bought? Or take the money and report the plot anyway? It's suicide!"

"It's a contingency plan, in case our one-man army comes a-cropper. It can use refinement. That's one of the reasons for this meeting, my fellow general. I'm a man of strategy, *le grand dessein*. Tactics are your strong suit."

"Stick your flattery up your arse."

An unpleasant man.

"Consider it stuck." Cadoudal drank.

"So you've abandoned your Viper, at a cost of two and a half million francs. I never knew you for a spendthrift."

"He's a bargain, if he comes through. Remember, we have France to gain. I haven't given up on him; but I'd be a poor commander if I put all my ammunition in one wagon."

"What of Moreau?"

"I expect him tonight."

"I don't like sleeping with the enemy."

"He's our friend—for the moment. We haven't so many we can afford to quibble. He can be dealt with when the time comes. Meanwhile he's as fiercely anti-Bonapartist as—"

"The Comte d'Artois?"

"I think we're agreed the count is a nincompoop."

"D'Enghien, then."

It was the first time the name had been mentioned aloud among those dedicated to the Restoration. Pichegru was nothing if not direct.

Le Duc d'Enghien, son of *Le Comte* d'Artois; soon, with God's grace, King Louis XVIII.

"Just so. His gouty father is hardly in a position to prevent our going round him."

"The young duke is *hors de combat*. He'd rather shoot partridges in Germany than reign in France."

Cadoudal smiled again. He fished out the splendid ring and held it up.

Pichegru stared. "Is it genuine?"

"The man who brought it said I could have it appraised, but he wouldn't recommend it. Fouché is omnipotent."

"Who brought it?"

"Our mercenary friend." He put it away. "So far as I know, our benefactor, the duke, is the only one who knows the Viper's true identity."

"So the royal partridge-killer is ambitious after all."

"So it would appear. I consider the token an open license on Bonaparte."

"You brought me all the way from that floating turd in the Atlantic to show me a bauble?"

"To find out if you're still in our camp."

"Hardly necessary. The dogs who piss on France aren't fit to live. You know, of course, I taught Bonaparte his military history at Brienne. Had I known what he'd do with it, I'd have caned him to death on the spot."

"*Bon.* I wanted to assure myself you were resolute."

A tap came to the door.

Cadoudal slid a pistol from that day's edition of the *Gazette* and rose to ask who was calling.

"Another visitor, General." It was the voice of his host, Monsieur what's-his-name.

"Did he identify himself?"

"I'm not such a fool as that, you Brittany buccaneer."

A new voice, this, deep with authority. The tone of yet another general, albeit one from the other side.

"You needn't show the man in. He's shown himself."

In civilian dress, Jean-Victor Moreau more closely resembled the lawyer he'd once aspired to become than a former Revolutionary officer. Tall, ovoid, with the huge plum-colored eyes of a figure in a Renaissance painting, he kept his lips tight as if to prevent bile from spilling out.

Cadoudal put away the pistol and offered Cognac.

"I don't drink with cream puffs."

"Let's not start out calling names like boys in a schoolyard," Cadoudal said. "We're allies, we three. Adversaries sharing a tent."

Moreau kept his coat on. He swept aside the tails and sat down. "I don't make friends with them either."

"That's the last thing you have to worry about, filth," Pichegru said.

"*Silence!*"

When Cadoudal roared in his top-sergeant's bellow, the walls rang. The others started, then kept still.

He resumed his normal tone. "How those creatures in Paris would rejoice to hear their enemies squabble. We share a common goal; or I assume we do. You haven't changed your mind, Moreau?"

The Jacobin's lips pressed tighter. "As well change the shape of the earth. Every day the Corsican chips away at the Republic. He's banned the *Marseilles*; the very anthem of the Revolution, and is conspiring even now with the pope to restore the Church in France. He'd have Our Lady of Victory spread her legs in return for a foreign alliance. I should have run him through when we fought together in the field."

"Excellent! We're not such polar opposites after all."

"I didn't say that. We couldn't be farther apart. I want to replace Bonaparte with a defender of the Rights of Man. You want to plop a tyrant back on the throne. It would be as if the last twelve years never happened."

"Not precisely," Cadoudal said. "To try to put it all back the way it was would only lead to another revolution. If those years did nothing else, they taught us to avoid the same mistakes. Pichegru?"

"We seek a constitutional monarchy," said the other Royalist; although it was clear from the expression on his coarse face he hated speaking civilly to a rebel. "A parliamentary government, like the English."

"A Cromwell manipulating a puppet? Decidedly not."

The Royalist generals exchanged glances.

Cadoudal leaned forward in his chair. "I was told you were ready to discuss an accord."

Moreau showed his teeth then.

"I heard the same, from Madame Hulot, my wife's mother. She hates the upstart so fiercely she'd be willing to replace him with Caligula. She's a venomous hag, and she talks too much to all the wrong people. If you arranged this conference on her word, it's useless."

"But surely your personal animosity—" Cadoudal began.

"Carries no weight. I lost to the Russians and Austrians at Cassano because the reinforcements I needed were stranded in

Egypt with Bonaparte, with the French fleet at the bottom of the ocean. That Oriental adventure cost the lives of hundreds of good men. That's when we broke ranks. But I'm not one of you."

"Then why did you come?"

"I was curious. I wanted to see if you'd given up your mad dream in the light of recent events, and were prepared to recognize the rightful Republican government in return for an alliance against the Consulate. Now I see a cream puff is a cream puff through and through." He rose.

"Where do you think you're going?" said Pichegru.

"Not here. There's a stench."

Cadoudal rested his hand on the *Gazette*, beneath which rested his pistol.

"Before you leave, I need your word as an officer you'll say nothing of this meeting to anyone, or of our presence in France."

"Unnecessary. If it gets out I'm in Paris, I shall stand in front of a firing squad. I'm off to the country."

"Your word, I said."

"At gunpoint?"

Cadoudal withdrew his hand. Moreau jerked his chin in a nod.

"You have it—and much good may it do you. If Fouché doesn't know you're on French soil, he's not the same man I knew in Lyons."

"Godspeed, General."

After Moreau left, Pichegru sprang to his feet and refilled his glass. "Was that wise?"

"I'm not the monster he thinks me. In any event I can't shoot him in my host's home. All shelter would be closed to me. Rest easy, Jean-Charles. He knows nothing specific." He took out his watch. "However, it's time we relocated. If we're to be targets, it's best we keep moving."

"Can we proceed without Moreau?"

"That was a rude shock; I was confident in my sources. But we still have two strings to our bow."

"An invisible viper," Pichegru said, "and a gang of untried troops wearing the uniform of the enemy. When the overture begins, I want a seat near the exit."

40

Bonaparte tugged at his waistcoat. "This needs letting out again. I grow fat in the saddle as usual."

Constant, his valet, considered that they were camped only a few leagues outside Paris, on a training exercise; his master could hardly have taken on weight overnight. But he said nothing.

The First Consul finished buttoning the garment, which was indeed snug at his middle, and thrust his arms behind him for Constant to help him into the plain green colonel's tunic he wore on campaign. The valet brushed away dust and lint and set the bicorne hat on the commander's head.

Now he resembled his image in paintings and lithographs, one of the most famous in the world. He took the small shaving mirror off its nail on the tent's center pole and turned it this way and that, inspecting himself from hat to knee-high boots.

"Yes, absolutely portly. Disgraceful."

"You'll look healthy to the men."

Bonaparte turned and twisted Constant's left earlobe; his most painful way of showing affection.

"I warn you against too much diplomacy. I may make you an ambassador."

The time was 7:00 A.M. In the palace and on the field, he was usually up long before then, breaking his fast on the sprint, but he'd been until nearly four o'clock dictating letters to his platoon of secretaries; lecturing the pope, correcting the latest draft of the Civil Code, and imploring Josephine to balance her household accounts.

But he showed no fatigue when General Lannes, his aide-
de-camp, entered the tent and saluted.

"What is it, Jean?"

"A visitor from Paris. Police Prefect Dubois."

"Indeed. He's getting to be a gadabout. Send him in."

Dubois took the aide's place, removing his hat.

"What the devil's that?" said Bonaparte. "It looks like an over-
size snuffbox."

"A design of my own, Citizen. I found the other too grand for
my humble office."

"Let's see it."

He handed over the cap with the low cylindrical crown.

The First Consul turned it over, inspecting the manufacturer's
label, and ran a finger round the sweatband. "It doesn't provide
much protection against the elements."

"Neither did its predecessor, once it was saturated with rain or
snow. This one sheds water like a duck."

"It's certainly lightweight. Do you intend to outfit all your
officers similarly?"

"Not without your permission."

"Do so, if you like." He returned it. "At least no one will mistake
a city policeman for an admiral. Surely you didn't come all this way
to discuss haberdashery."

"Something new has happened, Citizen."

"Report." He folded his hands behind his back in a posture
aped by many of his officers.

"It's General Pichegru. He's in France. Moreover—"

Bonaparte lunged, unlinking his hands, and clapped a hand
over Dubois' mouth.

The Prefect was shaken to the core. Apart from the occasional
excruciating twist of an earlobe, the First Consul and he had
never before made physical contact.

"Leave us, Constant."

The valet packed away his master's toilet kit and stepped out. The hand withdrew from the Prefect's lips.

"Don't interpret his dismissal as a stain on his character. The man's a model of discretion; but the less who know, the better for all. What's your source?"

"A Royalist named Bouvet de Lozier, in the Abbaye Prison. We swept him up with others after Cadoudal went missing. It was pure luck, Citizen; an officer in his charge asked him playfully what he knew about Four Nivose. He said, 'Ask away.'"

"A cream puff in truth. Is he reliable?"

"We checked his background. He was a close confidant of Georges Cadoudal's before the Royalist general left for England. Under threat of close questioning—you understand, Citizen, what I mean by—"

"Yes, yes. Fouché missed his calling. The Inquisition would have embraced him. Continue."

"He said Pichegru has met with Cadoudal and Moreau in Paris."

"Impossible! Moreau bleeds in tricolor. He hates Royalists more than I."

"They convened in a house in the city. We have the owner, a man with known Royalist sympathies, under watch."

"Arrest him."

Dubois circled his hat through his hands.

"The Police Minister thinks that if the man is harboring Cadoudal, any action there would alert our quarry and drive him farther underground."

"Did Fouché explain what his people were doing when Pichegru left Guiana? Fishing, perhaps?"

"I can but guess. A man traveling alone is hard to track."

Bonaparte smiled, showing his splendid teeth.

"You're a good policeman, Nicolas; you never criticize a colleague outside your own office." The smile evaporated. "However. This is *two* men the Minister has managed to misplace among his papers

and plunder. Pichegru was one of my instructors at the military
school in Brienne, did you know that?"

"It's in his file."

"Fouché and his files. I indulged him, gave him Bastille Day.
The Vatican negotiations were at an impasse, so I welcomed the
reprieve. But what has he done with it? It's possible, Dubois, to
raise a capable man too far above his station."

Dubois said nothing.

Bonaparte groped inside his tunic, extracted a sack of peppermints, and popped one into his mouth. Crunching:

"Arrest the owner of the house and search it. Take it down
to the foundation if necessary. We'll erect a statue in its place:
Charlemagne Christianizing the Saxons. I don't see how a papist
Royalist could object."

"May I ask what I'm looking for?"

"Evidence tying the swine to Four Nivose. Manufacture it if
you must, but see that it stands the test of logic."

"I should report to the Minister first."

"By all means. We can't have our top men falling out like
thieves. Embrace and kiss, but be quick about it. I want Cadoudal,
Pichegru, and Moreau before a squad of musketeers.

"No excuses this time," he added, his eyes gray as ice. "Unless
you want to take their place."

Fouché raged.

Part of his fury was directed at Dubois, who'd stabbed him
from behind. But mostly it was at himself for handing him the
dagger.

It was the rule of his life never to place his responsibilities ahead
of self-interest. But after swallowing the bitter bile of Bonaparte's
wrath for losing Cadoudal on the threshold of Paris, he'd been so
eager to redeem himself he'd assigned his most reliable informant

to watch the house where the three conspirators had met, and sent Dubois to report to the First Consul while he put on a show of keeping to his post. Of course the man had made himself the hero of the affair, and Fouché the goat.

He'd been forced by circumstances to violate his cardinal maxim in order to adhere to it.

Dubois, the devil, appeared unaware of the storm surging behind the Minister's placid facade. The Prefect stood awaiting instructions with his preposterous hat under one arm.

"Be especially thorough," Fouché said evenly. "Assign your most destructive crew to the house. If Cadoudal isn't inside, be certain it will never again shelter anything so large as an underfed rat."

"So the First Consul said. I'll give it to Limodin. He needs to flex his joints after so many weeks reading reports."

Fouché looked him in the eye. "A word of advice."

"Yes, Citizen?"

"Take care not to give too much responsibility to the men around you. You run the risk of their letting you down or showing you up."

Dubois looked puzzled. "Thank you. I won't forget."

Fouché studied him; undecided whether the man's seeming transparency was in fact a veil, or transparency itself. He regarded both as dangers.

Directly after the deeply unsatisfactory meeting with Pichegru and Moreau, "Citizen Couturier" slipped another social notch. Georges Cadoudal in a few weeks' time had moved from a plush bed in a country estate to a cot in the back of a Paris fruit shop, where rats passed in and out like shoppers at a bazaar.

The proprietor was a Royalist, although not so ardent he neglected to charge his guest a rental fee that would have put him up at the finest inn in Paris, if he could but risk it, with additional charges for extras:

A bottle of undistinguished claret, three francs;

A tin of snuff, a franc;

That day's edition of the *Moniteur,* five centimes.

He'd resisted the wine the first day, but after one hellish night with bedbugs (Revolutionaries, judging by their ferocity) he relented, to ease his misery. The snuff settled the urge for tobacco without smoke to give himself away, and he absolutely could not live without the newspaper. He read every word, looking for his own name.

Its absence brought no comfort. The press survived or perished on advertising and circulation, and when there was no news, it made some up. Silence suggested government pressure, which meant his presence in Paris was no secret; withheld from public knowledge while the net tightened.

Or perhaps not.

A rabbit cowering in a hollow log fed on his own fears, and they were bitter sustenance.

He was in hiding. So was Pichegru, and Moreau was out of the picture. These were no positions for generals.

"Merde." He swigged claret, waiting for the heat to crawl forth from his stomach and burn off the pestilential itches that pricked him from neck to ankle. They made a man wonder if Fouché's racks and screws were any worse.

Moreau's desertion was a great setback, a devastating loss. Cadoudal had hidden his emotions from Pichegru. However misguided his purpose, the sour Jacobin had represented the possibility of hundreds of recruits to the Cause. Pichegru, mercurial creature, might have flown the coop if he'd sensed Cadoudal's despair.

Dim, close quarters stoked a man's worst fears. His idea of salting Bonaparte's Hussars with Bourbon loyalists seemed as absurd as

Pichegru had said, a dream smoked up on the influence of opium and classical literature. Seeking for something else to occupy his thoughts, Cadoudal found something worse: the certainty he was undone.

This conviction started as a rustle, a mouse gnawing through plaster; or a Police Ministry spy carving an eyehole through the wall with a knife. More likely it was the sound of his host, whispering secrets to someone in the shop. He was not a whispering man; his delivery boys cringed from the volume of his mildest instructions.

Cadoudal knew better than to pass off this sensation as idle anxiety. His instincts had seen him into middle age in a pursuit that slew many in their youth.

He was on his feet in an instant.

He assumed his disguise, a stained cotton jerkin and the floppy leather hat of a market porter, shouldered the rucksack containing all he owned, and ran into the street, upsetting the owner's display of peaches on the pavement. They bounced and rolled. He stepped on one, turning his ankle when it spun out from under his heel. A blade of white-hot pain shot to his knee, but he seized a stick from an old man goggling at him, knocking him down, and used it to vault himself into the back of a passing cabriolet.

"Go!" He thumped the floorboards with his stick.

The driver turned a face as ugly as his passenger's, with a nose broken like a twist of pipe and a strawberry mark crimsoning him from cheek to collar. "Where to?"

"Anywhere! Use your lash!"

"Not so fast, Cadoudal." A new voice.

The speaker mounted to the seat from the other side of the vehicle, jerking a pistol from under his coat. He was in civilian dress, but all policemen looked the same.

Cadoudal's pistol was in hand. He shoved it into the man's ribs and yanked the trigger. The report was muffled by clothing and flesh. A burning stench filled the cab.

The policeman cried out, dropping his pistol, and buried his hands in his belly. Cadoudal heaved his weight against him, tipping him out into the street.

The vehicle was moving now, picking up speed; the horses had caught the scent of spent powder and burnt flesh and broken into gallop. More plainclothesmen ran alongside, weapons drawn. Cadoudal scooped the unfired pistol from the floor and shot at the man nearest. He yelped and fell behind.

But the cabriolet was slowing. Either the driver had regained control or yet another policeman had climbed aboard and taken over. The Royalist dropped both pistols and braced himself to jump.

A flash of metal and his nose collapsed, crushed by a swung pistol. *Mon Dieu!* Was the world made of police?

His last thought before the darkness.

41

Georges Cadoudal was the last of the active conspirators to be captured, questioned, and sent to Temple Prison to await judgment. Jean-Victor Moreau preceded him there by only a few hours. Although technically not a conspirator, the former General of the Republic was damned by his associations.

He had remained at large less than a day after his meeting with Cadoudal and Pichegru. Bouvet de Lozier, the Royalist being detained in the Abbaye Prison, had provided the information under the mildest of tortures.

Jean-Charles Pichegru, former General of the Army of Restoration, lasted nearly a week. Then he was dragged from his bed in the house of a Royalist sympathizer named LeBlanc. He was still in his nightshirt when a city policeman threw him down the steps of the Temple, the oldest operating prison in Paris.

Chief Inspector Limodin, who had stopped Cadoudal's flight with a pistol across his face, conducted his prisoner to the Quai Desaix, where Nicolas Dubois took charge of the interrogation. The Royalist sat on a hard chair with his shackled hands dangling between his knees, blood dripping from his smashed nose and down his chin to form a puddle on the floor.

The Prefect's demeanor was best described as protean.

With superiors like Bonaparte and Fouché, he was the humble servant of the people, decorous and self-effacing. Interviewing witnesses who were not under suspicion, he was a polite fumbler. When discussing police business with subordinates he was the quiet commander, patient but firm.

At home he was a meek husband, in awe of the mother of his children and a bit afraid of her. To his children he was kindness incarnate, warm and comforting, and generous with the First Consul's peppermints.

Cadoudal would never meet any of those men.

"Piece of shit! Assassin! You crippled one of my officers and murdered another, a man with a wife and three children! The firing squad's too good for you. I shall kill you myself!"

He snatched the leather hat off the shackled man's head, threw it aside, and stuck the muzzle of his pistol under Cadoudal's chin, tipping his head back while the bleeding reversed itself and spilled down his throat, choking him.

This was the Dubois no one saw outside his office where he preferred to conduct questioning. Of all those close to him, only Limodin knew it existed. The chief inspector sat in his customary chair, smoking his pipe and recording everything on folded sheets of foolscap.

He knew, too, although he never said it aloud, that *this* Dubois was the real Dubois. In this he was truly alone: The Prefect himself only suspected it.

Now, an arm's length from the man in custody, Dubois thumbed back the pistol's hammer and pulled the trigger.

The pin snapped on the empty chamber. Cadoudal lurched, wetting himself.

"The weapon of the man you killed, *Monsieur Merde.* The one you used to maim another."

"I acted in my own defense. How was I to know they were policemen?"

"You're the most wanted man in France. What did you expect, an honor guard?"

"You've made a mistake. My name is Giles Couturier."

Dubois stuck the muzzle deeper into the tender flesh on the underside of Cadoudal's chin, tilting his head back as far as it would go. "Stay with that story and I shall break your neck."

He swallowed blood and snot, licked his cracked lips. He broke. "I am General Georges Cadoudal."

"With what army?"

"The King's."

"No such person exists."

He lifted his chin. "You're wrong. We await the arrival of a Bourbon prince."

"Which one? They breed like rats."

Cadoudal said nothing. Both eyes were swollen nearly shut. He watched Dubois through half-moon slits.

"Did you plot to assassinate the First Consul and plop this prince on the throne?"

"No. Unlike Bonaparte, we're not murderers."

"Who is *we*?"

Nothing.

"Your friends were more helpful. Moreau and Pichegru said you met with them to plan the assassination."

"There's no such plan. The object has always been to seize the upstart and hold him hostage until the government surrenders and agrees to the Restoration. Once that succeeded, Bonaparte would be released—and exiled, of course."

"You nearly exiled him to pieces on Christmas Eve."

"I had no part in that."

"Your agents François Carbon and Pierre Saint-Réjant named you as the engine behind Four Nivose. The infernal machine that destroyed buildings and tore thirty-five people to ribbons wasn't designed merely to detain the First Consul."

"I never granted those fools permission to kill."

"You admit you knew them."

"I didn't say that."

"Your friend Pichegru—"

"I don't know any of these fellows you're talking about."

Dubois changed hands on the pistol and swept the muzzle across the prisoner's right temple. Even Limodin flinched.

The chief inspector wondered about the Prefect's motives. A forced confession was hardly necessary. There would be no trial in the usual sense of the term, and therefore no defense, only prosecution followed by muskets. He wondered if Dubois weren't trying to satisfy himself of the man's guilt before turning him over to Fouché and his methods.

Dubois' tone softened.

"Come, come, General. We know all your friends. They gave you up like that." He snapped his fingers. "Your actions today left a young widow and three orphans."

"Next time send bachelors."

Cadoudal braced himself, Limodin, too; but no more blows came. The Prefect stood patting his empty palm with the pistol.

"Where is your assassin?"

"What assassin?"

But the prisoner had hesitated an instant before responding.

"The man responsible for two murders that we know of just outside Paris, and two assaults. The man who crossed the Channel from England on the third day of Germinal, and who's been working his way toward Paris ever since."

"He must be traveling by turtle, whoever he is."

"He was delayed by a mishap. Also there's a war on. The country's aswarm with soldiers. He's a cautious man, this Meuchel. Does the name resonate?"

Another brief pause.

"I don't know any Germans."

Dubois had scored; Limodin could see it on his face. That line of questioning had intrigued the chief inspector. He'd been told of the events in Pontoise, but in none of their discussions had either of them expressed certainty that the violent stranger was part of the Royalist plot; Cadoudal's hesitation had confirmed it.

The Prefect was either a brilliant detective or *un fortuné fils du chienne*: one lucky son of a bitch.

Dubois turned to Limodin. "Drop this man in the dungeon like the festering turd he is. I'm off to report to the Minister of Police."

"Should I send for a doctor?"

"When our friend with the explosive pistols is more than just a name."

Georges Cadoudal ceased to exist within twenty-four hours of his capture. His riddled body was buried in the Temple Prison cemetery without a stone to identify it. Under strenuous questioning by Ministry experts, he'd mumbled *"Le Vipère"* through broken teeth. Immediately it replaced Meuchel as the name of Fouché's quarry, and the Royalist general was consigned to the firing squad.

Because of his former service to the Republic, and because under torture he kept to his claim that he'd rejected the overtures of Cadoudal and Pichegru, General Moreau was spared. He was returned to exile in French Guiana.

General Pichegru was discovered dead in his cell and declared a suicide: Self-strangulation was the official cause.

There remained only the Viper.

42

The man the Frontenacs knew as Marechal was alone in the parlor. He drank tepid chocolate, shaking his head over his *Moniteur*.

He hadn't thought Cadoudal quite that much of a fool. The long silence and his own uncertainty had flushed him from his English sanctuary, straight into Fouché's clutches.

News that the general and two of his co-conspirators had been arrested and dealt with had enraged the Viper nearly as much as Bonaparte's no-show on Bastille Day. The upshot would be to reawaken the country to the plot, making it more difficult still for him to approach his target.

But it wasn't all bad. Heightened security meant more armed men and more unfamiliar faces, and less suspicion when another stranger joined the rest.

Collecting the remainder of his fee once the thing was done would prove as much of a challenge as the thing itself. It would mean meeting with the Cutthroat Club in England and blackmailing them in person. By then, of course, he'd be hunted throughout Europe.

However, even that had its benefits. He'd be spared the emotional letdown that so often followed a completed mission. He'd dreaded that: after the exhilaration of the hunt and the triumph of the kill, naught but depression, deep and black. Despair almost to the point of suicide.

He reread the other item that had caught his interest: the latest details of a state celebration.

On 28 Messidor, the month of harvest (June 16 by the Gregorian), emissaries of Pope Pius VII had signed the Concordat of Rome, agreeing to re-establish the Catholic Church as the official faith of France.

With a single blow, Bonaparte had won the spiritual and po-litical support of the Vatican and robbed the Royalists of their strongest argument for Restoration. They could no longer depend on the popularity of their cause.

The end of the so-called Age of Reason set bells ringing in all the reopened cathedrals and demanded a public celebration on 10 Thermidor, the first *decadi*, or official day of rest, in the month of heat. The announcement was made on Bastille Day. Government offices and all factories would be shut down and the gates of the Tuileries opened to the public.

The First Consul and his wife would be present, greeting their fellow citizens from the balcony.

Chaucer-Molière-Meuchel-Marechal folded the newspaper. He sensed a trap. But it was an opportunity he couldn't afford to overlook.

The time had come for the snake to strike the eagle.

"Are you sure you won't join us, Monsieur Marechal? It's a great day for France."

Jean-Baptiste snorted at his wife's remark. "You mean it's a great day for Rome. The next thing you know, the First Consul will name a priest to his cabinet."

Their lodger postponed the inevitable argument. He was sit-ting on the edge of his bed with the door open and his arm in a boot, vigorously shining the leather with a horsehair brush. "Thank you, Madame. I overtaxed myself on the anniversary of the Day of Liberation. I'll stay here and look to my things, if you don't object."

"You are our guest," she said. "But promise me you'll get some fresh air. It will speed your recovery."

"You're very kind. I'm feeling quite well, though a bit tired. I will take your advice later."

After the street door closed behind the couple, he waited a full minute, then rose and shut his door, latching it and bracing it again with a chair. He opened the valise he'd commissioned in London and threw aside the clothing he hadn't unpacked.

It was the work of a moment to cut through the leather stitching with his dagger and remove the false bottom. He lifted out the bundle he'd placed inside in the back of the luggage-maker's shop in London.

He went to work with scissors, needle, and thread, items borrowed from his hostess ("You bachelors are so self-sufficient!"). When he finished, he dropped his empty courier's belt into the valise, kicked it back under the bed, and returned to the bundle.

He'd folded everything with a soldier's precision, but inevitably there were wrinkles. He shook out the worst of them and stripped. Moments later, he tucked the tails of a white shirt into white knee-breeches, buttoned on a waistcoat, white also, slipped into a swallow-tailed blue woolen tunic faced with red flannel, tugged on the freshly polished boots, and fastened a pair of white gaiters over them. Only the ordinary shirt and nondescript boots came from his usual wardrobe; everything else had been hidden under the panel in the valise, including the white ornamental belts he buckled in an X across his chest.

These items, once glimpsed, were what had led to the death of the luggage maker's son in London.

Finally, he took the bearskin shako he'd ordered from the tailor in Paris out of its tall pasteboard box and inserted the scarlet plume in the tricolor cockade that held it in place. The hat added a full twelve inches to his stature when he put it on. He adjusted the chinstrap and studied his reflection in the cheval glass that stood in the corner.

He overlooked nothing: Front, profile, back, peering over his shoulder. Crown to heels, epaulets to buttons. The pound and franc notes he'd sewn into the linings betrayed no telltale bulges. He plucked a grain of lint from his collar, bit a stray thread off a sleeve. Bonaparte was a martinet and so were the officers who served him. It would be disaster to attract the attention of a puffed-up major and get himself put on post.

From thick sidewhiskers to neatly trimmed nails, he was the model of a grenadier of the Consular Guard, assigned to the protection of the First Consul.

The finishing touch, military decorations, came from a slim leather case he'd packed with the uniform. Why *shouldn't* he wear them? They weren't forgeries of paint and tin, or items procured from a pawnbroker. They were plated with fourteen-karat gold and glazed enamel.

And they'd been pinned on him the first time by none other than Napoleon Bonaparte.

43

"World war?" Dubois scowled. "It's inconceivable."

Fouché looked uncomfortable, but not with the conversation. He hated waiting, which was what one did in the Tuileries, and he preferred street clothes to his dress uniform, which was too stiff with gold thread to settle back on his shoulders when he shrugged. All the other trappings of wealth and position met with his approval.

"You heard him as well as I."

"But is such a thing possible?"

"Bonaparte has never been wrong on the subject of war. I'd rather catch this Viper than put it to the test."

"Viper. *Quel théâtre!*"

"Keep your voice down, Dubois. We're withholding that morsel from the public. Our late friend Cadoudal was fond of such drama; in that he was not unlike the First Consul. Under other circumstances they might have been friends."

The confession that the Royalist general had hired an assassin to kill Bonaparte had come surprisingly easy once the Prefecture had turned Cadoudal over to the Police Ministry; he still had eight fingernails when he'd cracked wide open, spilling all he knew about this Viper. Fouché thought the Breton must have been proud of the shilling-shocker name he'd concocted, or he'd have held out longer.

"I still think we should have released the information," Dubois said. "Someone might hear something, and report."

"Too slim. Our quarry won't go about introducing himself as a venomous serpent, or by any of the other names he's used in the past. If we go buzzing round like a swarm of nervous bees, it will put him on his guard. Let him think we believe the plot is broken."

"He won't buy it. He hasn't eluded us this long by being careless."

"He was once, outside Pontoise; twice, if you count his dalliance with the doctor's widow friend. History has a habit of repeating itself."

They awaited Bonaparte in the room leading to the balcony. Like every room in every palace, it was freezing in winter and sweltering in summer. The walls sweated and there was a perennial damp spot on the carpet. Dubois stuck a finger between his stiff uniform collar and his neck, separating them with a noise like skinning a rabbit.

"Stop fidgeting. You're not a boy at Mass." Fouché kept his voice below the hearing of the other government functionaries, whose presence added to the beastly heat. Foreign Minister Talleyrand alone appeared unaffected by the conditions, starched and powdered in his Bourbon Court dress, whispering in the ear of Third Consul Ducos; making mischief the way a worm spins silk.

"What else can I do but fidget?" said Dubois. "You've set a dangerous trap, using the First Consul as bait."

"There was no help for it. Bastille Day came too soon, and now that we're at war there's no telling where Bonaparte will be in a week; storming Gibraltar personally, perhaps. If he stays out of public view, friend Viper will only bide his time until he resurfaces. Once a tick gets its head under your skin, it can only fester indefinitely. Better to burn this one with a cigar-end before he acts."

It had come about this way:

Fouché was still too much the Revolutionary to welcome a re-alliance with the Church; but once the nature of the plot had begun to unfold, he'd urged Bonaparte to commemorate the Concordat with a public ceremony.

"Really, Fouché?" The First Consul had sat drinking coffee at Malmaison, still wearing his green colonel's uniform and famous bicorne. The dust of military maneuvers frosted his boots. "I'd thought the Massacre of Lyons had only increased your thirst for the blood of the clergy."

"Times change, your excellency. It's a poor politician who resists changing with them."

The persuasion hadn't taken as long as getting him to skip Bastille Day; the Strong Man of France had railed against playing the coward before cowards, but Fouché had won his point, as he usually did, through stubborn tenacity. Bonaparte's deeply ingrained impatience was the Minister's best ally in such discussions. Of course he'd leapt at this fresh opportunity to appear in public and lay to rest any doubts about his personal courage.

"Very well, Fouché. Have that splendid uniform of yours sponged and pressed. You'll join me on the balcony."

Dubois was still reluctant, and stifling in his own dress uniform, crowned by his snare-drum hat. "I just wish there was a better way. Staking the man you're pledged to protect, like a goat, isn't police work."

"You'd circulate descriptions and sketches, which is; and it would prove feckless. What details we have would apply to every third man in Europe. Cadoudal knew nothing of his background; even the name he gave in England, Molière, was a confessed fiction. As for Meuchel, my inquiries have failed to turn up anyone of any rank with that name in the Austrian Army. We could arrest every Meuchel we find, but that takes time we don't have, and we wouldn't have our man."

"The First Consul has doubles to stand in for him on public occasions when he hasn't the time," Dubois said. "Anyone can wave from a balcony and present a target."

"I've more than a hunch he wouldn't fool the Viper. I did succeed in persuading the First Consul to pull in a division of grenadiers from the northern frontier to assist the Consular Guard. They're not needed on the Channel."

"Won't our snake notice the extras and smell a trap?"

"To go the other way, so soon after unraveling Four Nivose, would make him more suspicious yet."

"A shell game. I wonder how you keep track of the pea."

"You're unpracticed in espionage, Dubois. All your men are in place?"

"At every entrance, among the crowd, on the rooftops. Yours?"

"The same. Let's hope they don't shoot one another."

"At least we have a witness who can identify our man."

"By now he won't look anything like him," Fouché said.

"I think my people can spot a false nose and a wig."

"There are a hundred ways to dissemble your appearance without resorting to opera. He can lose or gain weight, shave his head, grow a beard, alter his gait, even disguise his height."

"All the more reason to be grateful for Eslée. He's seen him. Limodin thinks the Widow Deauville might become hysterical and give us away; but then Limodin hasn't met her. I have, and I'd take the risk, but the doctor refused to cooperate if we put her in harm's way. At all events I trust him."

"He lied once."

"He was honoring his oath. This affair can do with a little honor."

"Where is he?"

The Prefect popped open his watch. "The officers I sent

should have brought him here by now. I can't think what's keeping them."

"We begin well."

The streets were jammed. The morning was sultry already. The stench of sweat mingled with unwashed flesh, sour wine in goatskin bags, and penny cologne. It made the Viper's head swim.

The crowds, at least, made way for him, respecting the uniform crowned by the tall bearskin. Nevertheless progress was slow. Carriages and cabriolets made less speed still, crawling along a pavement clotted with bodies.

Such doings were nothing without mishaps. A driver, red-faced with frustration or drink or both, unfurled his whip, making contact with a pedestrian, a tactical error possibly caused by bad aim. The crowd dragged him, bellowing and struggling, off his seat and into its midst. Uniformed officers from the Prefecture pushed their way toward the commotion, blasting their tin whistles.

A most typical Paris celebration.

The Viper had allowed for delays. He entered the teeming palace grounds with time to spare. He glanced up at the balcony, its tricolor bunting tied back to expose the as-yet vacant interior, and stepped through an arched passage into the main corridor. The grenadiers flanking the arch, spotting the insignia of a captain, saluted. If his features were unfamiliar, they assigned the fact to the fresh reinforcements brought in from the east. The city police deferred to their judgment; such was the effect of martial law under a Republic. He returned the salute and mounted a marble staircase to the second floor.

"Captain!"

He spun on his heel on the landing, snapped to attention, saluted. "Yes, sir!"

The colonel, he was pleased to note, was unknown to him and

probably recently transferred from another branch of the army. His whiskers were black, his eyes set close, perpetually suspicious. They were alone in the corridor.

"What's your division?"

"The First, *mon Colonel*. Fourth *Tirailleur*, serving under General Delaborde."

"Where the devil is your saber?"

He made a show of surprise, slapping his hip. It was another thing he couldn't fit into the false bottom of his valise. He was prepared for that contingency, and here was the man to supply the solution.

"I—the belt must have come loose in the jostling outside. Sir."

"Things have come to a pretty pass when a drunken rabble manages to disarm a grenadier of the Guard."

"Yes, sir."

"And what do you intend to do about it?"

"I thought, sir, I would borrow yours." With a snap of the wrist, the dagger slid from his sleeve into his hand. He took two steps and swept it underhand into the colonel's belly.

Stab wounds initially aren't painful; the victim feels only a sudden push. The blade was withdrawn by the time the man looked down and saw the red blossom on his white waistcoat. The Viper switched to an overhand grip and drove the point through the colonel's left eye into the brain.

He was dead immediately, with minimal bleeding. His killer stepped back to let him fall.

The corridor remained empty but for them. He unbuckled the colonel's sword belt and strapped it round his own waist, the saber swinging in its ornate scabbard. He'd hoped for something more plain, but a gift was a gift.

He moved swiftly, wiping the dagger on the colonel's tunic and putting it away under his own, next to his pistol. Then he dragged the dead man by his ankles through an arch into an unlit and obviously unused chamber.

Sheets covered the furniture. He hauled the corpse into a corner far from the velvet-cloaked windows and covered it with a sheet he snatched off a chaise. Anyone glancing inside the room would see only another unidentified shape under a dust cover.

A platoon of boots stamped down the corridor. He retreated farther into the dark corner and waited, breathing shallowly, as the troops passed, their sabers rattling like crockery in their scabbards. When the sound faded, he took his hand off his pistol.

He breathed normally. His pistol held but one round, and it wasn't intended for common soldiers.

Dubois, standing beside Fouché, found himself humming along with the military band playing in the courtyard: one of those whirling, crashing, catchy martial airs that had followed French regiments from Paris to Cairo and back. It seemed a bizarre choice to commemorate the end of a holy schism. But he was an innocent in affairs of state.

Certainly the country's spiritual rebirth was good for business. Opportunists with rucksacks strapped to their backs worked their way through the crowd gathering under the balcony, waving prayer books hastily printed on coarse paper and bound with shoddy, hawking them like confectionery. They had many takers.

Watching from a casement window, Dubois recognized some pickpockets working in the other direction, hoping to lift purses not yet lightened by the entrepreneurs; but such things weren't his concern today.

Would that they were.

In time he grew weary of the bumping brass and rattle of drumsticks. His head throbbed in beat with the band. Sweat drenched his armpits. His mouth was dry as cotton.

"Excuse me, Minister. I need to find water."

"Um-hum." Fouché surveyed the grounds below through gold opera glasses.

Despite his parched and exhausted condition, Dubois kept alert, searching the invited throng growing within the marble chambers for the squad of officers he'd sent to fetch their witness. It wasn't like Limodin to be late.

He put a hand on the arm of a passing footman. "Could you tell me where I might get a drink?"

"There are wine merchants outside, monsieur."

"I was unclear. I want plain water."

The man seemed impatient; then appeared to notice the Prefect's pallor.

"Wait here, please. I'll send someone with a carafe."

"Thank you."

The lackey was gone less than a minute when Dubois saw the reason for his haste. A galvanic current surged through the crowd indoors. Bonaparte was coming.

44

It was like a great gust of wind parting acres of grain: The air freshened, the hum of conversation changed pitch, then fell away. The First Consul and his lady came round a corner arm in arm, trailed by aides-de-camp; all generals in ropes of gold braid, silk sashes, and decorations from the field. Glittering spurs that had never bit into horseflesh jangled at their heels. The crowd opened a path, applauding from the sidelines.

Bonaparte surrounded himself with titans. The Grenadiers of the Consular Guard had been selected for their height; their heeled boots and great shaggy hats made them seem tall as trees. The First Consul was a man of average height, but the sight of him in that company had led to the popular misapprehension that he was short.

He was dressed elegantly but simply in contrast to the pomp around him, in a scarlet coat with gold embroidery, skin-tight breeches, and boots that glistened like mirrors to his knees. His celebrated wife was a wisp of pale vapor in silk and muslin, her only jewelry a gold pin on one shoulder and a matching chain round her throat. Her storied auburn ringlets, worn short, exposed well-shaped ears. Her habitual tight-lipped smile was painted in place.

The Strong Man of France slowed from time to time to show his excellent teeth and exchange a few words, his lady to extend a languid hand to the fortunate; but the party moved briskly down the broad corridor. Dubois uncovered as it passed. No one took notice of him.

Which was just as well. He couldn't manufacture the saliva to return a greeting. He put on his hat. Where was Limodin with Dr. Eslée?

"Your water, monsieur."

"Thank you so much." He snatched a silver pitcher and a crystal goblet from the tray that was offered him, filled the goblet, emptied it greedily, filled it again and drank.

"A thousand thanks." He put it back. "It wouldn't look well for the head of the Paris Police to die of heatstroke."

The servant seemed not to have heard him. He was watching after the grand receding party. "He's a great man, isn't he? A true immortal."

"Yes. Let's hope."

The man dressed as a grenadier saluted as the Bonapartes passed, all but invisible inside their circle. He fell into step at the end of the last row of guardsmen. The others seemed to take no notice, intent on the couple in their charge.

The Tuileries was a rabbit-warren, riddled with groins, vaults, and side passages by order of the Medicis. Grenadiers were posted at entrances every few yards, with far less impressive men standing nearby, some in drab police uniforms, others in civilian dress.

If a trap had been set for him—for which he was constantly on guard—it was hardly airtight. The sentries ignored him as he passed, looking for suspicious activity among the grandly dressed guests drifting along in the party's wake.

They had either too little imagination or too much: They sought the extraordinary at the expense of the ordinary.

His boots were a half-size too large, but he'd made them fit with socks too thick for July. He'd bought the boots for just the price of resoling. The customer who'd left them with the cobbler had failed to reclaim them. They were the least expensive items on his person, and better than too tight. There would be running involved.

The Viper remembered his military training. When a commotion took place at one of the entrances, he kept his eyes front. He overheard the exchange in passing.

"Soldier, I am Chief Inspector Limodin of the Paris Police, in command of these officers. I'm under orders to bring this man directly to Prefect Dubois. Here are my papers."

"I have my orders as well, monsieur," said the sentry. "I answer only to an officer of the grenadiers."

"*S'il vous plaît.* It's urgent."

A third voice, this, vaguely familiar; the Viper had heard so many since. He turned his head a quarter-inch and locked eyes with Dr. Charles Eslée of Pontoise.

"From the cellars of the Vatican, your excellency. With the pontiff's compliments." Foreign Minister Talleyrand, once again in favor, tucked his stick under one arm and filled a heavy gold goblet from a tall black bottle with an escutcheon on the label.

Bonaparte said, "I wasn't aware he'd been in contact."

"A case arrived just yesterday, by special diplomatic courier. I thought it would be a pleasant surprise. Was I wrong?"

"On another day, perhaps." He unlaced his arm from Josephine's and took the goblet. "We'll send him a good French vintage in return. My blood's Italian, but I'm not prepared to admit France's vines are inferior."

"I'm told these barrels were put down under Lorenzo the Magnificent."

"Maybe he couldn't bear to look at them. I'll challenge the pope to a tasting next time I'm in Rome."

"Madame?" Talleyrand produced an identical vessel and held the bottle ready.

Josephine shook her head, smiling still. She despised the club-footed Foreign Minister.

Bonaparte lifted his goblet. Talleyrand filled the other goblet and raised it. "To a permanent understanding with the Church."

"An understanding, anyway."

They drank. The First Consul made a wry face.

"As I suspected."

"I find it full-bodied."

"So is German beer; but I wouldn't recommend it for an occasion of state." Bonaparte set his goblet on a tray held by a convenient footman.

Fouché approached.

"The public is eager, excellency."

"They generally are, when there's an excuse to drink. Where is Dubois?"

"I can't say. It's not like him to be—"

"Here!" The Prefect appeared, breathless.

Fouché's smile was bitter. He'd been interrupted in the middle of an obsequious insult to his colleague.

"How goes the snake hunt?" Bonaparte's smile died short of his eyes. He'd been told the latest details.

"Nothing so far, Citizen First Consul. I've someone coming who can identify the party. He's in the charge of my chief inspector."

"He's fashionably late."

"The streets are a nightmare."

"Let's hope they're the same for our friend," put in Fouché.

"Wine, Dubois?" Bonaparte tilted his head toward Talleyrand's bottle.

"Thank you, no. It disagrees with me in this heat."

"I thought you pale. I myself am seldom hot since Egypt. If you'd served with me there, you'd have a fire laid every day. Ah, Delaborde. Your men look splendid."

The general in command of the First Division of the Consular

Guard had joined them. Splinters of silver glittered in his side-whiskers. "Thank you, your excellency." He saluted smartly. "A rough lot, some of them, fresh from the frontiers."

"Good. A Paris post leads to sloth." Noise swelled from the crowd outside. "Don't overload the balcony, General. It's old and rotted with Bourbon neglect."

"I trust it will hold men enough to discourage a villain." Delaborde raised his voice. "Grenadiers!"

The Viper couldn't tell if Eslée had recognized him.

The chief inspector's body came between them on the instant their gazes met, waving his arms in furious argument with the obstinate grenadier at the entrance; he hoped it was distraction enough.

They'd seen each other for a fraction of a second, and it was human nature to place the uniform before the face. He had to place faith in his sidewhiskers, the healthy tan he'd acquired since leaving the doctor's care. Regardless, he must not risk a closer look.

Fate spared him that.

"Grenadiers!"

Delaborde's parade-ground bellow set the escort moving toward the balcony. The Viper fell into step with it.

His position at right rear put him first in the march, the ranks routinely breaking position from back to front. He trotted in double-time, the others in his line falling in behind. Their boots struck the floor in unison, chug-chug-chug. He came within a meter of a slight figure in a scarlet coat, standing beside a woman in white.

Bonaparte was no longer the gaunt brigadier general of 13 Vendémiaire, with hollow cheeks and long lank hair, but his person was undeniable. He often employed doubles to stand for him in public; this was not one. As it was with all famous men, once in his presence there was no doubt. Here was the great brainy forehead, the stray lock falling upon it, the straight, prominent nose, the obstinate chin, and those gray eyes, which could burn like flame or chill like ice, depending on the humor of the individual who commanded them. There wasn't a parlor in Paris that didn't display that image in paint or marble, or a newspaper in London that didn't feature it in insolent caricature.

The old hoodoo was still in effect: The power of his presence was like a blow to the solar plexus. The fact irritated the Viper; tempered further the steel of his resolve.

"Company—halt!"

The last line of soldiers slid into place and stopped with a crash of heels. Silence slammed down, louder than the shouts of the crowd outside, every eye on the balcony. The false soldier stood with his hands at his sides, thumbs in line with the seams of his breeches. The dagger was once again up his left sleeve; a precaution only, in case the pistol misfired or if he had to fight his way free in the aftermath. There'd be no time to reload in any event.

"You, there!"

He kept his gaze in the middle distance. Training alone had stayed him from flinching when Bonaparte barked.

He smelled peppermint. The First Consul approached.

Now he stood directly in front of him, half a head shorter, studying the decorations on his breast.

"Toulon. Italy. Egypt." He pointed at each in turn, as if selecting chocolates from a box. "You've seen much of the world, Captain."

"Yes, sir." He kept his eyes level.

Bonaparte touched the smallest medal, lifting it at the end of its ribbon.

"Thirteen Vendémiaire. I don't often see these. You were in the square?"

"Yes, sir. I was on temporary detached duty to the artillery."

"Name?"

"Débiteur, your excellency. My Christian name is Aleron."

"At ease."

He spread his feet and folded his hands behind his back. His right thumb touched the butt of the pistol under his tunic.

"A soldier's name, Aleron."

"My father's, your excellency."

"Josephine!"

That wraith approached, trailing silk and muslin like billows of white smoke.

"Allow me to present Captain Aleron Débiteur, a hero of the Republic. *Capitaine* Débiteur, Madame Bonaparte."

The Viper turned her way, holding out a hand in a white glove. The woman, whiter yet, laid hers on it. It was weightless in his palm.

"We have so many heroes these days," said she, "but it's rare for my husband to single one out. I congratulate you, Captain."

Her smile was mocking, he thought. Tiny fissures showed in the enamel at the corners of her eyes. He smelled her perfume, as light and airy as the woman who wore it; and like her, one of a kind. The cost of its manufacture would have outfitted a regiment.

"Thank you, Madame. It's a great honor." Kiss her hand? No. He let it lie where it was until she withdrew it. He refolded his behind his back.

"I don't forget faces," Bonaparte said. "We exchanged some words while we were waiting for the guns to arrive."

"Yes, sir."

"Forty Gribeauval twenty-four-pounders. Four hundred sixty-two enemy casualties, most of them slain."

The Viper said nothing, seeing a dead woman with one leg, the other still twitching across the courtyard. She'd been clutching a bundle of straw for her hearth. The memory haunted his nightmares.

"You're injured recently. I can always tell."

"I was in a military hospital in Marseille until a few weeks ago. Sir. I caught a Mameluk lance in Egypt, took fever, and came back aboard a merchant vessel. This is my first assignment since returning."

Few questioned a lie leavened with truth.

Bonaparte gave no sign that his Oriental disaster, the troops he'd abandoned in order to steal France at gunpoint, troubled him. He turned to Josephine.

"Vendémiaire was the Royalists' last stand. The defeat drove them from military action to base butchery."

She shuddered. "Don't remind me, Bonaparte. I want to forget Christmas Eve."

He turned back to the grenadier. "Quite a day, Captain. A whiff of grapeshot, like pepper in a drunk's face."

"Yes, sir. Quite a day."

"Débiteur. I'm sorry, but it doesn't ring a bell."

Snap!

A brown sparrow of a man in a uniform too grand for him shut the lid on his watch; an impatient fellow with a moustache like a furry insect, wearing a hat that suggested a cake pan. He was preoccupied with something other than the conversation. Something or someone was late.

The First Consul laughed. He reached up and tweaked the Viper's earlobe.

"A man indeed! A good augur for the day."

Capitaine Débiteur flushed and reached for his pistol.

45

"That's the man!" It was a shout.

The Viper recognized Eslée's voice; he might not have if he hadn't seen the doctor in the corridor outside.

He shoved the muzzle of the pistol into the belly of this Corsican, this mass murderer, this betrayer of his own army, and pressed the trigger.

As the hammer dropped, he felt a shudder:

Bonaparte's shock, communicated directly through the pistol into his hand.

Simultaneously there was a blur of flesh, slicing downward. A gasp of pain.

No spark was struck. The man in the flat hat had jammed the edge of his hand between the hammer and the powder charge. The firing pin had torn the flesh.

The Viper uncoiled, twisting loose the weapon and compounding the injury. The hammer fell a thirty-second of an inch, without detonating the powder. He recocked it; but Bonaparte wasn't there. His grenadiers had wrestled him to the floor. Their bodies were in the way.

Hacking was required. He switched hands on the pistol and grasped the haft of the late colonel's saber with his right: shrill scrape of metal on metal as it left its scabbard.

Another hand—God, was the world made of hands?—clamped his wrist, yanking it upward. Blood spilled onto his wrist. It belonged to the man in the flat hat.

The saber fell, clattering to the marble floor. But the hand that held him was slippery with blood. The Viper twisted free. He switched hands again, but the pistol was not for this man. He flicked his left arm, bringing the dagger into play. He made an underhand stab for the gut; but an arm in a uniform sleeve got in the way. The blade slashed fabric, sliced tendons. Flat Hat cried out.

The cry distracted one of the grenadiers shielding Bonaparte on the floor. He looked back over his shoulder, supporting himself on one knee and leaving the First Consul exposed. The Viper's gaze locked with Bonaparte's. They stared at each other as if across a battlefield.

He aimed for the heart, squeezed the trigger. The copper cap cracked, powder ignited. The grenadier threw himself across Bonaparte. The leaden ball struck him in the middle of the back, collided with bone, and burst, spraying razor shards through vital organs. He died instantly.

To the crowd on the ground, the report was lost in the thunder of drums and crash of cymbals; but on the balcony, the echo of the double explosion, the thick smoke of the discharge, and stink of sulfur stoked confusion. The Viper raced across the balcony, dropping dagger and pistol to grasp the railing, and hurled himself over the balustrade. The crowd, seeing movement, cheered the First Consul; but their cries trailed off as the figure hung from the railing by both hands, gathering himself for the drop. He let go.

He hit the cobblestones hard, pain splintering up both ankles. One at least was shattered; but he found his balance and broke into a run before the pain could set in.

The crowd opened a path for the man wearing the uniform of the French Army. He dove into it.

Dr. Charles Eslée, acting on professional instinct, stepped toward the Police Prefect, who was bleeding from both his hand and his arm; the grenadier who'd stepped in to save the First Consul was emphatically dead. But Dubois pushed the physician away, clawing for his own pistol.

General Delaborde was bawling orders.

Musketeers of the Guard stood on the balcony, shouldering their weapons. Those armed only with sabers had bundled the First Consul and his wife—the latter sagging heavily in her husband's arms—to safety. Bonaparte's face was black with rage.

Dubois' pistol fell from his hand. His slashed wrist had no strength. He picked it up with his other hand; the action of the moment sent pain into the background.

The musketeers shouldered their weapons but held their fire.

"Why don't you shoot?" Fouché had joined Dubois and Delaborde at the railing.

"Impossible," said the general. "Too many innocents."

"What of that? Are we going to let him slip through our fingers twice in one day?"

"With respect, Minister, I'm in command."

"To hell with your respect!" Fouché leaned forward, cupping his skeletal hands round his mouth. "Citizens! Stop that man! He's slain the First Consul!"

Delaborde opened his mouth to say something; didn't.

The shout rang across the crowded courtyard.

"*Jesu.*" Dubois would have crossed himself if his hands weren't otherwise engaged. The whispered word alone was more significant than the pious celebration: The Church had returned to France.

The Viper ran out from under his tall bearskin.

The crowd continued to make way for the man in uniform, hobbling now but desperately still in motion.

The gates were open. Even if they'd been ordered closed, the press of people would have prevented them from swinging.

Once outside the palace, he'd find a horse. Once outside Paris, he'd smear mud on his military dress and find another Pontoise; some quiet village, anyway, get medical attention for his ankles, shave his whiskers, don peasant's clothes, find transportation—kill for these things if anyone resisted—and take the smugglers' roads to the Channel. The mariners who crossed it regularly made no distinctions between human contraband and goods; they demanded payment only. His tunic and waistcoat were lined with currency, which would buy him passage to England.

The Cutthroat Club would refuse him the rest of his compensation; but they'd pay to prevent him from betraying them to their own authorities, who frowned publicly on foreign intrigues while supporting them in private. They'd be made to serve as examples.

Later, when the Viper was forgotten, or thought dead, he'd resurface and return, if only to preserve his record.

Dieu! It was like wading through splinters of glass. This was the price he paid for mixing work with desire. Bonaparte was the only mission he'd ever accepted for reasons beyond pure profit. The man had slain starving Parisians to protect the same corrupt Directorate he'd displaced later at his own convenience, cast lots with the lives of the men who followed him in Italy, and abandoned them in Egypt. The Viper had embraced the chance to kill him, savored the irony of making money on the deal.

Bellowing came from the direction of the palace. He couldn't make out the words at first.

Of course there'd be shouting. The volume would be great, to equal the extent of the failure to capture him. Then he heard the words, carried mainly by repetition from the crowd:

"Stop him. . . ."

"Slain . . ."

"Slain the First Consul . . ."

"Slain Bonaparte!"

"Butcher!"

"Where is he?"

A shout in his ear, this. It was the uniform; the man thought the man wearing it was chasing the assassin.

It was a chance. "Outside the gate!" he cried. Faces turned that direction. The gate was fifty meters away.

His legs were ablaze with pain. He gritted his teeth, sucking air between them, pumped his knees. It was worth amputation to get through that gate.

Forty-five meters.

"Stop that grenadier!" Another shout from the balcony. "He's the killer!"

A hand seized his arm.

He twisted free, stumbled forward. Hands clawed at his tunic. He twisted loose with a shrill tearing of wool, almost lost balance, caught it running. To fall was to be flayed alive. He tore open the tunic, buttons flying, clambered out of the sleeves. He left his pursuers holding only part of the uniform of a Grenadier of the Consular Guard—and six thousand pounds sterling sewn into the lining. He'd pay twice that for forty meters more.

In that moment he surrendered his last protection.

Even a mob sure of its purpose hesitated to desecrate the Tricolor. Those who wore it had flung the ogres from the frontiers, chased them all the way back to their corrupt capitals, bearded them in their dens, and forced them to sign over their territories to the Republic, then returned laden with treasures for the people of the pavement to admire.

But a man stripped to his waistcoat, running for his hide, was no soldier, no invincible.

A deserter.

A coward.

A Judas in the costume of the Republic.

"Slain . . . Slain the First Consul . . . Slain Bonaparte."

"Slain Bonaparte!"

"Seize the assassin!"

"Kill him!"

Hands clawed at him, tore his shirt sleeve at the shoulder. He groped for dagger, saber, pistol. All gone. A hand horned with calluses closed on his right biceps. The arm went dead. Other hands plucked at his clothing, sundered the seams, dug their nails into flesh. For the first time in his life he understood fear.

Hands on his arms, on his legs, fingers raking at his eyes, at the corners of his mouth. Something snapped. White-hot pain shot to the top of his skull.

Then he remembered the arsenic in its sausage-casing, stitched under the skin of his right hand. He bit at the heel, for the mercy the capsule would bring; but his jaw wobbled, couldn't get a purchase. It was broken.

He tried to call out.

For what, help?

In any event he had no voice; a brutal grip closed his throat.

So this was despair.

It tasted like brass.

His feet went out from under him. He hadn't fallen; he was lifted off the ground, tipped onto his back, borne away in a rip current, turned over and over, a pig on a spit. His torn sleeve came away like the skin from an orange.

That led to inspiration.

They pulled apart his waistcoat, another two thousand in notes spilling from the lining, ripped away at his shirt and breeches, jerked the boots from his feet, snatched at his underdrawers.

He was naked.

Nothing more to tear now but flesh.

They passed him from hand to hand, from the tallest to the shortest, ever downward. The sky cast over with red faces, rained curses stinking of garlic and sour wine. Then they let go with a team shout.

He fell three feet onto cobblestones. His lungs emptied. He lay gasping. Then the crowd bent over him and went to work in cold earnest.

Clumps of his hair were torn out by the roots. Fists pummeled his face until the burning stopped and he could no longer feel the blows, even when the cartilage in his nose crumpled like pie crust. He began to strangle then, drowning in his own blood and mucus. Feet kicked him, feet shod in stiff hide and hobnails, some in fine leather: Mobs didn't distinguish between classes. He heard straw crackling in a hearth; his ribs breaking. A foot found his groin. His stomach turned. Another collided with his head, and he heard the bellow of the beast no more from that ear, a half-mercy.

Something flashed in the sun. A butcher's long-handled meat cleaver. Where had *that* come from? It slashed down and across, left to right, right to left, like a scythe mowing grain. Things came away from his face, his head, his body. Armless and leg-less, he twisted and thrashed, writhed, tried to coil in on himself, opened his shattered jaw wide, hissed. His back arched. His torso convulsed, right, left, right again, slower, slower.

Still.

46

"'Torn to pieces.'"

"*Oui.*" Chief Inspector Jules Limodin smoked his pipe. He was sitting in his place opposite Dubois at his desk.

The Prefect grimaced. "You hear someone threaten to tear so-and-so to pieces, and think it comical. The reality is nothing to laugh about."

"It's the same with tarring and feathering," Limodin said. "I saw it happen once, in Corbeil. A dentist; nobody of any account. But I wouldn't suggest such a thing now, even in jest."

"There should be a law against large gatherings."

"There may be soon. I understand the First Consul has finished the Civil Code." The chief inspector puffed a gale of smoke. "You were reckless, you know."

Dubois glanced down at his arm in a sling. "I would do it again—albeit with certain modifications."

He'd acted automatically, jamming flesh into the mechanism of the Viper's pistol. Ironically, that small injury, patched as it was, still pained him more than his wrist, which was a more serious matter; he'd wear the cast for several more weeks, and would remember 10 Thermidor every time he looked at the scar, the only decoration he was likely to bear for performing the duties of his office.

Not that he was likely to forget. The mare the Royalists had blown to bits on Christmas Eve had presented an aspect less grisly than the assassin's remains once Paris had got through with him.

"What kept you, by the way?" he asked Limodin. "Two seconds

later and Dr. Eslée's warning would have been moot, and the First Consul dead instead of that poor grenadier on the balcony, now a martyr to the Republic."

"The crowds, and a stubborn sentry at the door. I had to stamp on his instep finally to get Eslée inside." He removed the pipe and glared over the bowl. "I was under military arrest for twelve hours."

"He was doing his job. So were you. So was I. Don't expect a rise in salary."

"I wouldn't know what to do with one. I neither drink nor gamble and I don't keep a mistress."

Dubois steered the discussion away from an indelicate subject. "How are you getting along with the hat?"

Limodin wore a duplicate of his superior's round flat cap, at an angle that seemed jaunty for him. The item was now part of the official uniform code.

"It covers my head. One can't ask for anything more of a hat."

"You're a hard man to please."

"Not so hard. Doing what I'm paid to do comes close." He puffed. "What do you suppose possessed the Police Minister to cry out that Citizen Bonaparte had been killed? All he had to do was order the crowd to stop the man in flight."

"Our people don't command easily. They require a reason to act. They're our greatest weapon, especially when they're in high dudgeon. They brought down three governments, and in this case they spared France the price of a firing squad."

"Irony. The Viper was counting on escaping into the cover of that same crowd after his work was done."

"You think more like a criminal than a policeman, Jules."

"I resent that."

"It's true."

"All the more reason to take issue."

They fell silent. The courtyard outside was quiet. The troubles with England had passed for the time being. All the troops were back in their garrisons.

"It's been three weeks," Limodin said. "Have we learned anything new?"

Dubois shook his head.

"There's no record of an Aleron Débiteur having served in any branch of the army under any rank. I'm not sure he was even French. He had more accents than a peddler has wares. The English have no record of him. They disavow him entirely; small surprise. The Austrians and Germans followed suit. No one we interviewed at the military hospital in Marseille recognized his description, so what he told the First Consul about serving in Egypt is in question. At the time he claimed he was recovering in that facility, their most serious case was a corporal with dysentery. Can you imagine shitting to death for your country?"

"There should be a medal for that: A golden turd surrounded by laurels."

The Prefect hardly listened. Even his lieutenant's congenital inelegance could not penetrate his thoughts.

For an instant, he'd stood face-to-face with the man all France had been hunting for weeks, staring into a cold mask with gray-green eyes as dead as a snake's. There had been no mercy in that face, nothing human. He crossed himself.

Limodin saw the gesture. "Something?"

"Nothing. I may never get used to this quiet." He frowned. "*Débiteur*. A man with a debt to pay. Our friend's last alias, which may be significant. Perhaps he thought he owed Citizen Bonaparte something: a reckoning. He told Eslée he had a friend who served under Bonaparte on Thirteen Vendémiaire, and expressed disapproval of firing upon one's own countrymen. I think we know this man had no friends. He was speaking of himself."

"Perhaps."

"He wore a decoration for that action, and another from the

Egyptian campaign, awarded under whatever name he was using then. If he *did* take part in the massacre, and *was* stranded in Egypt by his commander, his motives may have been personal. Had the Cutthroats suspected that, he'd have cost them much less money."

"That was his mistake. If he'd done it for the money alone, he might have succeeded. The job is the job; holy crusades are for knights. I once sank fifty francs on a prizefighter who lost his head and attacked his opponent in white heat. He was on the canvas after three rounds."

"You said you don't gamble."

"That lesson cost me fifty francs."

Dubois surveyed his desk, clear of files for the first time in months. They occupied crates on the floor awaiting delivery to the state archives.

"The raw truth of the matter," he said, "is we may never know who the Viper was."

"Just as well. There wasn't enough left of him to bury under a stone."

AFTERWORD

Although the Viper is my invention, most of the principal characters in this novel lived, and the details of the Christmas Eve Plot are as reported. Had it not been for an unsatisfactory scarf and a drunken coachman, there might never have been an Emperor Napoleon or an Empress Josephine. If you think that's not such a bad thing, imagine how history would have gone if any of the governments that preceded theirs had survived.

The English, whom I admire, are nevertheless guilty of recreating the myth of St. George, holding out virtually alone against the dragon Bonaparte. The reality is far less heroic. They acted, first, to prevent the contagion of Republicanism from reaching Britain, and second, to secure their economic and political interests on the European Continent—but seldom in direct conflict with the armies of France.

With the exceptions of Lord Nelson's navy and the Duke of Wellington's Iberian campaign, England was idle for most of the Napoleonic period, letting its allies take beating after beating and substituting its treasury for cannon, bankrolling plots by others against the government in Paris. I gave the Cutthroat Club a name; however, the cabal existed, comprised of a mad king, a corrupt Parliament, and nobles with holdings on the Continent. Its sole aim was to reverse the will of the French people and enslave them once again to the Bourbon Court, preferably shedding everyone's blood but its own in the process.

No one could invent a Joseph Fouché. Napoleon's Minister of Police was J. Edgar Hoover, Heinrich Himmler, and the KGB rolled into one, ruthlessly wielding limitless power over his fellow citizens. He schemed, first, with the Bourbons, then with the Revolutionary Committee of Public Safety, then the Directorate, then the Consulate, then the Empire, and with the Bourbons again after the Restoration.

He's always been with us in some form. You see him whispering in the ears of chancellors, premiers, ayatollahs, and presidents. Today, eyeglasses and a business suit—and the cooperation of a self-serving press—make him seem ordinary and harmless, but he's responsible for much of the world's evil. Forget Waterloo: Allowing this creature to remain in power as long as he did was the Corsican's biggest mistake.

Police Prefect Nicolas Dubois was a competent administrator, in charge of Paris' first organized police force. He was also a brilliant detective. Despite ridicule from above and below, his idea to reassemble the pieces of the cart and mare killed on 4 Nivose provided the first break in the investigation, which Dubois continued to pursue despite jealous lack of cooperation on the part of the Police Ministry under Fouché. It's a matter of the ups and downs of changing government that both men were eventually dismissed from office at the same time.

The direct results of what began with the Christmas Eve Plot are known to history.

On the night of March 14, 1804, three brigades of police and three hundred dragoons crossed the Rhine, arrested Louis Antoine, the *Duc d'Enghien,* a member of the Royal House of Bourbon, and brought him back to France. He was charged with conspiring against the Republic with Georges Cadoudal and others in order to place himself on the French throne. Under questioning, the Duke confessed that the British Parliament paid him 4,200 guineas a year for his cooperation in bringing down the Consulate. Following a military trial, Bonaparte signed an order of condemnation and the Duke was executed by firing squad.

Two months later, in an effort to provide a line of succession and discourage further attempts on the First Consul's life, the Republican Senate declared Napoleon Bonaparte Emperor of the French. The Royalists had succeeded in restoring the monarchy; ironically, the monarch was the very man they'd schemed to destroy.

The Republic was dead. *Vive la République!*

—Loren D. Estleman

BONAPARTE CHRONOLOGY

The following includes facts salient to *The Eagle and the Viper:*

1769
August 15: Birth, Ajaccio, Corsica.

1784
September 15: Enters École Militaire in Paris, France.

1785
September: Graduates military school at 16, commissioned Second Lieutenant, Royal Artillery.

1793
September–December: Commanding artillery, retakes Toulon from the Royalists, is promoted to general.

1795
October 5 (13 Vendémiaire): Fires cannon into a mob intending to storm the Tuileries Palace and oust the corrupt Directorate from power.

1796
March 2: Marries Josephine de Beauharnais.

1797

January 14: Wins the Battle of Rivoli, completing a series of stunning victories, seizing Italy from Austria and annexing the country to France.

1798

July 1: Captures Alexandria, Egypt, from England.
August 1: English Admiral Nelson wins the Battle of the Nile, stranding French troops in Egypt.

1799

November 9–10: Leaving the French Army in Egypt, returns to France, overthrows the Directory, and is appointed head of the nation as First Consul.

1800

December 24: An explosive "infernal machine" aimed at his assassination (the "Christmas Eve Plot") destroys most of a Paris street, killing and maiming innocents, but failing in its intention.

1804: Crowned Emperor of the French.

RECOMMENDED READING

More than 200,000 books have been written about Napoleon Bonaparte. (My own modest library contains about two hundred.) A complete bibliography is a near impossibility, even if I had time and life enough to read them all. Here are a handful I found useful in writing and vetting *The Eagle and the Viper*:

Cassin-Scott, Jack. *Uniforms of the Napoleonic Wars in Colour, 1796–1814.* Dorset, UK: Blandford Press, 1973.
   The book is what it claims to be, and extremely helpful in describing military dress during this martial period; a rainbow should have this spectrum.
   (NOTE: Please don't blame Cassin-Scott for the policeman's cap I eventually gave Prefect Dubois; the design belongs to a later Paris. I had difficulty picturing him in any other headgear.)

Chartrand, René. *Napoleon's Guns 1792–1815: Heavy and Siege Artillery.* Botley, Oxford: Osprey, 2003.
   Surely a Napoleonic novel with only one battle scene, and that a flashback, is a rarity; but being able to identify the cannon that were likely used to quell the riot of 13 Vendémiaire (Gribeauval twenty-four-pounders) provided verisimilitude. This is an excellent source for Bonaparte scholars and firearms aficionados.

Clayton, Tim. *This Dark Business.* London: Little, Brown, 2018.
   This book appeared after I'd finished *The Eagle and the Viper*, but Clayton's premise is nearly identical to mine, and deserves mention.

England's campaign to disguise its many attempts on Napoleon's life and its self-serving motivations are the subject of this book, and the author cites names, dates, and details of the ongoing conspiracy (beginning with the Christmas Eve Plot) all the way to King George III and William Pitt, the bipolar, paranoid British prime minister who greenlighted the attempts and drank himself to death shortly after Napoleon conquered all Europe during the Battle of Austerlitz. Clayton makes the case that the UK managed to sell the fallacy of the Corsican's power-hungry persona and England's role as his courageous nemesis well into the twenty-first century. (Significantly, he points out that the term "propaganda" came into general use in this connection, coined by its employers.)

Cronin, Vincent. *Napoleon Bonaparte: An Intimate Biography*. New York: Morrow, 1972.

First published in Great Britain in 1972, Cronin's book is meticulously researched and reads like a thriller novel. It's especially useful for the personal information: Napoleon's appearance, dress, habits, relationships, preferences, and dislikes. It was in this history, when I was in college, I first learned the rudimentary details of the Christmas Eve Plot, and conceived of *The Eagle and the Viper* on the instant.

Durant, Will and Ariel. *The Age of Napoleon*. New York: Simon and Schuster, 1975.

The Durants—the Lunt and Fontanne of world history—claimed to have written this one as an afterthought, to pass time while waiting for the Grim Reaper. Most of us would have chosen less rigorous pursuits; but Napoleonic literature would have a decided gap without this 800-page bagatelle. They devote a significant number of pages to Cadoudal and his co-conspirators, most remarkable considering the breadth of their subject: the world from pole to pole, from the French Revolution through the re-burial of Napoleon's remains in Paris more than fifty years later. Their labor helped me triangulate the versions presented by Cronin and Schom. (See below.)

Forssell, Nils. *Fouché: The Man Napoleon Feared*. New York: AMS, 1970.

This book first appeared in 1925, revised three years later on the basis of newly discovered information, and remains unparalleled on its subject. Monster that Fouché was, Forrsell (or his translators; his opus debuted in Swedish) chronicles his life and career with remarkable objectivity. Not until John Toland's massive *Adolf Hitler* did anyone to my knowledge dissect and examine a thoroughly evil man so clinically. This was rare in the somewhat emotional field of biography in the early twentieth century. Without Forssell I could not have written this book.

Ludwig, Emil. *Napoleon: The Man of Destiny*. New York: Boni & Liveright, 1926.

Ludwig's immensely readable tome was a runaway bestseller: Al Capone, the Napoleon of Chicago crime, is said to have read it while imprisoned in Alcatraz, and compared his career and island exile to the Emperor's. It also suffers from some emotionalism. Ludwig was a Bonapartist, and it's obvious he was infatuated with his subject. This isn't great scholarship, but it's largely accurate, and as much fun to read the fifth time around as the first. "What is Paris saying?"; his recurring trope. Irresistible.

Markham, Felix. *Napoleon*. New York: New American Library, 1963.

This is the *Shane* of Napoleonic biography. Just as Jack Schaefer's frontier retelling of the story of David and Goliath brought American western mythology to generations of schoolchildren under the Scholastic imprint, Markham's compact biography can be found in most university bookstores, introducing Napoleon to whole new audiences. He adds nothing to established history, but serves it up in a reader-friendly format, a trade-mark shared by bestselling American history scholars Stephen Ambrose and David McCullough. It has seldom if ever been out of print.

Markham, J. David. *Napoleon for Dummies.* Indianapolis: Wiley, 2005.

I know what you're thinking: What a friend said when he saw my shelves. "Really?" But it's a handy place for a morsel needed in a hurry. Markham pompously lectures Napoleon on where he went wrong, from his marriage to Josephine to the Battle of Waterloo. He'd have been stood before a firing squad in a hot Paris minute.

Roberts, Andrew. *Napoleon: A Life.* New York: Penguin, 2015.

At this writing, Roberts' is the latest on its subject, the first to bene-fit from some 200,000 of Napoleon's letters that were previously unre-leased; a jaw-dropping figure, considering the many thousands already available and all his other works, politically and militarily, undertaken during his fifteen years in power. The result is a balanced account, criti-cizing Napoleon where his errors are clear and complimenting him in the many cases where his decisions contributed to the welfare of his country, of Europe, and of the world. A monolithic and entertaining history, enlivened by Napoleon's own words.

Schom, Alan. *Napoleon Bonaparte.* New York: HarperCollins, 1997.

When I acquired this one, it was the most recent popular biogra-phy of Napoleon. There have been many since, proving that the man is still fascinating: At sixteen he was a lieutenant of artillery; a general at twenty-four; at thirty, he ruled France; at thirty-six he was Master of Europe; and he was dead at fifty-one, an age when most world leaders are just getting started. Schom's style is easy-go, and he's earned it by dint of years of close study and detective work. He corrects Cronin—discreetly, without criticism—on a number of details concerning the Christmas Eve Plot, and helped clear up some confusion for me when I compared his findings with those of other scholars.

The above are secondary sources. For the personal details of a titanic personality, nothing compares to consulting with his intimates. I present the following without publication details; they're seldom out of print, and available in many editions:

Armand de Caulaincourt, Duke of Vicente. *With Napoleon in Russia.*

Caulaincourt was a member of Napoleon's cabinet and his general factotum for years. His memoirs of lengthy conversations with the Emperor aboard a sledge during the retreat from Moscow in 1812 provide the sort of revealing details and reminiscences that can only be confided during a long, tedious journey in flight from disaster.

Constant, Louis. *Recollections of the Private Life of Napoleon.*

As quoted in the present book, "No man is a hero to his valet." Although this *premiere valet de chamber* would abscond with 5,000 francs from the French treasury during Bonaparte's first exile, this memoir suggests he worshipped his master. Three massive volumes catalogue his character, opinions, toilet habits, and physical appearance in a way no man could who had not seen his subject frequently naked.

C. F. Méneval. *Memoirs of Napoleon Bonaparte.*

Méneval was Bonaparte's private secretary for many years, and commander-in-chief of a small army of scribes who struggled to keep up with his dictation: His employer was known to keep many letters going simultaneously, to his wife Josephine, the crowned heads of Europe, U.S. President Thomas Jefferson, his many mistresses, and generals in the field. Méneval examines his subject in meticulous detail throughout three highly readable volumes.

Emmanuel de Las Cases. *Life, Exile, and Conversations with the Emperor Napoleon.*

The Comte de Las Cases immigrated to England during the French Revolution, and became fluent in English. Napoleon brought him along to his final exile on St. Helena, to translate his memoirs—and, I suspect, eavesdrop and report on the conversation of his British captors. These four hefty volumes are the closest thing we have to a Napoleonic autobiography; although it's been criticized as "sweetening" the truth, I subscribe to Las Cases' claim that Napoleon sought to create the United States of Europe, making war to preserve peace. When the European Union was founded in the twentieth century, he ought to have received credit (as well as the idea for the Chunnel; which in Napoleon's case was conceived in an effort to invade England without naval interference). Las Cases' detractors dismiss him as an opportunist, enduring the hardships of "that God-forsaken rock in the Atlantic" in order to write about Napoleon and become rich. I can hardly fault him that; I'd like to do it myself.

Latimer, Elizabeth Wormeley. *Talks of Napoleon at St. Helena.*

Actually, Wormeley was the translator; the author was General Baron Gourgaud, who accompanied Napoleon into his last exile; but Wormeley's is the name that appears on the spine of the 1903 edition. (Forgivable: Her familial connections with Napoleon's British enemies, personal contact with surviving Bonapartes, reported in footnote, are invaluable, as much for their balance as for the information provided.) Quoted at length, the deposed emperor reflects on his life and career, including the murderous scheming of Cadoudal, Moreau, and Pichegru. Although he makes no mention of the Christmas Eve Plot, he refers to the "infernal machine," demonstrating that the affair was still in his thoughts after fifteen years.

So many books about Napoleon; so little time.

ACKNOWLEDGMENTS

For whatever may be found laudable in *The Eagle and the Viper,* I have a remarkable unsung association of bright and witty colleagues to thank.

Many years ago, in collaboration with her late father, Fred, Mary Ann Verdi founded a fortnightly writers' group in her home in Beverly Hills, Michigan. It's still going.

The membership was crucial to the development of this book. These talented writers include Peter Barlow (who also suggested the title), Mike Brogan, Lee Helms, James O'Keefe, Frances Patricia (Pat) Olson, the late Phil Rosette, John Hus, and Mary Ann Verdi-Hus. The act of reading one's writing aloud to a group is a technique I recommend; in that milieu, when a word or phrase is off, it makes a dull thud in one's own ears that's often missing when read in solitude. *Then* there is the bonus of intelligent feedback from a learned and experienced audience.

I mention also our late dear friend Frank Wydra, a brilliant writer and former member. Although he didn't live to lend aid to this book, his support, professionally and personally, helped to make this world worth writing about. We toast his memory regularly, as we do Phil Rosette's; and express wishes for the recovery of our chum Len Charla from serious illness; his suggestions during the reading of an early draft helped jump-start the final version.

The publishing personnel I've been privileged to work with shun attention (perhaps to avoid being inundated with manuscripts they'll never find time to assess); however, I want them to know how grateful I am. My longtime agent—who I *know* prefers to remain in shadow—tops that list.

As always I thank my wife, author Deborah Morgan, for wise counsel, constant support, and the occasional kick in the tail. This gifted author and accomplished editor provided criticisms and suggestions that helped me apply the final polish to a project that had been many years in the making. In her light I have grown beyond my imagination.